To Steve & Mary Jo
Ho ho ho!

David Berry

LAST KID BOOKS
by David Benjamin

The Life and Times of the Last Kid Picked

Three's a Crowd

A Sunday Kind of Love

Almost Killed by a Train of Thought: Collected Essays

Skulduggery in the Latin Quarter

Summer of '68

Black Dragon

They Shot Kennedy

Jailbait

Bastard's Bluff

Woman Trouble

Fat Vinny's Forbidden Love

Witness to the Crucifixion

Choose Moose

Dead Shot

The Melting Grandmother and Other Short Works

Cheat

Also by David Benjamin

SUMO: A Thinking Fan's Guide to Japan's National Sport

Christmas in a Jugular Vein

David Benjamin

LAST KID BOOKS

Copyright © 2024 David Benjamin
Illustrations Copyright © 2024 Greg Holfeld

Last Kid Books
309 W. Washington Avenue
Madison, WI 53703

First Edition
November 2024

All rights reserved

No part of this book may be used or reproduced
in any manner whatsoever without written
permission from the author.

Printed in Wisconsin, United States of America

For more information or to order books:
visit www.lastkidbooks.com

Library of Congress Control Number: 2024922825

ISBN-13: 979-8-99171679-1-1

A NOTE ON THE TYPE

This book was set in Athelas, a serif typeface designed by Veronika Burian and Jose Scaglione and intended for use in body text.[1] Released by the company TypeTogether in 2008, Burian and Scaglione described Athelas as inspired by British fine book printing.

Printed and bound by Park Printing Solutions
Verona, Wisconsin

Designed by Little Creek Press and Book Design
Mineral Point, Wisconsin

To Patty Brill
who got it all started

"Christmas ought to be brought up to date," Maria said. "It ought to have gangsters, and aeroplanes and a lot of automatic pistols."
—John Masefield, *The Box Of Delights*

*Suddenly it's Christmas,
The longest holiday.
When they say "Season's Greetings,"
They mean just what they say.
It's a season, it's a marathon,
Retail eternity.
It's not over 'til it's over
And you throw away the tree.*
—Loudon Wainwright III

*We gotta send Santa Claus back to the Rescue Mission.
Christmas don't make it no more.
Don't you know that murder and destruction
Scream the toys in every store…*
— Frank Zappa

Preface	1
The Little Red Dot	8
Interview with the Virgin	10
Real kids, real silence	13
If the Romans had had "smart weapons"	16
"A Christmas ring-tone"	19
You better watch out!	22
A Christmas email	25
The frisking of the Magi	29
A viral Christmas story	33
The manger incident	36
A 3-D Christmas	40
"I didn't come from these people"	43
An inconvenient Christmas	47
"We four kings of Orient are …"	50
The Ballad of Skagway Phil	55
Christmas comes to FEMA	59
The Night Before Christ … Mouse?	64
Christmas through a glass, darkly (Next Year, Bring Guns)	66
"This show's gonna be huge!"	69
Christmas Doggerel, 2015	80
He's ba-a-a-ack!	81
Christmas Doggerel, 2016	86
Santawocky (Christmas Doggerel, 2017)	88

" ... Darkness is cheap, and Scrooge liked it ... ". 90

A Christmas miracle (Christmas Doggerel, 2018) 94

The skeptical shepherd. 96

An American Christmas, 2019. 110

The stranger in the stable. 112

What color the child? (Christmas Doggerel, 2020) 118

The fourth ghost. 120

Christmas: It's not all shmaltz and treacle 128

A Murray Christmas to all 132

It was a dark and stormy Christmas
(Christmas Doggerel, 2021). 157

Have Yourself an Analog Christmas 158

A definition of winter 167

Yuletide blowback. 171

How George wrecked Christmas 175

Nobody says. 197

About the Author 217

Preface

"And in thy dark streets shineth"

Purely in terms of narrative drama, the Christmas story—the Nativity scene—is kind of a drag. In uttering this heresy, I seek not to disparage the beauty of the Bethlehem tableau. Luke's lyricism is undeniable, especially in the Revised Standard version:

> *And Joseph also went up from Galilee, from the city of Nazareth, to Judea, to the city of David, which is called Bethlehem, because he was of the house and lineage of David, to be enrolled with Mary, his betrothed, who was with child. And while they were there, the time came for her to be delivered. And she gave birth to her first-born son and wrapped him in swaddling cloths, and laid him in the manger, because there was no place for them in the inn.* (Luke 2:4-7)

A really nice image but a quick re-read reveals where Luke went wrong.

You can't help but notice that the whole "no place in the inn" crisis is an afterthought, as though Luke snapped his fingers, bopped his head and—like a comedian who'd blown his setup—said, "No, wait, I forgot this part."

By comparison, Matthew might have done a better job as a narrator if he hadn't skipped over the crowd scene at the manger and gone straight to the gory aftermath, when Joseph took Mary and the baby and escaped to Egypt while Herod ran amok:

> *Then Herod, when he saw that he had been tricked by the wise men, was in a furious rage, and he sent and killed all the male children in Bethlehem and in all that region who were two years old or under, according to the time which he had ascertained from the wise men.* (Matthew 2:16)

This version gives the audience a little more drama, including the fingering of the Magi as stool pigeons. But if you look closely, this tale is a letdown because there's no pursuit of the fugitives. Herod is closing the stable door after all the oxen have skedaddled. In Matthew's chronology (with which he could have fiddled because there's no historical record available to fact-checkers), Joseph and the family have safely lammed off to Egypt long before Herod begins his slaughter of the innocents. The story would be vastly more thrilling if Herod's troops were hot on the trail of the Christchild at the same moment when his stepfather and virgin mom, desperate to escape the murderous king in the midst of his infanticidal frenzy, whip their aged steed into a fatal froth and hide under a bridge with their dying horse while Herod's minions thunder above.

Admit it. This version sounds a lot more fun.

My contention is that since well before the birth of Jesus, the canons of good storytelling have entailed some measure of conflict and suspense, spiced with a surprise or two. Homer's *Iliad* and *Odyssey*, which predate the Nativity by eight hundred years, are full of this juicy stuff.

However, until Charles Dickens took it on, Christmas was a static narrative theme. Dickens' stories of the season, especially *A Christmas Carol*, inspired a vast literature of Christmas by infusing them with suspense. More significantly, Dickens created a template for stories of the season with three "modern" elements.

Above all, Dickens made clear that Christmas had become, by the middle of the nineteenth century in the Western world, a secular celebration embraced even by people whose faith isn't Christian. Dickens' genius lay not in the fact that he acknowledged and lent lip service, every holiday season, to the dichotomy between the sacrosanct and the mercantile but in the fact that he ignored the argument. Dickens staged a tumultuous clash of values and delved into the human search for meaning but did so by barely suggesting its religious overtones.

Moreover, he recast Christmas with a sense of humor.
And ghosts!

In response to his uncle Scrooge's "Humbug!" Fred conveys ideas that could have been intoned from a liberal, twenty-first-century Anglican pulpit:

I am sure I have always thought of Christmastime, when it has come round—apart from the veneration due to its sacred name and origin, if anything belonging to it can be apart from that—as a good time; a kind, forgiving, charitable, pleasant time; the only time I know of, in the long calendar of the year, when men and women seem by one consent to open their shut-up hearts freely, and to think of people below them as if they really were fellow passengers to the grave, and not another race of creatures bound on other journeys. And therefore, uncle, though it has never put a scrap of gold or silver in my pocket, I believe that it has done me good, and will do me good; and I say, God bless it!

Dickens' second key is the element of darkness. Dickens understood intuitively that the chill and desolate aspects of Christmas—one of the shortest, bleakest, coldest days of the dying year—give resonance, depth and drama to this strange holiday's redemptive power. After all, every year on December 25, we celebrate the poorest prophet in religious history by blowing a fortune on toys, clothes, jewelry, perfume, cranberry sauce and electric shavers.

I've always thought that the carolers whom Scrooge shoos from his doorstep should be singing "Good King Wenceslas," a carol icy and spooky enough to have been composed by Jack London.

Sire, the night is darker now, and the wind blows stronger,
Fails my heart, I know not how; I can go no longer.

Mark my footsteps good, my page, tread thou in them boldly.
Thou shalt find the winter's rage, freeze thy blood less coldly.

Dating all the way back to Herod's reign of terror and even the shadowy innkeeper who banished Jesus to the stable, the Christmas story has had antagonists. But in Ebenezer Scrooge, Dickens created an archetype for yuletide villainy—pinched, mean, miserly and heathenishly contemptuous of the holiday spirit. Scrooge embodies, exalts and gives witness to Christmas' dark side—the poverty of the Cratchits, the debtors' prisons, the union workhouses, the treadmill and the Poor Law. This contrast deepens the story beyond the feast day's superficial message of sweetness and light.

Dickens' mischief in *A Christmas Carol*—and the element that endeared me to the story from an early age—is that Scrooge, both before and after his redemption, is the story's most interesting character and one of the greatest in all of literature. Walt Disney once said that a movie is only as good as its villain. Scrooge, the apotheosis of that dictum, is the voice of a "war on Christmas" that has been smoldering since at least 1843. When I first saw Reginald Owen as Scrooge in the 1938 film, the line that captivated me and sent me to the library to memorize it was Scrooge's imprecation against "every idiot who goes about with 'Merry Christmas' on his lips."

In this curmudgeonly lyric, I found grist for my imagination. I could picture a hooded blackguard hidden among shepherds, lurking malevolently over a helpless newborn in the windswept stable. Dickens had conjured an ambiguous Christmas with ghosts in chains and jolly spirits hiding Ignorance and Want beneath their velvet robes. Immediately, the fictional possibilities of the season appeared to me endlessly variable.

Dickens' third vital element is change, another requisite of good fiction.

For a story to work, to be credible, to involve the reader,

the central character ought to be different at the end from the way he or she was at the beginning. *A Christmas Carol*, *How the Grinch Stole Christmas* and Natalie Wood and Maureen O'Hara coming to "believe" in *Miracle on 34th Street* are all tales of transformation.

When I was in grade school, I was affected by all these stories. I also read O. Henry's classic *The Gift of the Magi* and Robert Benchley's wonderful *A Good Old-Fashioned Christmas*. Later, every year, Dylan Thomas' *A Child's Christmas in Wales* and—before it was made into a movie—Jean Shepherd's masterpiece, *Duel in the Snow or Red Ryder Nails the Cleveland Street Kid*. What I learned, subliminally, but it stuck with me, was that you can write about one of the most familiar themes in human experience but there's no rule that you have to color inside the lines. Indeed, if you want to grab your audience, the more you emulate Dickens, expose the prickly underside of comfort and joy, the more you startle, frighten and transgress—or, in Benchley's case, giggle—the more likely your story will be remembered. The more likely some impertinent kid will scrounge through the library to read and memorize the most outrageous of your dastard's outbursts.

As this anthology indicates, I've always been fascinated with Christmas, both when I was a devout little boy in Catholic school and later as an apostate storyteller in constant quest to spin tales of the unexpected. I wrote my first intentional Christmas stories, "The Little Red Dot" and "Next Year, Bring Guns," when I was sixteen. Miraculously, although the vice-principal of my high school strongly preferred that I not write anything for my school newspaper, editor Patty Brill snuck these two pieces into the Christmas issue of *The Lance*.

Since then, I've tried to compose a new Christmas story every year. During my tenure as editor of the *Mansfield* (Mass.) *News*, I contrived to fill our fat holiday issue with Christmas stories written by kids in every grade of the town's schools. The results were a joy to the world.

The astute reader will note that the stories here contain an occasional undertone of politics. This is appropriate. When Scrooge cites the "useful course" of debtors' prisons and the Poor Law, he's broaching one of that era's heated political issues. Going back further to the *first* Christmas story, the reason that Mary and Joseph were transients without lodging in Bethlehem was that they'd been uprooted from their home in Nazareth to obey orders from the emperor Caesar Augustus as part of a Roman tax census. Nowadays, when Christmas rolls around, the pious propagandists of Fox News tirelessly claim that the liberal establishment's "war on Christmas" forces everyone to use euphemisms like "Happy Holidays." However, such intentionally neutral secularisms predate the existence of Fox News by decades. I'm not sure when corporations and greeting card publishers adopted "Season's Greetings" and similar religion-free nostrums in an apparent effort to avoid offense to non-Christian Christmas celebrants, but it happened before I was born.

Dickens never proposed a substitute for "Merry Christmas," but he was instrumental in expanding the feast day's meaning to embrace and spread goodwill to everyone regardless of their faith—or absence thereof—just as Jesus welcomed among his fellows and followers Romans and Samaritans, fishermen and Pharisees, beggars, lepers and whores. He only spared from his love the sort of profiteers who would exploit the joyful birth of a Savior to rake in the shekels.

Among my Christmas stories, technology also emerges as an occasional theme. This trend is the product of my union with Junko Yoshida, one of the world's truly prominent technology journalists. She has recruited me not only as her lifelong copy editor but also as commentator, now and then, in her publications, first *EE Times* and, more recently, *The Ojo-Yoshida Report on High Technology*. George Leopold, one of Junko's colleagues, commissioned several of my Christmas pieces—notably "A Christmas ring-tone" and "A Christmas email"—for light reading in *EE Times*' holiday issue. There's even a piece memorializing the brief resurrection of 3-D, a video technology that has died at least three deaths since the first 3-D flick, *The Power of Love*, was released in 1922.

Finally, as I strive here to justify the stretching and twisting that I've applied to our most familiar holiday motifs, I'm obliged to return to Luke. The lyricism of Luke's Nativity is the rare remaining relict—in my mind—of my parochial education at St. Mary's School in Tomah, Wisconsin. Since those grade school days, Jesus and his Gospel have evolved in my perception—and my reading—as an almost exclusively "literary" theme. In the two thousand years since his mythical birth, Jesus has become one of Joseph Campbell's most oft-invoked and many-faceted heroes with a thousand faces. The Jesus narrative from birth to death has been altered, glorified, massaged, protracted and diddled by authors from Ernest Renan and Lew Wallace (*Ben-Hur*) to Pär Lagerkvist (*Barabbas*), Nikos Kazantzakis and even—God help us!—Tim Rice (*Jesus Christ Superstar*).

The literary magic of Luke's immortal paragraph is its poetic economy. So much is left unsaid—and unseen—that the enterprising storyteller has countless gaps to fill, passages to invent, carols to interpolate and verses to steal. As I edited this anthology of yuletide deviations, I was surprised to note that I had written eight different variations on the sacred scene in the Bethlehem stable. I actually had nine, but one was so redundant that I spiked it. I suspect that, as I continue to dutifully craft my annual Christmas story, I'll give in again to temptation and resort to Gospel parody. Scripture is, after all, a template for every storyteller and, for both writer and reader, an inexhaustible wellspring of imagination, mystery, agony and wonder.

Were he still with us, Luke might not approve of my impious tinkering. Charles Dickens, I suspect, would be, at least, tolerant. After all, he gave us Scrooge and a bunch of other yuletide yarns. Dickens clearly regarded Christmas as a rich theme worthy of exploration, expansion—illumination—by authors following his example. I share with Dickens, I hope, the conviction that the more Christmas stories, the more varied, whimsical, spooky, even transgressive, the better. It is our best, our most beloved and our most complicated festival.

The Little Red Dot

(My first published Christmas story, slightly censored but restored here, appeared in the Robert M. La Follette High School Lance, *21 December 1966.)*

Last winter, around December 30, I was walking across a barren, snow-covered cornfield in the heart of Wisconsin. When I reached the center of the field, I stood still and—meditatively—turned 360 degrees to survey the unimpressive panorama.

Broken cornstalks and leafless trees.

But suddenly, far off in the distance, I saw a little red dot. I peered intently at it and, being curious by nature, I started to wonder what it might be. As I watched very closely, I noticed that the little red dot was getting bigger. It appeared to be coming toward me.

By and by, I noted that the little red dot was not simply a little red dot. Rather, it was some sort of little red being moving in my direction.

Knowing of no other type of being that would set forth in public in such a stark, blazing color, I assumed that it must be a little red human being.

Then, when the little red being was still nearly a half-mile away, I realized, in huge amazement, that this strange little red apparition was none other than that generous, fat, jolly, roly-poly, lovable Christmas fairy, Santa Claus. A gasp of surprise escaped my breast. Immediately, suffering again from my natural curiosity, I wondered what dear old Saint Nick was doing here, walking across a barren, snow-covered cornfield in the heart of Wisconsin.

My curiosity only grew when I saw that the little red dot of Santa Claus, which was by now noticeably larger, was accompanied by another dot, slightly bigger but brown.

Of course, I wondered what that could be.

In a matter of seconds, I realized that Santa was pulling the big brown dot behind him. In fact, Santa seemed to be having trouble with the ungainly object, whatever it was. Needless to say, I was by now—despite the cold—burning with curiosity.

Then, much to my chagrin, I perceived that, as only it could be, the big brown dot was, beyond the shadow of a doubt, Santa's sleigh.

I probably would have started wondering what Santa was doing pulling his sleigh across a barren, snow-covered field in the middle of Wisconsin but for the fact that I was wondering about something else. For, instantly after I realized that poor old Santa was dragging that heavy old sleigh all by himself, I started to wonder what it was that filled the sleigh. For, in truth, Santa's sleigh was filled, and incidentally, it was absolutely piled up with some far-distant, unrecognizable substance, which was also brown.

Soon, Santa and his sleigh were less than three hundred yards away, and I could make out everything pretty clearly. So, in a moment, I perceived that Santa's sleigh was stacked up mountainously with dead reindeer, eight of them, their antlers poking out every which way. I wondered what Santa was doing dragging around a sleigh full of dead reindeer.

Now, although Santa was visibly struggling mightily with the heavy sleigh and breathing rapidly, his approach was quite fast, and he was saying something.

Then, as I stood speechlessly watching him, Santa Claus plodded past me, not turning his head, icicles hanging from his bedraggled beard, mumbling angrily, over and over again, the words, " ... goddamn deer hunters ... goddamn deer hunters ... goddamn deer hunters ..."

Over and over again.

And so, Santa disappeared into the distance, muttering under his labored breath, slowly becoming a little red dot. I sure hope he made it back to the North Pole.

Variations on a Nativity theme (#1)

Interview with the Virgin

This time of year, Nativity scenes—many very elaborate—start popping up in front of every church. They feature real straw, hand-hewn mangers, lifesize papier mâché cows, sheep, shepherds, donkeys, Magi, Josephs, Christchildren, not to mention the Virgin Mary—who, to my surprise, stepped out of the creche the other day, nudged me sideways on the pew and sat down.

"I gotta get off my feet," she said.

I was speechless. She wasn't. She waved a weary hand at the Nativity (now lacking one key statue) and said, "What's wrong with this picture, huh?"

Before I could guess, she said, "I'll tell you what's wrong, Steve. What am I doing standing up? Or even sitting up? Since when does a woman who's just given birth—to an enormous kid, by the way (without benefit of Demerol!). And another thing! This virgin birth dodge? A failed concept. You ever try pushing the son of God through an intact hymen?"

I told her I wouldn't if I could.

"Damn straight!" she ejaculated. "This cockamamie idea that I was standing at attention, welcoming well-wishers ten minutes after birthing Jesus, is a male chauvinist myth. Truth is, Steve, I was flat on my back, puffing like a beached tuna. Listen, you've read Luke, right?"

"The Christmas story," I said. "Sure. It's beautiful."

"Yeah, nice story. Except for the parts Luke left out!" she said. "Like, for instance, where is it written that the labor took twenty hours?"

"Twenty hours?"

"That's right, Steve. Twenty miserable hours on a pile of donkey shit. Look over there!" She pointed again. "That's supposed to be a stable, right? So what's missing? The manure maybe? And the cats. Have you ever seen a stable anyplace that wasn't crawling with diseased cats? And look at the help I had! You see an obstetrician here? A midwife? Anybody at all?! Heck, I would've settled for a barber! What'd they give me? A carpenter! What was Joseph gonna do—cut the kid's cord with a jigsaw?"

I shuddered. "I never thought of Christmas so … clinically."

"Of course you didn't, you deluded sexist romantic! You're a man. Look over there. You see those shepherds?"

"Yes."

"Disgusting! Lying outdoors, sleeping with dogs, getting up with fleas, hip-deep in sheepflop. Have you ever smelled a shepherd? And every last one wants to handle my newborn babe! No wonder I wrapped the tyke in swaddling clothes, laid him in a manger and said, 'Everyone! Touch this kid and I'll shear ya down to your short hairs!'"

Mary went on, "Honest to God, if there was one of those slobs traipsing through the stable, there had to be fifty of 'em. I couldn't sleep a wink. Even when I wasn't nursing Jesus, fighting off shepherds and darn near suffocating every time the ox farted, there was the blinding light from that star. It was like a night game at Yankee Stadium. And look! See that Christchild statue over there?"

I looked again at the glowing image of the newborn Savior, spreading his pudgy arms to embrace the sufferings of humankind.

"Well, that ain't my Jesus. My baby was no blue-eyed, towheaded WASP, and he wasn't born a year old. He was shriveled and blotchy. His head was cone-shaped, bald as a duck egg—and if he'd had any hair, it would've been black as the ace of spades. Look at me! I'm an olive-skinned Jew, not Tuesday Weld. If I'd given birth to a blond, the idiot shepherds would have stoned me for witchcraft.

"And if the shepherds and that star and all those noisy angels singing elevator music, every minute day and night, and that chiseling innkeeper—if all that wasn't enough aggravation, these foreign kings show up and start passing out gold, frankincense and myrrh. Raising the kid's expectations. Give the infant Savior gold one year and he's gonna want gold every Christmas 'til the Crucifixion. And where we gonna get frankincense even if Joe can afford it on a carpenter's wages? Trust me, Steve, there wasn't a Neiman Marcus in Nazareth."

I sympathized with the Virgin. Certainly, the Nativity was less bucolic than we depict it in our modern iconography. "And then!" she cried. "The last straw!"

Her face turned crimson.

"I finally get Jesus nursed and quiet. I'm dozing off, and

suddenly this lice-infested peasant kid barges in. He's telling Jesus he's a poor boy, too, and he has no gift to give—as if somebody had asked him for one. So then he says, instead, he'll play his drum. His DRUM? So I try to tell this kid: No, not that! Get outa here, for Christ's sake! I just got the baby to sleep. But before I could move, the little psychopath is whacking the damn drum, *pa rum pum pum pum*—over and over and over—and pretty soon Jesus is wide awake, bawling his brains out! Silent night, my puckered ass!

"But then—God bless the old coot—clueless Joe finally comes through."

"Wha'd he do?"

"Well, Joseph was tired, too. He woke up, yelled, 'What the hell is that racket?'", put his foot through the drum and beat the brat senseless with his own drumsticks. And then ..."

Her face took on a beatific radiance.

"I started giggling," said the Virgin Mary. "I swear to God, that was the first time I'd smiled since that weird day nine months before when the Holy Ghost floated into my room and started feeling me up."

25 Dec. '98

Real kids, real silence

The wonderful thing about going back home for Christmas is the opportunity to get in touch with your family ... sort of.

Well, not really.

Returning to Wisconsin this holiday, I discovered that my once voluble nephew Bronx (not his real name) had sunk into a state of reticence bordering on catatonia. He's twelve. Meanwhile, his big sister Haiku (not her real name, either)—an eighteen-year-old college freshman—is just beginning to master the use of monosyllabic fragments when responding to adults. Until now, her discourse with her elders was so terse that a traumatized quahog, by comparison, was Rosie O'Donnell on a caffeine jag.

The father in question, my brother Bill (real name: Bill), has long been troubled by the silence of Haiku and now worries about Bronx's evident unwillingness to bare his soul, confess the longings of his pre-pubescent libido and seek Dad's wise counsel. What's wrong with kids these days?

I posed this question to my wife, Hotlips, who studied American family dynamics on Japanese television in the 1960s—which consisted largely of American TV dubbed in Nihongo. She learned through *Father Knows Best*, *Leave It to Beaver*, *Donna Reed*, and other sitcom classics that America was an idyll of intra-family intercourse. In such shows, everybody talked about everything. Nary a thought went unexpressed. Your typical TV kid in those halcyon days, after a short period of guilty anguish or low-intensity angst, would break down like cheap cardboard and stagger into Dad's den, desperate for a hug. Or he would head for the kitchen, dripping tears, to bury his face in Mom's (taffeta) apron. Every fistfight, strikeout, petty larceny, busted window, forged report card, sexual pang, surreptitious cigarette, self-serving fib, broken date, hazing incident or unsavory friendship would worm its penitent way onto the confessional lap of Ward Cleaver, Jim Anderson, Andy Taylor, even Danny Thomas and Lucas McCain!

Yes, don't you remember? The Rifleman, who killed three or four people in every episode, was a caring and sensitive psychotherapist.

In every show, every week, every kid would spill their guts. Totally! And the problem would be solved—shazam!—with kind words, moral platitudes and, once in a while, a little mild punishment. Lucas McCain would lay down his semiautomatic Winchester, fold Mark into his arms, kiss him on the head and then send him outside, with a few words of gentle reproach, to slop the hogs and straighten a few fenceposts.

Watching it on television, Hotlips thought this phenomenon

remarkable and a sign of America's higher civilization. The willing unbreasting of youthful secrets—rewarded by parental sympathy—never occurred in Japan.

I had to explain to Hotlips the substantial gap between romance fiction like *The Partridge Family* and reality. As I chose my words, I realized that the cruelest deception in that golden era of family TV lay not so much in mythical parents like Ward, Jim, Donna and the Rifleman but in Wally, the Beav, Shelley Fabares, Paul Peterson, Patty Duke and Opie. These fictional kids were the pinnacle of cathode surrealism. They were the fictional betrayers of the kid code because true kids, then and now, and forever after, like Bill and I when we were kids, and Bronx and Haiku today, cherish above all the blessings of silence and the shroud of mute invisibility. A kid doesn't bare his or her soul to other kids—ever (unless, of course, the kid's a girl and it's a slumber party). But even if you share the odd secret with your best pal, you never—not in a million years!—spill your guts to adults, especially parents. If grownups want your guts, they've got to pull 'em out by hand. These are the rules.

So, although I'm sympathetic with Bill's struggle to plumb the murky depths of his children's psyches, I was reassured by the stony resistance—to all efforts at adult probing—by Bronx and Haiku and even by their taciturn stepcousin Alan Ladd (not his real name). Parents of our generation, who seem habitually forgetful of their own youthful silence, tend to remember instead the false example set by Wally and the Beav. We fecklessly yearn for offspring who aren't the granite-faced enigmas we used to be, but more like the logorrheic blurters who populated the sitcoms of TV Land. I think this is because when we were kids, we—like Hotlips—looked up to TV kids. We were envious. We all wished we could be emotionally complex, impossibly articulate and cleverly scripted, like Billy Gray and Angela Cartwright. And we all wanted to tell our parents our rottenest crimes without getting screamed at, whacked, grounded and shunned. But we knew our own limitations and our parents' predilections. We knew that confession was bad for our health. Discretion was our shield, and *omertà* was our code.

I'm afraid that if Bill really wants his kids to strip their inhibitions and bare their souls, he'll have to do it the hard way. Strap 'em down to his workbench and plug in the Black & Decker belt sander he got for Christmas.

Or else ... wait 'til they grow up.

12 Dec. '00

Variations on a Nativity theme (#2)
If the Romans had had "smart weapons"

BETHLEHEM, Judea, Dec. 26, 0000 A.D. — A small stable was destroyed here yesterday, and an undetermined number of non-combatants killed or injured, after a remote-controlled missile, fired by Roman forces, missed by less than ten yards its intended target, an inn where a notorious Hebrew terrorist was reported to be spending the night.

The "smart weapon," launched from a Roman galley on the Sea of Galilee and guided by an unmanned radar-equipped "drone" seagull, was fired after reports that Barabbas, a Hebrew assassin long-sought by the Caesarean Intelligence Agency (CIA), had arrived in Bethlehem, apparently to disrupt the census recently ordered by Emperor Caesar Augustus.

"We had a solid tip from a reliable CI that Barabbas—who's a real bad guy—was at the inn," said Marcus Dubius, spokesman for the Roman occupation. However, after centurions arrived at the scene, they found only the destroyed stable and a crowd of shell-shocked Judeans who said Barabbas had left Bethlehem days before.

Because of the devastation caused by the "smart weapon," Roman officials have yet to determine the death toll in what is being called "an unfortunate military accident." According to Dubius, "As long as these Hebrew terrorists continue to hole up in heavily populated areas, there are going to be civilian losses like this. If more of the natives cooperated with their Roman liberators, we could flush out these fanatics and prevent such tragedies."

According to witnesses, a Galilean family, who had come all the way from Nazareth, was wiped out in the mishap. They had intended to stay at the inn—where they would have survived—but were shunted into the stable because they had failed to reserve in advance.

"There was no room at the inn," said innkeeper Rachel Goldfarb. "It's terrible what happened, but I keep telling people, you want a room, make a reservation. How hard is this?"

The family was identified as a carpenter named Joseph, his wife Miriam (or Mary) and a newborn son. Also killed were several unidentified shepherds, an ox, a donkey, at least five sheep and, in the words of one confused bystander being nursed for a head wound, "a heavenly host of angels." A drummer boy, whose presence in the stable was unexplained, was seriously injured and later died of his wounds.

One of the mysteries CIA officials have yet to fathom is the large number of people who appeared to have gathered in the stable, a circumstance that worsened the tragedy. "As far as we can tell, the woman was in childbirth just before the missile hit," said the Roman spokesman. "But these people have babies all the time. I mean, really, these Semites breed like gerbils. This is not the sort of thing that normally draws a crowd."

Among witnesses to the carnage, incongruously, were three prominent Magi who had traveled all the way from the East, apparently for the purpose of visiting this obscure stable.

They were crestfallen when they found the humble stall reduced to ashes and littered with smoking body parts. One of the kings, Balthazar, claimed to have followed "a bright star in the heavens" to the Bethlehem region.

Despite similar reports of an intense brilliance lighting up the night sky over Judea, Marcus Dubius, the Imperial Roman Press officer, scoffed. "They probably just saw the afterburner from the missile. These weapons burn pretty hot."

Melchior, another of the eastern Magi, said he and his companions had come, laden with gold, frankincense and myrrh, to celebrate the birth of a "Savior."

"Something in our hearts told us we must follow the [alleged] star, for the son of God was about to be born, thence to suffer and die for the sins of mankind," added Melchior. "We had no idea he was going to die this quick. What are we gonna do with all this leftover myrrh?"

Contacted at his palace in Jerusalem, King Herod, the local Roman satrap, said, "Well, this is sad, of course. My heart goes out to these folks."

Asked about reports of a Savior being killed in the stable, Herod said, "Frankly, I'm tired of hearing all this Messiah talk. If this country is going to move forward, we've got to forget about saviors and baptists and all these other Jewish fairy tales and start cooperating with the Romans. These troops came to liberate us, and we should be grateful."

In a related piece of good news, Herod announced that, out of respect for the family who died in the Bethlehem stable, he had postponed a plan to have every firstborn son in Judea slaughtered by soldiers.

"Just think of this as my little Christmas present," said Herod.

Herod—who was known and loved for his charming verbal flubs—did not explain what he meant by the word "Christmas."

Meanwhile, Roman authorities had ordered Bethlehem

residents to avoid contact with the media during the investigation of the incident. Those who violated this advice would be "flogged to death summarily, or crucified," according to Marcus Dubius. "In other words," he added, "it's business as usual around here, and people should go about their affairs normally."

Roman authorities offered no timetable for the completion of their inquiry. However, the site of the tragedy was quickly cleared. Within hours, the only sign that anything had occurred was a charred manger lying broken in the missile crater.

16 Dec. '03

A Christmas ring-tone

All through Christmas Eve, E.B. Scrooge had been on the phone.

Phones, actually—landlines, LANs, DSL, GSM, GPS, Wi-Fi, SMS, Skype, email, fax, you name it! He'd been downloading data, transferring funds, passing tips, calling in chits and harassing debtors since two o'clock in the morning. His workday followed a dizzying sequence that started with the first bell in Tokyo, then worked steadily west through Hong Kong, Singapore, New Delhi, Moscow, the Middle East, and onward. Scrooge chafed at the sluggishness of the Western markets, from London to Wall Street to São Paulo, all paralyzed by the encroaching birth of Christ.

"Humbug," muttered Scrooge.

Nonetheless, he'd kept every telecom link buzzing and Bob Cratchit pounding his keyboard right up 'til closing time. The only interruption had been his ne'er-do-well nephew spouting yuletide nonsense and—later—a group of soft-hearted merchants seeking contributions to feed and house the poor.

"Are there no dumpsters?" Scrooge had quipped (his one moment of holiday merriment). "Are there no subway tunnels?"

He dined as usual at Denny's, glued to laptop and headphones, setting up Asian conference calls after midnight. The only break in his routine was a glitch in his domestic cell phone, which inexplicably uploaded a weird image that resembled Scrooge's dead partner, Jacob Marley. No text message appeared—just a voice moaning, "Scrooge, Scro-o-oge."

Scrooge shrugged it off as a bacterial hallucination. "That's the last time I order the meatloaf at Denny's," he growled.

At home, Scrooge had just plugged his mobiles into chargers, set up his PC to upload email and switched his landline onto speaker when more weirdness struck. Suddenly, there was wailing and screaming on the speaker, then smoke, and then—*kaboom!* The power failed, the lights went dark, and out of the PC billowed a black cloud. A moment later, a ghastly specter resembling Marley appeared. He was wrapped in chains that consisted entirely of telephones—old Western Electric bakelite models, huge drop-a-dime pay phones, Princesses, Slimlines, Maxwell Smart's shoe phone, Dick Tracy's wristwatch, and a thousand mobiles ranging from the banana-shaped monsters of the eighties to the most delicate state-of-the-art clamshell. And they were all ringing, buzzing, babbling, displaying ads, snapshots, sports clips, weather reports and naked Playmates. Marley's phone-festooned phantom blinked, glowed and flashed blindingly, like a one-man Times Square.

Scrooge covered his ears and begged for this apparition to begone. This only prompted a scream so loud from Marley that he drowned out the phones.

Suddenly, silence.

"Listen, E.B.," said the creature. "I don't have much time. This eternal torture will start up again in a few minutes."

"What do you want of me, Marley?"

Marley said he had wrought this terrible chain in life and that Scrooge's chain was even heavier—and noisier. Scrooge argued that Marley had been a good man of business. Marley snapped irritably, "Mankind was my business. The common welfare was my business!"

Marley went on, "But where was I? Constantly on the phone. Look at me now. These two ponderous receivers are glued to my ears—literally. I can't get 'em off! I hear mortals brag that they're 'Always On.' That sounds fine until you realize, too late, that you can Never Get Off!"

Scrooge still didn't grasp Marley's point.

"What are you, stupid? Scrooge, I'm giving you one last chance to hang up the damn phone! To recover a vestige of your attention span. To eat one meal without interruption. Read a book! Have a conversation face-to-face with a human being! Or meet a woman without the Internet as your World Wide Pimp!"

In hopes of saving Scrooge, Marley promised visits by three spirits, the Ghost of Pagers Past, the Ghost of Mobile Telephony Present, and the (truly hideous) future Ghost of Wearable Electronics and Barcodes Tattooed on Your Ass.

That night, the three spirits worked a miracle. Scrooge vowed to mend his ways by reducing his telecommunications to one landline and a smartphone with an unlisted number. With tears in his eyes, he vowed to help Bob Cratchit raise his family and to save Tiny Tim's life.

Alas! Scrooge's best intentions didn't quite work out.

First thing Christmas morning, Scrooge flung open the window and called out to a boy passing by … then another boy, then twenty more boys, several girls and a wandering beagle. Everyone, except the dog, couldn't hear Scrooge's desperate pleas. They were all talking on their portables, composing text messages, watching TV on their displays or playing video games. Scrooge reluctantly grabbed the phone to call the butcher and have him send a big turkey to Bob Cratchit's house. But the butcher was using his message function to screen calls. Scrooge tried visiting a website, "bigturkeys.com", but discovered that it had gone bankrupt three years before in the dotcom crash.

Scrooge kept calling—all day. He couldn't reach anyone except the Tokyo Stock Exchange. Bob Cratchit's family ended up eating beans and weenies for Christmas dinner. Tiny Tim died a month later and—without Tim to save—Scrooge fired Bob Cratchit and outsourced his job to a phone bank in Calcutta.

On the other hand, thanks to being "always on," Scrooge got in on the ground floor when Verizon, Vodafone and Google merged with Deutsche Telekom and Halliburton. Then the new conglomerate partnered with Microsoft and bought controlling interest in the United States of America.

Finally, one of the lessons Scrooge had learned from his spooky Christmas Eve paid off. When America's new CEO, Bill Gates, appointed E.B. Scrooge the president of the United States, Scrooge remembered a prophecy made by the last Ghost.

He ordered barcodes tattooed on everybody's ass.

15 Dec. '04

You better watch out!

Lately, a typical day in the news cycle tends to dwell on thumbscrews and red-hot pokers. With ten shopping days 'til Christmas, for example, the *New York Times* featured six torture stories—not counting the one about how Supreme Court nominee Samuel Alito thought doing a body-cavity search on a ten-year-old girl would take a bite out of crime.

So I wasn't surprised to hear about the apparent abduction of hundreds of children to a shadowy network of "black sites" north of the Arctic Circle. It was alleged that these kids, all of whom had records of "acting up" in school and "insubordination" in settings such as Pop Warner practice and Cub Scout Pack meetings, were subject—while being held at these secret locations—to physical and psychological duress tantamount to torture. In almost every case, these children suddenly showed up back at home after three or four days, accusing "jolly old Saint Nick" of being the mastermind behind their mistreatment.

Authorities at first dismissed these charges against Santa as "tall tales" fabricated by agnostics as part of "the war on Christmas." However, a rash of abduction claims—and their eerie similarity—eventually triggered investigations.

One such case involved Robert "Little Bobby Shaftoe" of Upper Falls, Virginia.

Shaftoe claims that, on his way home from school, he was thrown into a black van, where he was stripped, bound, blindfolded, drugged, diapered, stuffed into a Doctor Denton's sleeper and transported for almost twelve hours, finally awakening in a bare cinder-block cell. For three days, teams of interrogators—all of them incredibly short, with pointy ears, wearing green outfits and bells on their toes—demanded to know if Bobby had been "naughty or nice."

Shaftoe said these "midgets," as he called them, grew furious when he insisted that he'd been "nice." Demanding that he confess to numerous "naughty" acts, the "midgets" slapped Shaftoe repeatedly. They kept him awake by flashing red and green lights blindingly into his cell twenty-four hours a day while playing, over and over again, the Beach Boys' Christmas Album.

After that, things got worse. Shaftoe was forced to look at nude photos of Barbie performing unnatural acts with Ken, G.I. Joe and Kermit the Frog. Once, a fat woman in a red dress with white fur trim put a leash on his neck and led him outdoors for a walk, naked, on the frozen tundra. All the while, she kept saying, "You are such a naughty, naughty boy. Aren't you a naughty boy? Admit it! You're naughty and nasty and filthy. You're a sick, twisted little bare-assed bad boy, aren't you?"

Eventually, terrified of another encounter with the fat woman, whom the "midgets" referred to only as "The Missus," Shaftoe confessed to stealing his sister Suzy's Halloween candy and lying about it to his parents. Just before his captors dropped him off in Upper Falls, they said that because he had confessed to "gross and habitual naughtiness," he was "gettin' nuttin' for Christmas."

Investigators have since determined that Shaftoe could not have swiped sister Suzy's Halloween candy. Shaftoe is an only child.

Inquiries into these mysterious kidnappings might have foundered if not for testimony from an informant known only to investigators as "Deep Stocking." In early contacts, Deep Stocking said he was not a "midget." "I'm a fuckin' elf, man. Look at the ears!"

Deep Stocking claimed membership in the North Pole's inner circle. He said he was in danger for his very life if his cooperation with authorities were ever revealed to the man fearfully referred to as "Manitoba Fats." These are excerpts from his statements:

"Every year, you got more kids everywhere, screamin' for more loot—really expensive stuff, too! But the North Pole is shrinking, man. And elves don't exactly grow on trees—even if there were any damn trees! Used t'be elf women were happy to breed like hamsters. Now, they all want careers! Still, we were keepin' up with demand until these upper-bracket tax cuts in the U.S. Man, the rich kids went totally ape. Used t'be some silver-spoon punk wanted an all-terrain vehicle from Santa. Okay, fine! But now the kid wants to drive the damn ATV around his own private twenty acres of national forest, wearing a lizardskin jumpsuit and a gold-plated helmet.

Used t'be your typical WASP princess wanted a doll with a wardrobe and a dollhouse. Now she wants a forty-room mansion in Bel Air, and she wants live people—we've been using illegals from Mexico and refugees from Haiti—to dress up in designer outfits, fix their hair and have tea parties with 'em. These brats are killin' us, man!

"Now, y'see, Fats' motto's always been 'Show me the money.' So we humor the greedy little narcissists. And, for public relations purposes, we also gotta throw a few candy canes and yo-yos to the poor kids. But we have a budget just like anybody. So the place where the squeeze hits is the middle class, like this Shaftoe moznik. If we can get kids like Bobby to admit he's been naughty, we can shave Santa's list, save a bundle and keep the goodies flowin' to the children of lobbyists, politicians and corporate CEOs—who underwrite our subsidies.

"Listen, Fats don't like to poke foreign objects into little girls' body cavities any more than you or I do. But his sleigh is only so deep, and those eight tiny reindeer ain't gettin' any bigger—or younger. He's doin' the best he can and—hey, this is the main thing, ya follow?—he's comin' across with what the market demands.

"Besides, once kids figure out that they might end up at Gitmo North with a lot of cigarette burns between their fingers, they'll eventually climb off Santa's lap and quit askin' for the world on a satin pillow. They might even go to church and find out how this mishigoss got started. If they do, then maybe Fats can cut 'em a break and lay off the rough stuff."

14 Dec. '05

A Christmas email

Dear Friends and Relatives:

Sure hope you'll receive this. Our server has been a little

balky lately, partly because of the big changes around the household. But more about that later.

We've all been in pretty good health this year. In fact, we're positive of that because of the vital signs surveillance module (VSSM) that came with our amazing home network. The VSSM keeps track of our temp, blood pressure, electrolytes, air and water quality, microbial infestations and bacterial load. And it puts out a piercing alarm whenever Dad's cholesterol tops three hundred, which is about three times a day. I've taken to carrying ear plugs at all times, just in case!

But golly. What a great system.

For those of you who haven't heard, last year, just before Christmas, Dad won a "major award" in an online quiz. The prize turned out that we were chosen as a test family for the Acme Total Home Interactive Networking Grid (THING), which—for the most part—is a real humdinger.

Except for a glitch or two.

Certainly, it's been a blessing to Dad because he doesn't have to run down to the basement and start swearing like a sailor every time the furnace goes on the fritz. The furnace is plugged in. Everything is plugged in! And lately, since Dad's been pretty much housebound, the THING video system has kept him occupied. He's able to simultaneously access sports, hardcore pornography and martial arts movies (he just loves this stuff) on our all-plasma, three-screen, picture-in-picture, digital-HD home theater. Around the clock! In fact, we haven't seen him out of his La-Z-Boy since before Veterans Day. Honestly, I'm not sure when or where he pees (excuse my French), and I can't find out by asking him. Since he logged into the embedded Sony Hypno-Vue anti-distraction vortex a month ago, he's less talkative than the interactive carrots in our Smart Refrigerator.

But we know (from the VSSM) that he's happy. And that's all that matters.

The best thing about THING for Randy, our youngest, is

the built-in one hundred-gigabyte MP3 music ecosystem, which he has not left—even one minute—for more than a year. I don't really understand how it works, but between his portable player and his PC, Randy apparently has a collection of almost 6.3 million songs. I can't imagine where he finds them all! Before he stopped talking to anyone else last February, he told me his goal in life is to listen to every single song, "even that old-timey crap by Mitch Miller and the McGuire Sisters" before he dies. After worrying about Randy's grades in school and wondering whether he would ever have a direction in life, it does my heart good to know he's living his dream.

And I'm sure that whenever we get out of the house again, the doctors at the emergency room can surgically remove Randy's earphones where they've been sort of absorbed into his head and correct that "fixed and dilated" problem with his eyes.

I honestly believe THING has given Ralphie, our oldest, a new lease on life. I can't tell you how glad I was to see him finally quit playing with that dangerous Red Ryder carbine-action two hundred-shot range model BB rifle with a compass in the stock. I lived in daily terror that he was going to shoot his eye out. Now, he devotes his free time—well, all of his time—to THING's online gaming system. I was a little concerned about his playmates during the six months he was glued to his PlayStation playing this exciting game called *Kindergarten Killing Spree*. Some of the players were, apparently, inmates in prison and patients in institutions. Also, I didn't really approve of him playing a game that was rated DD for "Deeply Disturbed." But since he switched to a new game, *Sort Out the Bodies Later, Bitch!* he's fallen in with a more wholesome online crowd, mainly from the office of the vice president of the United States.

Ralphie rarely takes a break from his video games, but that's copacetic with us because when he's not wreaking massive and unspeakable carnage in cyberspace, his behavior has been a little odd—like the time he ran out of the house screaming and disemboweled nine of the Bumpuses' hounds with his bare hands.

Luckily, now that we can't leave the house at all, the neighborhood pets are definitely safe from Ralphie. Ha ha.

Seriously, though, we've been pretty much stuck here at home ever since I swung my elbow carelessly in the kitchen and activated the "Panic Room" option on THING's remote control. This little "oops moment" sealed us indoors, prevented anyone from approaching within one hundred feet and shut down all outside communication, including emergency services. I guess this is one of those apps Acme's going to have to "tweak."

Not that I'm complaining! THING is really a wonderful innovation and totally secure—judging from the paramedics and SWAT team members who tried to crack it. Their bodies have been strewn on the lawn for two weeks now.

I have to admit, I'm feeling just a tad lonesome here, being the only one who actually knows that we're sealed up tighter than Melania Trump's sphincter. Dad, Randy and Ralphie all have their toys to occupy their every waking second. And—my apologies to everyone—I'm way behind on my Christmas shopping. This mean old THING won't even let me sneak onto the Lands' End website.

We're hoping here—well, I am, anyhow!—that the people outside (I notice a few FBI jackets and some people who look like National Guard and Acme Technical Support) will figure out a way to outsmart THING's security. I sure don't have the first clue what to do. Golly, I'm just a high-tech dummy! But we'll be running out of food and water just after New Year's. And I'd hate to miss the January white sales.

Most of all, I'd love to be able to do the laundry and flush the toilet again. The men of the house don't seem to mind, but frankly, the smell is starting to get on my nerves.

So, Happy Holidays everyone! If you're in our neighborhood,

drop by the old homestead and see how the "siege" is going! If you stand by the big oak tree and wave, we can just see you through the titanium mesh.

Love and kisses,
The Parkers

22 Dec. '05

Variations on a Nativity theme (#3)
The frisking of the Magi

JUDEA, ca. 0000 A.D. — Three elegant but dusty figures, astride camels, approach a frontier outpost somewhere in Palestine. Several burly men wearing the insignia of mighty Rome halt the travelers. One soldier speaks.

"Mornin', fellas. This is a security checkpoint. We're with the Transportation Security Administration of Rome, Judea Branch, Bethlehem Barracks. I'm Captain Lucius Suspisius. And these are my trusty sidekicks, Gropus, Friscus and Delaeius. We're gonna have to inspect your bags."

"Oh no, that won't be necessary," replies one of the travelers, whose silken raiment is a muted purple in hue. "We three kings of Orient are."

"King, shming," the lead centurion snarls. "Everybody gets inspected."

Melchior, the spokesking, acquiesces. "Very well, but please. We're in a hurry."

"Aren't we all?" says Suspisius. "So, you boys traveling for business or pleasure?"

"Oh, neither. We are westward leading, still proceeding—toward the perfect light, that we may fall prostrate at the feet of the Angel of Angels, Savior of Mankind, Lord of Hosts and newborn King of Israel."

"King of Israel?" says Suspisius, nervously. "Not so loud, pal. The only king in these parts is Herod. And he's not the type to welcome competition. If he thought there was a newborn king in this valley, he'd have us out impaling babies 'til we couldn't lift our sword arms."

"Oh, no, you misunderstand. We seek to worship not an earthly king, but he who rules over all of Heaven and Earth—a holy child born this day of a virgin mother."

Suspisius sighs. "Guys, look around. This is Judea—the armpit of the Middle East. All we got here is sheep, shepherds, sheep, dirt, fleas, lice, sheep and a lot of Hebrew terrorists with daggers and ax handles, not to mention the sheep. Did you ever stop to think you might've gotten a bum steer? I mean, of all places, how'd you end up here?"

"Oh, that's simple," says Melchior. "Over field and fountain, moor and mountain, we are following yonder star."

"Yonder star? Where?"

"Yonder."

"Really? I never noticed. How 'bout you, Friscus? Delaeius? You ever see yonder star?" The guards shake their heads.

"But that's impossible," says Melchior. "It's brighter than day, with choirs of angels bending near the earth to touch their harps of gold and sing that glorious song of old."

"Well, we work the day shift," says Suspisius. "And after we knock off, we tend to drink heavily. I've seen my share of snakes, pink elephants, little green men. But angels?"

"Well, never mind," says Melchior. "We're in a hurry. Remember?"

Suspisius makes a decision. "Okay, listen, you guys are a little strange, but you seem harmless. We're gonna let you through, but we still have to give your luggage a little once-over. Let's see that satchel there. You mind opening that up? Okay, that's—wait a minute. What is that stuff?"

"This. Oh, just a little frankincense. A gift for the holy—"

"Frankincense? What's it for?"

"Oh, well, you set a match to it, and it exudes this lovely—"

"Hold it, King! You're hauling combustible materials into

Judea during a period of Orange Alert? How much you got there?"

"About a pound, I guess."

"Whoa! Don't you know you can't carry more than 3.2 ounces of flammable or combustible fluids, pastes or powders, secured inside an unlocked TSA-approved terra-cotta container bearing the seal of the regional director of the provisional Roman government? This jewel-encrusted casket doesn't qualify, King. I'm gonna have to confiscate your ralphincense."

"Frankincense."

"Whatever. Let's get this over with, whaddya say? What the hell you got up there on your camel, guy?"

Balthazar looks alarmed. He says, "Myrrh. Actually, it's a little myrrh tree."

"A tree?" asks Suspisius. "You're taking a tree to Bethlehem?"

"Well," Melchior says softly, "Myrrh produces an aromatic resin useful for making perfume, potpourri—"

"No, no, no, no," says Suspisius. "You think they'd let me keep this cushy day-shift gig if I started letting people strew uninspected agricultural items all over the landscape? Haven't you guys ever heard of hoof-and-mouth disease? Smallpox? Cholera? Lepers!?"

"But, but," spluttered Melchior, "myrrh is just a fragrant unguent."

"Yeah, you look like a fragrant unguent, pal. What's with the lavender kimono anyhow? Listen, the agricultural inspector is due in a month. Meanwhile, your myrrh stays right here on that shelf, along with all the other loco weeds, toadstools and love-apple plants."

Suspisius next glares at Caspar. "You!" he bellows. "Open your pouch!"

Caspar obeys and Suspisius looks within. "Well, this I recognize. How much gold you got here, King-boy?"

"Perhaps ten ounces, perhaps—"

"Never mind," says Suspisius. "What we've got here, obviously, is a financial instrument whose value exceeds one thousand *aurei*. You can't enter Judea with that much gold. Think of the economy, King!"

"*Aurei*?" asks Melchior. "What's an *aurei*?"

"Funny you should ask, 'cause it looks like you've got about five thousand worth of 'em in here," says Suspisius. "And their journey to the West ends right here. Yo, Gropus, looks like Herod's gonna have a happy New Year, after all."

"Wait!" cries Melchior. "You're taking our gold and giving it to Herod?"

"That's the rule. Besides, Herod needs the money. Would you believe he blew his whole year's imperial allowance on a gal named Sal?"

"But you've seized everything. All our gifts to the Christchild. Though we are monarchs, we go destitute into Bethlehem."

"Listen, King. This here's the Roman Empire. You think Caesar got rich and powerful by letting foreigners cross borders with financial instruments big enough to gag a dromedary?" asks Suspisius. "Which reminds me: How long since you deloused those mangy camels? And by the way, your shoes. You got any metal in your shoes?"

"Well," says Melchior, crestfallen, "the stitching is spun silver."

"Okay, take 'em off. Leave 'em behind."

"Barefoot?" wails Caspar. "Barefoot into Bethlehem?"

"Please, have mercy," begs Melchior. "It's supposed to say in the Bible that we came bearing a veritable king's ransom. But now, Holy Scripture will be a lie. The Savior gets nothing from the Magi."

"Ah, he's better off, trust me," says Suspisius. "You give the little *pisher* all this stuff, pretty soon he'll start putting on airs like you guys—acting like he was King of the Jews or somethin'. Not good."

"Yeah," says Delaeius. "Around here, that's the sort of attitude could get you crucified."

12 Dec. '07

A viral Christmas story

When the electronic engineering team at VeebCo formulated the most elegant and revolutionary design ever conceived for a veeblefetzer, they were too excited to contain themselves. They were seen dancing in their lab coats and attempting handshakes far too complicated for any white man to execute successfully.

Word of the breakthrough leaked upstairs to the executive suites. Before the engineers could put their embryonic design back under wraps, a pride of marketing lions, their eyes glistening with yuletide greed, had descended upon the lab.

VeebCo's chief veeblefetzer engineer, Fred Frawley, met this onslaught by urging caution. "All we have is a prototype," he insisted. But he could not conceal the fact that this prototype could run circles around the SuperVeeb, a design that only fourteen months before had taken the veeblefetzer market by storm.

"It still has a few bugs. It's too costly to mass produce," said Frawley. "We haven't tested it in real-world conditions."

But marketing VP Vance Velvett was undeterred. "Great!" he said. "De-bug the hell out of this beauty! Test it, streamline it, slap on a paint job and have it ready by Christmas. Okay, big fella? Go for it! Let's roll!"

"Christmas?" protested Frawley. "It's already September. We couldn't begin to do all that by Christmas."

Velvett, however, was on a roll. "We'll call this baby UltraVeeb. Every kid in America is gonna be so excited they'll be threatening their moms and dads with hunger strikes and suicide attacks if they can't get their very own UltraVeeb from Santa. This is gonna be VeebCo's crowning glory!"

Crawley tried to calm Vance Velvett. "Even if we solve all the materials and production problems, we can't possibly build enough units before Christmas!"

Vance Velvett asked, "Are you sure?"

Frawley said, "Absolutely!"

Velvett said, "GREAT! This could turn out better than PlayStation 3, better than Wii, better than—be still, my heart—Tickle Me Elmo! We could be hip-deep in the greatest 'hot toy' shortage in holiday history. Picture it! Lines of parents stretching twice around Walmart at three in the morning. Moms mugging one another in the KayBee parking lot. Riots. Massacres! The first family on the block with a mint-edition UltraVeeb will have to hire SEAL Team Six to keep the neighbors from storming their rumpus room!"

The engineers appealed to VeebCo CEO, Wilbur "Veeb" Ewbank. He was torn between the immutable realities of R&D and a stockholder "community" clamoring for another consumer-product "home run." If Ewbank couldn't come through, the board would cut him off at the knees. He'd be forced to retire with barely forty million dollars and the villa in Monaco to his name. And VeebCo would probably have to close its last two domestic factories in Akron and Baltimore.

Vance Velvett assured the CEO that the mere announcement of UltraVeeb would double VeebCo's stock price. Production shortfalls could be finessed, as long as one UltraVeeb came off the line by Thanksgiving. Ewbank had no choice. He gave UltraVeeb the go-ahead.

The only skeptics were the engineers, who somehow had to squeeze ten gigabytes of veeble power—without adding cost—into a SuperVeeb chassis.

By Thanksgiving, America was buzzing over a half-dozen "consumer-generated" YouTube videos (with suspiciously high production values) that depicted kids veeblefetzing with such grace, speed, pleasure and sensuality that several megachurch evangelists spoke up to condemn UltraVeeb as the handiwork of the Devil.

Other VeebCo marketers advocated a bigger ad budget beyond Vance Velvett's daring viral YouTube marketing approach. But Velvett stuck with word of mouth as the lead strategy. "People don't trust ads," he told his team. "They hate corporations, and they've given up on TV. But they believe each other's Internet posts implicitly even though they know everyone on the Web is operating under a phony identity. They know that most other people—in real life—are idiots, but on the Web—somehow—everybody's Walter Cronkite. It's never been easier to sell something—anything!—in America. I tell ya, guys, I have found God, and his name is Google!"

On Sunday after Thanksgiving, the first UltraVeeb queue appeared outside a Toys R Us in Atlanta. Within forty-eight hours, an estimated 5.6 million American parents were calling in sick to stake out the veeblefetzer departments at Kmart, Sears, Best Buy, Target and every other consumer electronics outlet in the U.S.

Two days later, Frawley reported that the lab was unable to make a workable UltraVeeb for less than $26,000. They wouldn't get close to the Christmas deadline.

"GREAT!" exulted Vance Velvett. "Thank your whole team. Now, take the rest of the holidays off. You did a magnificent job!"

A moment later, Vance Velvett was ordering VeebCo's software engineering division to patch together a SuperVeeb upgrade that would turn it from semiautomatic to automatic. The engineers hesitated, worried that the upgrade—although technically feasible—might result in power overloads and flux degradations that could be hazardous. Frawley's hardware team agreed emphatically with this warning.

Quickly, Vance Velvett called Legal, who concluded that

the cost-benefit analysis favored the SuperVeeb upgrade by a factor of 3:2, which Accounting computed as a net positive revenue balance of $410 million.

"No-brainer," concluded Velvett. "We've got a projected inventory of twenty-five million SuperVeebs to unload. You guys either put out the upgrade or empty out your desks."

The next day, VeebCo announced that everyone queuing up for an UltraVeeb console would be able, immediately, to buy an "Extra SuperVeeb-Plus," with an add-on automatic-firing capability, titanium flux suppressors and stratocast stabilization—all for only $299. Best of all, each purchase would entitle the buyer to a FREE trade-up to UltraVeeb, redeemable as soon as the temporary production backup ended in "early January."

Everything fell beautifully into place. Within six hours, twenty million Extra SuperVeeb-Pluses, with software mimicking the future performance of UltraVeeb, the ultimate veeblefetzer, flew off the shelves.

It wasn't until late morning on December 26 that the first cost-benefit casualty, a nine-year-old boy in Enid, Oklahoma, named Timothy "Tiny Tim" Cratchit, was horribly disfigured by shrapnel from an exploding Extra SuperVeeb-Plus.

14 Dec. '07

Variations on a Nativity theme (#4)
The manger incident

BETHLEHEM, 0000 A.D. — The Virgin Mary noticed that the rude shed behind the inn was growing uncomfortably crowded. She said, "Joseph, for God's sake, make yourself useful. Clear out some of this riffraff. You might want to start with that freak in the red suit and patent leather boots."

Joseph roused himself for action, but before he could move, the red-suited weirdo had squeezed right up to the manger and put his nose, remarkably like a cherry, right up to the newborn Christchild. "Cute li'l tyke ya got here," said the intruder.

Then, he stood up straight and introduced himself. "Claus," he said. "Santa Claus." He handed Joseph his card, which included a blizzard of nicknames—Saint Nick, Kris Kringle, Father Christmas, etc. and a nonsense address: North Pole.

"But I'm in a hurry. Have to make my rounds, you know. Ho ho," said Claus.

"Ho ho?" asked Joseph.

"Continents to cover before I sleep. And my coursers are champing at the bit," he said, mysteriously. "So, what's your pleasure? What do I pull from my bag for the kid?"

"Coursers? Bag?" asked Joseph. "What's a continent?"

But the crimson-garbed visitor was busy. "How about a nice string of jingle bells to hang over his crib? They love that," said Claus. "Or maybe a set of alphabet blocks? Perhaps a candy cane for him to suck? Oh, I've got it! A security blanket—à la Linus!"

"Linus?" asked Joseph, still clueless.

"Linus!" said Claus. "Yes! 'A Charlie Brown Christmas!'" Vince Guaraldi. An all-time yuletide favorite. You'll recognize it if I hum a few bars."

Claus then began to actually hum, slightly off-key. He was stopped abruptly by Mary, who had picked up the restless babe and swaddled him protectively to her breast.

"I don't know who you think you are, but you're bothering the son of God, the Savior of mankind, the everlasting light, the hopes and fears of all the years—"

"—are met in thee tonight!" Claus broke in, musically. "I know that one by heart."

"Know *what* one by heart?" asked Mary, now as flustered as Joseph.

"The carol," said Claus. "'Oh, Little Town of Bethlehem.' I know 'em all. Fact is, ma'am, I know Christmas backwards and forwards. I should! I'm freakin' Santa Claus. Ho, ho, ho and all that! Y'understand?"

Mary didn't think the intruder was showing the proper respect—or sanity. "I think you'd better leave," she said. "This is a holy night."

"I know that one, too," said Claus. "Oh, Holy Night, the stars are brightly—"

"Hey!" snapped Mary, losing her composure. "You're ruining the mood here, lardass. Why don't you just roll up your beard and hit the road?"

Claus paused, his droll little mouth drawn up like a bow. "Road? Mary, I don't need roads. I've got a miniature sleigh with eight tiny reindeer. And they fly!"

"Well, then, loudmouth," said the Virgin, "why don't you just take a flying—"

Suddenly, noticing something in the corner of his eye, Claus turned with a jerk, and laying a finger aside his nose, he shouted, "You guys! Who're you?"

One of three regally-dressed newcomers shoved a shepherd aside and said, "We three kings of Orient are. Bearing gifts we traverse—"

"Gifts! Finally! Now *that's* the Christmas spirit! Ho, ho, HO!" bellowed Claus merrily, frightening the oxen. "Whaddya got?"

The kings did their best to present their offerings of gold, frankincense and myrrh to baby Jesus, but Claus horned in, laughing like a bowlful of jelly. "Gold! Terrific! Nice choice, Melchior," he said. "Joe, you'll want to take this right to the First National Bank of Nazareth and start up a nice Christmas Club account for the kid."

Claus was less enthusiastic about the other gifts. "Guys, really! Frankincense for a newborn? I'm a grownup, and I got no use at all for this stuff. And myrrh? I don't even know what the hell myrrh is," said Claus. "Listen, boys, this is not rocket science. The golden rule of Christmas shopping is age-appropriate giving. Caspar, for instance—two words. You listening? Teddy bear!"

Among the worshippers there arose such a clatter that even Claus finally perceived what was the matter. "Hey, don't beg me to stay," he said, a right jolly old elf. "This is my big night. By the way, Joseph, hey! You gotta put a chimney in this dump. I had to come in through the front door. Look at me! I should be tarnished with ashes and soot!"

"I thought you'd never leave," said Mary. "I only pray that, after you go, we can restore the somber and reverent spirit of this blessed occasion."

"Somber? Reverent? Gimme a break," said Claus with a wink of his eye and a twist of his head. "Without me, Christmas ain't Christmas, toots. If me and the elves don't work overtime all year, all this poor kid is ever gonna get is frankincense and Fruit of the Looms."

The Virgin looked Claus proudly in the eye and said, "This babe, Jesus, son of our Lord, will be loved and worshipped throughout the world for all time. Great choirs will sing his praises. Empires will tremble. Temples and cathedrals will be built in his name."

"Choirs?" scoffed Claus. "Churches? Empires? Is that all ya got?"

"My Jesus will rise into Heaven and sit at the right hand of God," Mary persisted.

"Oh yeah? You know where I sit every year?" said Claus. "Smack-dab in the middle of Macy's, on top of a mountain of holiday loot—from Thanksgiving 'til Christmas Eve. You may have the Lord of Hosts and a flock of angels bending near the Earth, but I've got Walmart, Neiman Marcus, Toys R Us and Victoria's Secret. You may have Christ, lady, but me—I've got *Christmas,* lock, stock and Rudolph."

He stood for a moment, swollen and arrogant in the tiny ox-shed, looming over the babe in the manger. Then he turned to leave, shouting as he did so, "Hey, kid, you with the drum. I need a little exit music! Something befitting my station. Here, try this: *Pa rum pum pum pum*. Yeah, that's good. Keep it up 'til I drive out of sight.

"Happy last-minute shopping. Stores are open all night!"

10 Dec. '08

A 3-D Christmas

PARIS — For more than fifty years, the frustrating drawback to the broad adoption and popular acceptance of 3-D entertainment in motion pictures and television has been the simplest device among all the technologies that make 3-D possible—those annoying one-size-fits-nobody cardboard spectacles.

As anyone who has ever watched a 3-D film knows, 3-D images appear blurry, off-register and discolored unless filtered through special lenses. With these cheaters, however, this Christmas season's 3-D films are so dazzling that strong men swoon and toddlers wet their pants. However, these "glasses"—literally unchanged since the dawn of 3-D cinema in the 1950s—are clunky and inconvenient. Video industry experts agree that consumers will shun 3-D television if it requires them to keep a supply of ill-fitting disposable spectacles tucked somewhere in the family rec room.

Indeed, in a recent trial in Düsseldorf, Germany, one test subject was a man already tormented by a chronic tendency to misplace his remote control. On the second day of his test run, he lost track of his viewing specs. His reaction is recorded as the first known incident of "3-D rage." According to police, the apoplectic Düsseldorfer trashed his own living room and kicked his dog, a schnauzer named Fritzi, so violently that Fritzi coughed up two TV remotes that had been lodged apparently for months in his tummy. Only the timely intervention of neighbors prevented the furious TV viewer from battering his wife with a set-top box.

Such tragedies, however, are now unlikely thanks to a joint announcement here today at an international optics conference sponsored by the Consumer Electronics Alliance (CEA), the Motion Picture Association of America (MPAA) and the International Congress of Cosmetic Elective Surgery and Specialties (ICCESS).

"The need for those ugly 3-D glasses can be eliminated with a relatively easy, quick and inexpensive surgical procedure, declared the alliance's spokesman and ICCESS president, Dr. Alphonse Argus.

Dr. Argus explained that, in this procedure, a crack optical surgeon snips two tiny nerve ends and then inserts into each pupil a special electronic 3-D receptor. After a few healing days of blurriness, the patient can see 3-D video without a filter. Dr. Argus crowed, "Suddenly, any film or TV show augmented with 3-D technology explodes before the eye with a vividness, clarity and depth that virtually blows the viewer's mind.

In early trials, according to ICCESS, reactions have ranged from mere delight to an almost catatonic state of euphoria, which required several hours of recovery. "It's like a really good acid trip," said Dr. Argus, "if anybody here is old enough to remember that."

Dr. Argus noted one drawback to this surgery: the snipping of nerves leaves the patient unable to see the regular world all around in three dimensions or in color.

Dr. Argus deemed this "minor bug" a "blessing in disguise." He said, "Look, right now, the humdrum, or unpleasant, or downright unsightly visions of daily life appear to the human eye in rich color and infinite depth. This is quite impressive in an objective sense, but what are you really looking at? Your wife and kids never change. Your house, your breakfast, the traffic on your way to work, your desk, the drunk in the alley behind your office building. All this dreary rigmarole is a tragic waste of depth perception."

On the other hand, Dr. Argus continued, humanity's

richest experiences, "heart-rending movies like *Free Willy* and *Mamma Mia*, and deeply moving TV shows like *Love After Lockup* are relegated to a form that's flat and lifeless, denied the vivifying depth that our eyes lend to everything else. This is a cruel trick of nature and terribly unfair.

Dr. Argus hailed the collaboration among consumer electronics purveyors, Hollywood studios and the "angels of mercy" in the optical cosmetic surgery profession as "a historic breakthrough in visual evolution."

"Finally, ordinary sights will look—appropriately—like a re-run of *I Love Lucy*. But the moment a visually-augmented patient steps into a theater—either in the cineplex or at home—he will truly enter a magical otherworld of 3-D wonder, Dolby sound, HD resolution and ultra-Technicolor so intense that he will never want to return to stark reality."

According to Dr. Argus, ICCESS is poised to set up as many as 14,000 vision adjustment clinics in major cities throughout the "3-D viewing world." The clinics will be subsidized by grants from Hollywood studios, film production companies, television networks and major electronics manufacturers so that indigent TV viewers and filmgoers unable to afford the cost—roughly $12,000—of surgery can receive their 3-D implants veritably free of charge.

The first clinics will open this year on Black Friday in Los Angeles, New York, Paris, Tokyo and Indianapolis "so that our first lucky patients can watch 3-D video on Christmas morning."

"TV and movies are among the most democratic art forms ever conceived," said Dr. Argus. It's our duty, as believers in human rights, to ensure that everyone on Earth who wants and needs the personal fulfillment of 3-D video can undergo this vital—eye-opening—optical upgrade without regard to race, creed or economic circumstances."

Even in the traditionally gullible consumer electronics trade press, there are a few skeptics. One reporter, for example, challenged Dr. Argus. "Snipping nerves and impairing normal depth perception just to watch TV? Doesn't that violate the Hippocratic injunction to 'first, do no harm'?"

Replied Dr. Argus, "Well, is it really harmful to see dull things through dulled eyes if it means—on the other hand—that you can watch the delightful antics of Jessica Rabbit and wry expressions of George Clooney in three dazzling dimensions?"

"Besides, seriously," he added, "we're talkin' cosmetic, elective surgery, a practice that pretty much repealed the Hippocratic oath when the first silent movie star had her face lifted, and the first burlesque queen suddenly showed up with tits the size of volleyballs."

Dr. Argus finished by saying, "Certainly, sacrificing a lifetime of mundane depth perception for the sake of being able to see the next great Pixar-animated feature film exactly as God and Jeffrey Katzenberg intended, well, that's a tradeoff no sane consumer could pass up, especially during Christmas shopping season. Now, thanks to Hollywood, Silicon Valley and the compassionate caregivers in the worldwide nip-tuck community, nobody ever has to make so cruel a sacrifice."

22 Dec. '09

"I didn't come from these people."

GREAT NECK, N.Y. — Ever since I heard of him last summer, John Barnes has been a sort of hero to me.

According to news reports, Barnes is "a quiet, polite, unemployed man who ... had long felt different from the people he was told were his parents and siblings." He believed he had solved the mystery of these feelings when he came across the story of a little boy—the same age as John Barnes—

who'd been abducted from a Long Island grocery store in 1955. The missing boy, Steven Damman, was a mystery until he reappeared fifty-four years later in Kalkaska, Michigan, in the form of John Barnes.

Barnes said of his Michigan family, "I just knew I didn't come from these people," and then announced to the world his realization that he was the long-lost Steven Damman.

Boy, do I know how John—er, Steve, feels! The first time I had the exact same sensation of having been snatched by a masked man and dropped into the wrong clan, I was no more than five years old. My gene pool blues only got stronger as I got older—especially after I learned how to read and found out there were others just like me.

Among the most prevalent and compelling themes in fiction, from Tom Jones to Benjamin Braddock, is the character who feels misplaced and misunderstood among—supposedly—his own. There is no more vivid John Barnes moment than the scene in *The Graduate*, just after Benjamin has received from his doting but totally clueless parents an unsolicited, undesired scuba outfit. We watch Benjamin as he flipper-walks through throngs of mute, antic kith and kin into the swimming pool—where, finally, he finds solitude clinging to the drain hole and breathing compressed air.

John Barnes, wrenched from his Long Island roots and trapped in an unfamiliar, unfamilial family in the alien Midwest, was a real-life Holden Caulfield. He might have been one of a dozen disconnected, anguished characters created by Zola or—more poignantly—Dostoyevsky. He was Prince Myshkin. He was Raskolnikov. He was the underground man who knew not where he truly belonged, only that he did not belong here, among these objectionable people, whoever they were and whoever they thought he was.

The first real John Barnes moment in my memory was a Christmas day in Wisconsin. Every year, my alleged family on my mother's side would assemble somewhere to celebrate the holiday as populously as possible. And this was a family capable of staggering populosity. Mom had seven sisters and four brothers, all of them married and fiercely fecund. The venue that year was Uncle Bob and Aunt Aggie's four bedrooms and one abused bath in Necedah. Two-thirds of an overstuffed living room was occupied by an immense Christmas tree shedding needles like dandruff. The floor was invisible beneath shoals of trampled wrapping paper, ripped recently from several dozen disappointing fifty-cent Secret Santa gifts bought in bad taste by indifferent cousins.

Aggie's small kitchen was a fleshy melee of Grandma, aunts, aunts-in-law and cousinettes elbowing amongst one another as comestibles flew through their hundred hands from counter to stove to counter to table to counter to kitchen sink and back around all over again—ham, turkey, chicken, pork, potato salad, baked beans, macaroni salad, Waldorf salad, creamed corn casserole, green bean casserole, green Jell-O with shredded carrots, orange Jell-O with fruit cocktail, red Jell-O made pink with cream cheese, yellow Jell-O with little flecks of God-knows-what, and pies, cookies, cakes, cobblers, crumbles, marshmallows smothered in Dream Whip—on and on—filling every space, spilling over, landing face-down. *Clank*. *Splat*.

A narrow, inadequate serving table lay under siege by every cousin tall enough to tip over a bowl. The kitchen linoleum was slimy with a residue of snow melt, bacon spray, baby drool and mayonnaise. Uncles had claimed the beer supply and commandeered the dining room, occupying every movable chair, leaving women and children to either eat on foot or on the floor among the dogs, between pools of spilled Kool-Aid.

The sound in the house was a boozy male roar over a motherly threat drowned out by the bickering, squealing, wailing and puking of fifty underbred, overdressed infant hillbillies, every one allegedly blood of my blood, gene of my genes.

Outdoors was no escape. By three o'clock in the afternoon in the dead of winter, the sun was already months ago. The swift dusk of the Great White North hastened into a darkness so dense that it triggered claustrophobia and so cold that the moon recoiled into a pinpoint.

Repelled by the mob destroying the buffet, I backed up 'til I hit a wall, then rested by a hall tree and stood awhile in uffish thought. Observing my aunts as their hair went fright-wig in the kitchen steam and their voices grew froglike from screaming at kids, listening to the burps, farts and vulgarities generated by a herd of uncles, watching my cousins as they ate off paper plates with bare hands, gnawed chicken bones like jackals and smeared grease on their Sunday clothes, I was for the first time in my life the self-orphaned Huck. I just knew I didn't come from these people.

A year later, at Grandpa Schaller's up on Superior Avenue, I found refuge from the annual chaos. That Christmas Eve, I had scored a stack of Big Little Books. In T.J.'s big old house, where I had lived for a year in mute terror of my mother's father, I knew places to hide. So I did—poring through fat tales of *Mandrake the Magician*, *Buck Rogers*, *Bronc Peeler*, *Red Ryder*, *Little Annie Rooney* and the *Swiss Family Robinson*. As it turned out, there were a few cousins as weary as I of the yuletide riot. They found me, and we hunkered together in silent conspiracy, our lips barely moving as we turned the pages and basked in comic book corruption.

Those holidays from Hell imbued me with a lifelong horror of buffet-style dining and a keen appreciation of a warm corner and a good book. It's easier to appreciate the ordeal of Gregor Samsa if, dubious of your siblings and appalled by the madding crowd of random family, you have experienced Christmas as Kafka the Kid.

This, I suspect, was how it was for John Barnes, who, by the way, after everybody's DNA had been swabbed, cultured, autoclaved and analyzed, turned out to be John Barnes.

30 Nov. '10

An inconvenient Christmas

NORTH POLE — Senior Elf Pooky burst into Santa's office. His face was strained, his tone apocalyptic. "Santa! We gotta bug outa here!"

Santa could only respond with mute amazement as Pooky described the crisis. "Santa, we got leaks everywhere. There's water comin' through the floorboards. The Arctic Ocean is lappin' up against your sleigh. The North Pole is goin' under, Santa. It's global warming. It's killin' us, Nick."

Santa ho ho ho'd indulgently. "No, no, Pooky. Don't be silly. It's probably frozen pipes. Happens every winter," said Santa.

"Oh yeah?" screamed Pooky. "Well, tell that to the walruses who've moved into the elfs' quarters because they ran out of room on the ice floes—'cause there ain't no ice floes! Santa! We wouldn't mind, but wherever ya got walruses, ya got polar bears lookin' for food. And they think elves are appetizers. Nick, yesterday, Pinky got eaten."

Just then, Trixie Claus, Santa's nineteenth wife, burst into the room. "That's it, Nick," she said, "I'm moving back to the Playboy mansion."

Santa was thunderstruck. "Sweetheart, darling, honeybunch," he protested. "Haven't I given you everything? Sugarplums? Fur coats? That beautiful see-through negligee that you're wearing right now in front of Pooky, who's starting to drool?"

"Nick," said Trixie. "That round bed you got me. It's floating in two feet of ice-water. I lie down, look up in the mirror, I get seasick. I love ya, Nick, but I'm gone."

Trixie stormed out. Santa went pale and grabbed the elf. "Pooky, climate change or not, I need Trixie. She's the only thing keeping me warm. Where can we move to?"

Pooky rubbed his chin. "Well, we almost had that deal for a second workshop down in Alaska, But then you broke it off because the Inuits wanted casino rights."

"Inuits? What the hell's an Inuit."

"Eskimos, Santa. Y'gotta call 'em Inuits now. Santa, have you no grasp at all of politics?"

"Politics? Pooky, I can't get involved in politics. I'm Santa, goddammit."

"Well, Santa or not, you wouldn't let them build a casino next to your workshop, so the Inuits killed the deal. Now, thanks to your nonprofit Christmas spirit, we got no fallback."

"Well, get 'em back. Negotiate! Offer 'em a lifetime supply of candy canes."

Next day, Pooky returned in hip waders. "Okay, we got the Alaska property. But we had to give the Inuits a fleet of snowmobiles, a line of credit at Bloomingdale's, portable computers for all their kids, and the casino—with million-dollar slots, a sports book, Mariah Carey's floor show and a gentlemen's club. Laptops and lapdances, Nick."

"Whoa," said Santa. "Them Injuns drive a hard bargain."

"Inuits, Nick."

"Right. What you said."

"Anyway, they had us over a barrel, boss. And they remember you backing out last time," said Pooky. "You know the old Eskimo saying: 'Freeze me out once, shame on you. Freeze me out twice, and I'll slit your throat with a filleting knife.'"

Santa sighed. "This means no gifts for kids who are eligible for free school lunch, but ... what the hell. They can always get cotton underwear and No. 2 pencils from the Salvation Army."

"Okay then. All we need now is a new zip code," said Pooky. "I've been on hold for nine hours, but I finally got someone at the post office. Here."

A moment later, on Pooky's phone, Santa was trying to explain his problem.

"Look, fella," said a postal employee named Thelma. "In order to give you a NEW zip, you gotta tell me your OLD zip!"

"But there isn't an old zip. This is the North Pole, f'Pete's sake! I'm Santa Claus."

"Yeah, and I'm the Tooth Fairy. Look, Mac, what you need is a congressman."

Santa found himself on hold, where he stayed for almost an hour. Finally, a smoky voice said, "Hi there, constituent! This is John Boehner, incoming Speaker of the House. But, heck, don't think of me as the most powerful guy from Ohio since Warren G. Harding. Call me Woody. What can I do ya for?"

Loath though he was to deal with a politician, Santa told his tale, only to have Boehner reply, "Okay, enough with the kiddin' around, fella. Who is this, really?"

"I'm Santa Claus. St. Nick, in the flesh! Honest to God, Woody! Listen to this: Ho ho ho."

More laughter. "Well, I don't have time for half-ass impersonations. I'm the Speaker, y'know. But I'll connect you with the only guy in D.C. who believes in Santa Claus."

Another long hold and then finally. "Golly. Is this really Santa?"

"Yes."

"Golly! Well, I want, let's see, a Lionel train set. A new bicycle. And a nuclear plant over by Tulsa. And oh, about six billion dollars in subsidies for our hog farmers and cotton growers. And gosh, I'd really like a date with Michelle Pfeiffer or maybe that colored girl with the great hooters—what's her name? Tyra something?"

"I beg your pardon," Santa interrupted. "Who is this?"

"Me? They didn't tell ya? I'm the senior senator from Oklahoma, James Inhofe."

Santa was hopeful. If a senator couldn't swing him a new

zip code, who could? He said he'd been forced to evacuate the fast-sinking North Pole. Senator Inhofe exclaimed, "Move out of the North Pole? Jumpin' jeepers, Santa! You can't do that! Think of the kiddies."

"Well, we don't have much choice. The ocean is creeping up around our chins, sir. Polar bears are eating our elves, and killer whales are circling my workshop. My reindeer are treading water. Rudolph's nose shorted out last Tuesday. We're hanging by a thread here, Senator. Christmas might well be the first casualty of global warming."

There was a long silence, after which the senator said, "Well, I'll be hangin' up now, mister, whoever you are. You should be ashamed, pretending to be Santa."

"But I am Santa! And all I need is a zip code! Why won't you help?"

"Listen, pal. I may believe in Santa Claus, the Easter Bunny, Tinker Bell, the Virgin Mary, the *Protocols of the Elders of Zion,* Area 51, the Warren Commission and WMD in Iraq, but I'm no fool, and I won't be taken for one," said Senator Inhofe. "Everybody knows there's no such thing as global warming."

10 Dec. '10

Variations on a Nativity theme (#5)
"We four kings of Orient are ..."
(with Zero Mostel in the role of Joseph)

PARIS — By the time they reached the manger in the little barn behind the crowded inn at Bethlehem, the three kings were dog-tired and bleary-eyed from their journey. But when the crowd of shepherds, farmers and beggars saw the splendor of the kings' caravan and the richness of their raiment, they fell back, creating a path to the rude crib where lay the Christchild, wrapped against the cold in a strip of linen torn from his mother's clothing.

As the kings approached, they were amazed. The babe seemed to be wreathed in a celestial light. Their hearts soared, for finally they were certain that they had fulfilled their quest to behold the newborn King of the Jews. Refreshed by the child's beauty, they knelt before him.

The fourth king, as usual, missed the whole scene. Before he could catch up to the three other Magi, the crowd closed again, leaving him in the muddy street, trying to peer between the burly bodies of shepherds and the wings of archangels.

The fourth king wasn't surprised. This was the story of his whole trip. Even before joining the caravan of Melchior the Babylonian, Caspar the Persian, and Balthazar the Arab, he had lost his camel, which drowned crossing the River Eh, which separates the fourth king's small kingdom of Ih from the neighboring caliphate of Eh. Forced to ride a donkey, breathing dust stirred up by the camels of the other Magi, the little king often fell behind, once far enough to be overtaken by a band of wandering brigands, who stripped him of everything he carried, including his gift to the Christchild, a beautiful crystal ashtray. The thieves left him only his satchel and his flea-bitten steed.

Now here he stood, a prince in his own land, but in Bethlehem a nobody, ankle-deep in icy mud, shunted aside by riffraff and the heavenly host. However, he had no hard feelings. Besides, he reasoned, the baby wasn't going anywhere. Meanwhile, a nice nap couldn't hurt.

Laying his beloved afghan on a patch of straw beside the barn, the small king curled up and swiftly dozed. He would have slept all night except for a rumor that spread through the barn about the presence of a fourth king.

He awoke to the sight of a great husky man with a gray beard towering over him. The man scowled angrily down at him. "So, what do we have here?" he grumbled. "Another stinking, useless king? Where are you from, Shorty? And where's your crown? Where are your jewels, your sword, your silver breastplate?"

As the fourth king struggled to his feet, someone whispered to him, "It's Joseph. The father of the babe."

Before he could say he was the king of Ih, Joseph shouted, "Aw, hell, I don't care where you come from. What I really wanna know is how you guys got to be kings, huh? It can't be your brains. Lookit this one over here!"

Joseph waved a hand toward Melchior, monarch of Babylon. "You know what this one brings for the kid? A chest full of gold! *Oy gevalt*! To Bethlehem, the poorest town in the poorest part of the poorest province in the Roman Empire, he brings gold for a baby—who can't buy *nothing*! Gold? For Christ's sake (this was, by the way, the first recorded utterance of this epithet), he's a baby! All right, so maybe Melchior thinks Mary and me should buy something for him? So, who in Bethlehem we gonna get to make change—for a gold piece worth maybe 10,000 shekels? In this whole wretched province, you couldn't get together 10,000 shekels! Oy, but now, there's shekels. And we've got 'em. Me and Mary. And we head back to Nazareth. You think every thief and cutthroat on the road isn't gonna know this Mr. and Mrs. Shlemiel with the screaming baby are carrying a chest full of gold from Babylon? Hah! I should live so long. They'll know! And they'll kill us to get it! This Melchior? Maybe a nice king. But with baby gifts? He's a *putz*!"

Next Joseph directed his fire at Caspar, benefactor of frankincense. "Hey, I give it a chance. I light it up," said Joseph. "Pretty soon, my God in Heaven! Already, you got the smell of cow manure and chicken shit, donkey crap and sheep dung, plus the B.O. from what?—fifty shepherds and farmers and bums in here who wouldn't recognize a bathtub if it crawled over and bit 'em on the *tuchis*. And on top of this, you light up this frankin*farshtinkner*? And suddenly, above my baby's manger, you got this purple cloud of oh-my-God that smells like—*oy vay*! I can't even tell you—I'd rather a water buffalo sat on my face! So, Caspar! Your frankincense? Thanks, but *ptui*!"

Timidly, the little king asked, "And what, pray tell, sir, did Balthazar bring?"

Joseph's eyes flamed. "Myrrh!" he bellowed. "What the hell is myrrh? Does anybody know?"

Silence fell. Even the fourth king, although a king, had no idea. No one knew. Balthazar finally cleared his throat and tried to explain.

He said, "It's—"

"I don't wanna hear!" roared Joseph. "I gotta goddamn baby here! If the baby can't eat it, or suck on it, or wear it, I don't want it. Kings! Hah! They're worse than these *farkakteh* angels, with their blaring trumpets and their boring songs. You!"

Joseph was pointing at the fourth king. "Yes?" said the fourth king.

"Whaddya got for my kid?"

The fourth king, of course, had *bupkes*. He thought of explaining the trials of his journey, the dead camel, the intractable donkey, the band of brigands, the dust, the fatigue. But he knew that Big Joe was in no mood to listen to someone else's troubles. The fourth king knew he must leave without honoring the newborn son of God. Sadly, he began gathering up his few belongings—his satchel, his old afghan ...

"Now that!" shouted Joseph, snatching the moth-eaten afghan from the fourth king's hand. "Is what I call a gift!"

The small king was stunned. He reached to take it back, crying out, "Oh, no. That's just my old afghan, knitted by my grandmother."

Suddenly, the fourth king found himself smothered in Joseph's embrace. Joe lifted the little sovereign clean off his feet while raising the dusty afghan high for all to see.

"He brings me a family heirloom—to swaddle my shivering

child!" proclaimed Joseph. "Now, this truly is a king among kings! All hail—er ..."

Joseph had to stop. He said, "Say, who are you, little *shaygetz*?"

The fourth king, haltingly, replied, "Me? I'm, um, the King of Ih."

"Huh?" said Joseph.

"No, Ih."

"Eh?"

"No, that's the next country over?"

"Eh?"

"Yes. But I'm from Ih."

"Huh?"

"No. Ih."

"Ah!"

"No, that's up north."

"Well, never mind all that," said Joseph as he led the fourth king to the manger and handed the well-worn but precious afghan to Mary. "Just tell us your Christian name, little fella."

"My name?" said the king. "Well, I'm called Jesus."

Joseph rubbed his chin. "Nu," he said, "this is a nice name, Jesus. Mary, maybe we should name the kid after the only one of this whole mob who brings a gift we can use?"

Mary, who was expertly swaddling the child and laying him in the manger, replied, "Joseph, I don't know. It is a lovely name, Jesus. But I was thinking we should name him Sheldon, for my rich rabbi uncle in Capernaum. He could do the boy a lot of good when he's ready to break in as a preacher. A nice temple of his own on the seashore ..."

"Mary, come on!" said Joseph. "Who needs your uncle Sheldon? We got a pot of gold here. We got frankincense. We even got this cockamamie myrrh. It's gotta be worth somethin'. Besides, what kind of a name is Sheldon Christ?"

"Well, Joseph," said Mary, "maybe, for once, you've got a point."

"Good! It's settled. We call the boy Jesus," said Joseph, giving the fourth king one more hug. "Now, you boys! You mighty kings of the Orient! Melchior, Caspar, and what's your name! Don't tell me you forgot to bring beer."

20 Dec. '11

The Ballad of Skagway Phil

(With apologies to Robert Service and all those who cherish his memory)

To be read aloud, with gusto, between renditions of "Deck the Halls" and "O Holy Night."

Santa's elves were whooping it up at the Eskimo Bar & Grill
When, in from the cold, so brazen and bold, strode the
   dastardly Skagway Phil.

The arctic wastes had known few crooks as filled with venom
   and rancor:
Phil robbed a bank in Dawson, it's said, and then he ate
   the banker.
Legend has it Davy Crockett killed a b'ar when he was three.
Well, Phil did, too. But first, he raped the bear repeatedly.

Seeing Phil, the elves grew still. They set aside their hooch
   and beer.

The party was nipped, the Eskimo gripped by the hairy hand of fear.
Here was a mob as hard as a spike—of trappers and roughnecks and Inuit whalers,
But none had the nerve to look Phil in the eye. Their faces went pale and then paler.

The gamblers, the barkeep, the floozies in red all knew what Phil came to do,
For he had it bad, he'd always been mad for the lady that's known as Lou.
He'd seen her one night at the Eskimo, through the smoke and the roar and the stench,
And said, "I'd wrestle polar bears if only I could win that wench!"

Now, Phil could get most anything, by fist, or gun, or bludgeon,
But lovely Lou rejected Phil and said she wasn't budgin'.
So, brokenhearted, Phil departed, raging as he sallied forth,
Commencing a spree of butchery that terrorized the Great White North …

… 'Til, suddenly, he disappeared. The tundra seemed to swallow Phil.
Some thought his love for Lou had waned; some said he got too bored to kill.
Whatever the cause, Phil went unspotted for many a frigid Yukon year.
Nor was there either chum or sweetheart, missing him, to shed a tear.

Now, here he was, as mad as hell, his eyes aflame and bloody red,
He bellowed, "If I can't have Lou, I mean, by God, to shoot her dead!"

He aimed his Colt at Hans the elf, who meekly, trembling,
 said,
"But she ain't here no longer, sir. Lou found herself a man
 and wed."

From deep within his soul, Phil wailed and then he raised a
 mighty furor.
His gunfire winged the barkeep, scattered elves and
 smithereened the mirror.
He grabbed the helpless Hans's neck and bounced him off a
 distant wall.
The whole saloon was froze with awe. You could've heard a
 feather fall.

"I want her here," roared Phil, "or swear to God, I'll kill you
 all!"
When suddenly, a jolly elf, quite oversized (near six feet tall),
Burst through the doors, his tummy huge, his eyes aglow
 with life.
"I hear," he grinned and said to Phil, "you used to know my
 wife."

This stranger dressed in red, with snow-white beard,
 gave Phil a jolt.
He staggered back a step then, scowling, poised to fire
 his deadly Colt.
But wait! The words sank in. Phil realized it must be true:
This geriatric tub of lard was doin' the gal that's known
 as Lou.

The fat man said, "Pleased t'meetcha, Phil," and after the
 slightest pause,
"The North Pole's glad to have you here. We hope you'll stay
 because
We welcome everyone up here. We'd better! After all,
 I'm Santa Claus!"

DAVID BENJAMIN

The giant elf concluded then with a deafening series of guffaws.

It took a minute. Phil couldn't believe the dazzler he had known as Lou,
Who used to party all night and stay abed 'til two next day (with two),
Who dealt from the bottom and bartered her charms with a pair of Chinese bookies
Was sweeping floors and darning socks and baking ginger cookies.

She'd up and married a bourgeois myth, the middle-class' Christmas fairy.
She'd given up the sportin' life to make a lot of ingrates "merry."
More sad than mad, Phil said to Santa, "Claus, I have to murder you.
Lou broke my heart, that's bad enough. But worse than that, you've broken Lou."

For a moment of suspense, they all thought Phil would draw and shoot.
Santa had no gun, he had no club, nor even a dagger hid in his boot.
But old Saint Nick, unarmed, was still a cunning cottonpicker.
As Phil took aim, his gun hand steady, well, Santa Claus began to snicker.

With quiet laughter, everyone saw, his rolls of flab commenced to flow
Until, from deep within, there rose that great, familiar "Ho ho ho!"
And, as that sound grew strong and rich, the merriment began to spread.

The youngest elves couldn't help but giggle, sugarplums dancing in each head.

The dance-hall gals were next to crack. The barkeep loosed a tenor chuckle.
As Santa went on ho-de-hoing, the sternest scowls began to buckle.
Whalers grinned and roughnecks laughed and slapped each other on the back.
Though Phil frowned grimly at the scene, his seething hate began to slack.

Maybe his love for Lou, he thought, had only been infatuation.
After years of jealousy and mayhem, Phil deserved, perhaps, vacation.
The scene before him rocked with mirth. Elves and whores rolled in the aisle.
Even the barroom cat, named Blackie, seemed to crack a Cheshire smile.

Skagway Phil relaxed his trigger finger, then he holstered up his gun.
Blowing his sweetheart's brains out now no longer seemed to him much fun.
The piano began, and Phil retreated, bellowing out as he took flight,
"Merry Christmas to all, you lucky stiffs. You get to breathe another night!"

25 Dec. '11

Christmas comes to FEMA

The weary old man, who had visited disaster agencies all across the northern hemisphere, finally arrived in Washington,

D.C., and staggered into the office of Craig Fugate, head of the Federal Emergency Management Agency (FEMA).

Fugate was clearly surprised at the sight of his visitor, a portly senior citizen in a smudged and soggy red suit, his white mane filthy, his long beard tangled with bits of flotsam and jetsam, a strand of seaweed clinging to his neck. The old-timer carried an immense bag that reeked of decomposition.

"Whew," said the old man. "My dogs are barkin'! Mind if I sit down?"

Fugate quickly gestured his exhausted, bedraggled guest to a chair and asked what had brought him—obviously a long way—to FEMA.

"You don't recognize me?" said the visitor. "Damn, I must really be a mess!"

Fugate confessed that he didn't know the stranger, who replied, "Well, dammit, boy. I'm Santa Claus. Father Christmas. Jolly old Saint friggin' Nick!"

At this, the FEMA director stared with disbelief and said, "Mister, I haven't believed in Santa Claus since I was seven years old. Even if I did, I don't see any reason why Santa would show up here. This is FEMA, old man. Not FAO Schwarz."

The stranger leapt to his feet, wroth with indignation. "Don't see any reason why I'm here?" he sputtered. "Where do you think I came from, kid?"

"All right, mister," said Fugate. "If you really were Santa Claus—which I doubt—you'd be from, well, the North Pole."

"You're catching on, kid," said the visitor. "Now tell me. Have you ever heard of global warming? Do you know what happened to the North Pole this summer?"

Fugate paused to think for a moment. Then it hit him. "It melted?"

"No flies on you, kid," said the sarcastic stranger. "Now, lemme show you something."

Suddenly, with a burst of strength that belied his age, the old-timer lifted his sack and dumped a great stinking heap onto the director's desk. It seemed to consist mostly of blood-stained animal hide and antlers.

"My God. What is this?"

The stranger sighed bitterly, his eyes filling with tears. "It's Blitzen!"

"Blitzen?"

"Yeah," said the visitor. "This is all I have left of my eight tiny reindeer. The Big Meltdown wiped out everything, kid. Mrs. Claus? She sank like a stone."

Fugate looked perplexed. "Well, I guess I understand. But the reindeer," said the FEMA chief. "I thought reindeer could swim."

"Swim?" said the old man. "Swim?! When suddenly, the whole polar ice cap disappears and all you got is ice-cold water for a hundred miles in every direction? And the only boat in the whole North Pole is a leaky sleigh? Yeah, kid, we did swim. We swam our asses off after the damn sleigh went down. And some of us made it to land, kid. But you know what was waiting for us on the beach?"

Fugate made a guess. "Polar bears?"

"Hey, you're sharper than you look, kid," said the visitor. "So, you probably know what polar bears' favorite snack is."

"Reindeer?"

In response, the stranger grabbed the carcass off the desk and shook it in Fugate's face. "This is all I could salvage, friend. And I had to fight off two polar bears, a pack of wolves and a flock of seagulls just to save this much of Blitzen's hide," said the stranger. "And please! Don't even ask what happened to Rudolph."

Fugate didn't ask. The stranger told him anyway: "Ripped to shreds by a pod of killer whales."

"Oh my God."

The FEMA chief realized he was starting to believe this far-fetched story. He said, "Wait a minute. This can't be true. Who are you, really?"

The old man sighed. "Santa Claus, dammit. I'm Kris everlovin' Kringle, kid!"

Fugate insisted on some sort of ID to prove this unlikely claim. The stranger patted his pockets until he finally found a waterlogged wallet. From it, he pulled a limp, wet Social Security card. It read, "Edmund Gwenn."

Craig Fugate, a student of the history of Christmas, realized the implications. "Holy smokes," he exclaimed. "You really *are* Santa Claus."

"Well," said Santa, "I'm glad that's finally settled. Now, what are you people gonna do to help me out? I'm a hell of a lot more important to the U.S. economy than a few waterlogged summer cottages on the goddamn Jersey shore."

"Well, I can't argue with that, Santa," said Fugate. "What do you need?"

"First of all, pontoons," said Santa. "About ten acres of 'em. If this is gonna happen every summer, I'm not gonna keep goin' down with the stinking ship. And then, you gotta help me get my elves back. They're going to want a lot more money than I was payin' 'em before."

"Why more money?"

"Look, kid. My elves used to think the whole world was the North Pole. They were ignorant and happy as long as I kept renewing their *Playboy* subscriptions. But with this disaster, they're spread all over the place. And you know how the old song goes: *'How you gonna keep 'em up on the Pole after they've seen Toronto?'*"

"There's a song?" said Fugate.

"Listen, kid, you just get the ball rolling. Send me a few million bucks, a whole lot of pontoons and the Army Corps of Engineers. If your boys come through, I guarantee a merry Christmas for all the kids in the world in 2013."

"Wait a minute! 2013?" said the FEMA chief. "What about this Christmas?"

"This Christmas, fuggedaboudit. Look, kid. I'm only Saint Nick. My biggest miracle is getting eight reindeer to fly in formation one night a year."

Fugate felt a wave of panic. Wasn't there any way to save the impending holiday?

"Well, I offered the job to a few of my fellow saints. Christopher, Peter, Augustine, Francis of Assisi, Ignatius of Loyola, Joan of Arc—you know, the usual suspects," said Santa. "But we're talkin' a huge job at the last minute. I got no takers until …"

"Until?"

"Well, good old St. Patrick. He said he'd try," said Santa. "Typical Irishman. Loaded to the gills with good intentions but, well … also loaded to the gills."

The FEMA director considered the dilemma: "Okay. So, Santa's toyshop is at the bottom of the Arctic Ocean, the reindeer have all been eaten by whales and bears, and St. Patrick—not Santa Claus—is the one who'll be crawling down chimneys all over the world?"

"That's about the size of it," said Santa as he stuffed pieces of Blitzen back into his bag. "Not to mention, the only Santa suit Paddy has isn't red. It's green. My God, what if some poor insomniac six-year-old *sees* him?"

"But Santa, without you on the job, what are all the children going to find under the tree?"

"Under the tree?" said Santa. "Oy! Don't ask."

"Please, I gotta know," said Fugate. "What are my grandchildren going to get for Christmas this year?"

"Your grandchildren? For Christmas? From Patrick?" Santa shook his head, setting loose a brief cascade of dirt and seaweed. A small crab crawled out of his beard.

"What else?" he said. "Potatoes."

5 Dec. '12

The Night Before Christ ... Mouse?

(With apologies to Clement Moore and everyone weary of silly Christmas parodies)

(To be read aloud, with gusto, between renditions of "Jingle Bells" and "Santa Baby")
'Twas the night before Christmas, when all through the house,
Not a creature was stirring—save for one little mouse.
Inside of a chimney-hung stocking was where
A rodent named Rosie was nesting, and there
Her mouselings were nestled all snug in their bed,
Fat with the sugarplums on which they'd just fed.
Now, Rosie had gnawed a small hole in the toe,
So she could see outside and instantly know
If anything odd or untoward was the matter—
Like the din that arose, with a shout and a clatter.
Concerned it might waken her mouse girls and boys,
Rose ran to the window to check out the noise.
When what to her wondering eyes did appear
But a fat man in flight and a whole bunch of deer,
All of them looking as though they might dash
Right into the house in a blood-curdling crash.
But the fat man was nimbler than his girth might suggest,
And the reindeer paid heed to his every behest.
He shouted their names while swooping and swerving:
"Now, Dasher! Now, Dancer! Now, Marvin and Irving!
On, Comet and Cupid! Blitzen, step on the gas!
And Rudolph, goddammit, quit draggin' your ass!"
By maybe an inch, he steered from the wall
And dropped on the roof like a medicine ball.

Rose trembled with fear as the house seemed to sway
'Neath the weight of the fat guy, his deer and his sleigh.
They pawed and they trampled. They slobbered and snorted.
Then the fat guy in red took his bag and transported
The load through the snow on the slippery roof,
His every step loud as an elephant's hoof.
As Rosie turned 'round, in a timorous crouch,
Old Fats, in the chimney, came down yelling, "Ouch!"
How he'd squeezed himself downward, the mouse couldn't see,
But there he sat wincing and rubbing his knee.
His suit was still crimson, his head to his toes.
But the filth in the chimney had ruined his clothes.
He looked like the homeless men Rosie had known
Before she had moved to the 'burbs from downtown.
The fat man was up now. He took in the scene.
The parlor'd been readied. 'Twas spotlessly clean,
With twinkling lights, garlands, a beautiful tree,
The babe in the manger, as sweet as could be,
A wreath on the mantel, with ribbons of silk.
By the tree, on a table, ah! Cookies and milk.
Old Fatso, who saw food, abandoned his bag—
He went for the sweets like a drunk on a jag.
He'd emptied his plate, but he then wanted more
And even tried eating the crumbs off the floor.
His round little belly gave out with a roar.
But then he espied them, the stockings all hung,
And lusting for sugarplums, Santa Claus sprung.
Now, Rosie, who feared for her eight baby mice,
Jumped onto the fat man. In less than a trice,
She had latched to his face with all of her claws,
His cherry-red nose clutched tight in her jaws.
Santa, surprised, spun 'round like a top
And tripped on his sack. In one mighty flop,
He toppled the tree, his voice shrill with pain,

DAVID BENJAMIN

As balls, lights and angels descended like rain.
The family's father, aroused from his sleep,
Came into the room with a cry and a leap.
"What th' hell's going on?" he bellowed at Fats.
Screamed Santa, "They're killin' me! Call off your rats!"
Suddenly stage-struck, Rose let go her grip.
Amid the confusion, 'twas easy to slip
Through sputtering lights and broken pine boughs
Back to the stocking that served as her house.
The fat man still floundered, a whale on the sand,
'Til father and mother had lent him a hand.
Poor Santa stood reeling, his face flushed and bleedful,
So sad for himself that he was not heedful
Of two little girls who had come down the stair,
Aware that Saint Nicholas—Gosh!—was right there.
But as Fats stood there wigless, both tots were appalled
By the pissed-off old geezer, fat, sooty and bald.
The kids got their presents and went back to bed,
Their greed satisfied, their fantasies dead.
"Screw the chimney," growled Fats, and left by the door,
While Mom and Dad cleaned up. They worked until four.
But Rosie had had a grand Christmas lark.
So, as she settled back down in the dark,
She purred to her babes, who were all sleeping tight,
"Happy Christmas to all mice, to *us* a good night!"

25 Dec. '13

Christmas through a glass, darkly

(In memory of Paul Keeffe, La Follette H.S., Class of '67)

On a recent visit to New York, I got together with a lifelong friend, Pat Keeffe, who was in the first graduating class ('65) at Robert M.

LaFollette High School in Madison. Earlier in the year, Pat and his family had mourned the too-soon loss of Pat's brother, Paul, who graduated with me in '67. Paul was handsome, funny, charming and spectacularly unpredictable.

Pat recalled reading—with Paul—one of my first Christmas stories. I'd written it when I was barely sixteen and lost it until Patty (Brill) Hammes (also '67) dug it up from her high-school newspaper archives. Pat Keeffe somehow remembered the story by its title. I promised him I'd find it and send a copy. Since it holds up well after all these years—better than a lot of stuff I've written since then—I've added it to this anthology.

Next Year, Bring Guns

The clock was near to chiming two o'clock in the morning. For the third time that night, I flashed the ready sign to Amos. Catching the signal, Saunders nudged Amos, who had dozed off. The waiting, clearly, had not gotten on his nerves. I ventured to breach the silence.

"Use your head, Amos."

My exclamation roused several idlers, including Clow and Wesley, upon whose brute strength the operation depended.

Another ten minutes passed uneventfully. We began to worry if he would ever come. Had he smelled a rat and just passed us over?

Then, finally, Wiese stirred clumsily. His keen ears had picked up the distant sound of jingling bells. In a second, it came to Bedrich, then Eloiten. Then, the rest of us heard. This was IT. We all took a tight grip on our bludgeons, truncheons and bodkins.

Moments later, clomping, trampling, prancing and pawing pounded on the roof above us. It was HIM. Hyland's iridescent eyes glowed in the darkness. They were a dead giveaway. Obis made him put on his sunglasses. We all breathed easier.

A clattering and scraping echoed from the chimney. He

was coming. We could hear him grunting and puffing, cursing obscenely under his labored breath. I clutched my icepick.

Suddenly, the coveted bag clunked into the hearth. Graves, losing control, lunged toward it. In the nick of time, Sidman, Parmelee and Ross seized Graves by the ankles and dragged him back. I made a quick check of our hiding places. Not one of us could be seen. The plan was set. Then, all eyes flashed to the fireplace as he kicked the sack aside and landed, coughing, in a cloud of fine ash. With a bend and a twist, he was free from the chimney.

And there he stood, red and sooty and sloppy, his yellow buck teeth protruding from his stringy gray beard, his hand—coated with grime—resting on his monstrous belly. He reeked of B.O. and reindeer manure. He lay his finger up side of his nose and then thrust it inside. He dug out a booger the size of a Swedish meatball and smeared it across his bodice. Then, scratching his crotch and lighting a cigarette, he straightened to his full height—a great big fat mountain of fuming pork grease.

Luveta turned her head in revulsion. Rahl whispered to me, "How does a tub of lard like that get down a chimney?"

Dragging the bulging sack to his side, he looked casually around, smirking. His pig eyes settled on the milk and cookies. Food. An expression of greed crossed his brow. He reached, compulsively, for the goodies. He had taken the bait.

A scant second too early, Siert took the cue and leapt from cover. He threw himself onto the back of the beast. The red giant, like a grizzly flicking away a squirrel, shoved Siert off and—with a roar of Neanderthal fury—set himself.

Waving our bludgeons, flashing our stilettos and crying, "Ya-a-a-ah! Blood!" we attacked the crimson creature.

Amos, Varney, Courtney, Graves, Obis, Festus, Campbell, Vilhjalmur, LaMont, Merten, Sidman, Ross, Corbin, Gerard, Traugott, Cathmor, Tayloe and Saunders hit him low.

Clow, Wesley, Wiese, Bedrich, Eliot, Eloiten, Hyland,

Parmelee, Rahl, Asa, Grover, Clifton, Dowse, Townsend, Bagnall, Myers, Jim and I hit him high.

Gillman, Elijah, Madison, Gray, Nym, Luveta and Adonis hit him in the middle.

Eyes blazing, nose flaring, snot flying, slaver foaming from his mouth, he swung left and right, smashing heads. Time and again, we pierced his immense overcoat with our daggers and bounced our clubs off his polyethylene skull.

His colossal strength, with the split second of warning that Siert had given him, was winning out. He tossed our slight bodies like matchsticks. I saw Wesley splat into the wall at the end of the room. Corbin was squashed beneath gargantuan feet. He took a last drag on his Camel and put it out in Luveta's eye, sending her screaming out the door and into the blizzard. He strangled Grover with a flick of his wrist.

Inch by inch, he retreated to the hearth. With the precious sack of toys before him, casting aside our futile efforts to halt him and destroy his evil reign of avarice and materialism, he disappeared—with a mighty shove—up the chimney.

We took the defeat hard, as hard as we had taken it the year before, and the year before that, and the whole twelve years before that. Maybe we were getting old.

An hour later, licking our wounds, we all went upstairs to nestle snug in our beds. As we filed out, stepping respectfully over the bodies of our dead, I turned to my comrades and said, "Next year, comrades, bring guns."

1 Dec.'14

Variations on a Nativity theme (#6)
"This show's gonna be huge!"

BETHLEHEM, 0000 A.D. — Contrary to popular legend, the desk clerk at the inn—whose name was Yifat—was sympathetic to the bedraggled couple who arrived from

Nazareth and asked for a room. After giving them the bad news that the inn was full up, Yifat said, "Wait a minute! I just got word that these three Magi from God knows where are searching for the Christchild—I mean, really! These days, who's NOT searching for the Christchild? But they're running late, and I can see that your wife is *really* pregnant. Whoa! Is she gonna have a baby or a camel? Seriously, though, the Presidential Suite is sitting empty. So why don't I sneak you two in there at the regular room rate, at least for tonight."

The couple was about to jump at the deal when a man small of stature with large, soulful eyes, horseshoe bald with abundant sideburns, a wispy mustache and wet lips interceded. "Not so fast there, Yifat, my good man. Not so fast!"

He shook hands all around. "How are ya! My name is Glick, Isadore Glick. But you should call me Izzy. I'm what my friends call a facilitator, and you don't wanna hear what my enemies call me! Hah! Listen, I couldn't help but hear Yifat utter the words 'Christchild' and 'pregnant' in the same paragraph. And it hit me!"

"What," said the man from Nazareth, "hit you?"

"An idea! A brainstorm! The chance of a lifetime? No! This is the chance of an epoch," raved Izzy. "But we have to set the scene. I mean, guys are gonna be writing about this moment for centuries! Centuries!"

"Moment? What moment?" asked the befuddled innkeeper.

"Look, Mac," Izzy rattled on, "the Christchild has to be poor and humble from the very beginning so that the wretched of the Earth can relate to him. So, I was hoping that you might have, like, a dirty, drafty servant's quarters. Maybe with a view of the offal pit?"

Yifat was visibly offended. "Listen, stranger. I've worked my *tuchis* off to make this into a two-star hotel. I've got locks on the doors, glass in the windows, clean sheets once a week. If you've got your heart set on wretchedness and squalor, I can't help ya. It's either the Presidential Suite or there's no room at the inn."

"'No room at the inn.' That's good!" said Izzy, "I gotta write that down."

Yifat said, "So, I'm sorry, pal. There *is* room at the inn. How about you leave these nice people alone?"

Izzy Glick, true to his vocation, was undeterred. "Wait a minute," he said. "On the way here, I saw out back this filthy, broken-down, disgusting little outbuilding."

"Out back? That's the stable, fella," said Yifat. "We don't put people—"

"Whaddya got there?" Izzy was excited.

"What do I got? What does anybody have in a stable? There's the cow, a donkey, a few chickens and goats. And it's hip-deep in fresh manure. It stinks."

"Really? Manure? That's great! It's perfect! What about a manger? You got a manger?"

"Well, of course. What's a stable without—"

"What about sheep? You got sheep? We need sheep!"

"You want sheep?"

"We gotta have sheep," demanded Izzy. "We're talkin' the Lamb of God here. Think symbolism, Yeef!"

Yifat, who suddenly had a new nickname, paused to consider this lunatic request. "Okay, yeah. There's my cousin, Shlomo. He has a flock he keeps on the hillside east of town. We don't usually invite Shlomo to family gatherings. Nice enough kid, but well … he smells of sheep."

"So, you can get Shlomo and his sheep to the stable?"

"I guess so. But why—"

"And angels!" said Izzy. "We need some angels."

Yifat rolled his eyes. "C'mon," he said, "Do I seem like a guy who knows angels? Look, I'm Jewish. Do Jews even have angels?"

"I'm afraid we do." Joseph entered the conversation.

"Joe, that's your name, right? You know some angels?" asked Izzy eagerly.

"Well, one of 'em, sort of," said Joseph, a little sheepishly. He paused, blushed and went on, "Actually, this is a little embarrassing. Y'see, I'm not the father here."

Izzy went white. "Say what?" he said. "Aren't you the girl's husband?"

"Of course I am."

"But not the babe's daddy?"

"It's complicated," muttered Joseph.

"Well, this is terrible," said Izzy, crestfallen. "You're telling me the Mother of God sleeps around? In Nazareth."

"No, it's not like that," replied Joseph. "'Cause there was an angel."

"*Where*," asked Izzy suspiciously, "was an angel?"

"Well, I wasn't there, in the room, at the time," Joseph confessed. "But what happened, as far as I know, is that this angel comes down from Heaven, into my wife Mary's bedroom, through the ceiling. Poof. And right there, he imbues Mary with the Holy Spirit and pumps into her womb the miraculous seed of the son of God. Never laid a finger on her, either. She's still a virgin."

The innkeeper took a step back. "Your wife got knocked up by an angel? And she kept her clothes on? And so did the angel?"

"Yes, well ..." Joseph actually blushed. "That's what she says."

"And you swallowed that?"

"Hey," said Joseph, "she's sixteen, she's gorgeous, she's demure, and she's a nice clean Jewish girl. Look at me. I'm fifty if I'm a day. I got corns, calluses, hardly any hair. My back is killing me and I can't see any farther than I can spit. My prostate is a mystery and I'm lucky if I can get it up once a month. But I'm married to the best-looking babe in Nazareth County. Am I gonna ask questions about how the girl got ... er, filled with the Holy Spirit?"

"Wow," exclaimed Izzy Glick. "What a scene! What a story!"

"What a crock," whispered Yifat.

Izzy patted Mary—who couldn't speak because she was having a contraction—on the hand. "Don't you worry, kid. With me in charge of this production, you're gonna be able to tell folks back home that there were angels heard on high, bending near the Earth, to touch their harps of gold."

"Harps of gold?" said Yifat, barking a sardonic laugh. "This is Bethlehem, pal. We'd consider ourselves well off if we had even one harp carved out of a dead olive bush."

Izzy scowled. "What? I don't believe it. You've got no musicians in this one-camel town? This is an occasion that screams out for music."

"Well, we do have a few musicians, sort of," said Yifat, a little defensively. "There's my brother-in-law, Moishe. He plays the three-string lute. You could call that a harp. And, for a few extra shekels, I guess Moishe could bring along his brother, Meshech, who's dynamite on the three-hole wooden whistle! Oh, yeah, and then there's my neighbor's kid, Egon, the little drummer boy."

"Egon?" said Izzy. "Doesn't sound like a Jewish name."

"Nah. He's a Philadelphian. All the good percussionists come from Philly."

"Oh, really?"

Izzy waved off the prospect of Moishe, Meshech and Egon. "Never mind all that. Leave the music up to me."

Izzy grabbed a little boy, whispered in his ear, handed him a coin and sent him hurrying off into the Palestinian night.

"So, okay," said Yifat wearily. "Are we good now?"

"Not really. We need a crowd. Lots of ye faithful, joyful and triumphant, beholding and adoring. Earth has to receive Heaven's all-gracious king in style. God and sinners reconciling, the soul feeling its worth and all that jazz. Dig?"

"I guess I dig, but rounding up an audience in this town?" said Yifat, skeptically. "Look, I can probably get Shlomo to herd his shepherd friends over here—although the smell?

Whew! And if there's music? I guess a few people might drop in, even to a stable."

Izzy wasn't satisfied. "Shepherds and drop-ins. Is that all? You're gonna get angels, right?"

"Maybe."

Izzy Glick shook his head. "Still not enough. We're talkin' history here, Yeef."

Yifat's face lit up. "Well, I do have these reservations for three kings of Orient coming this way. But they were due a week ago. That's why the Presidential Suite was available. I was holding it for 'em."

"Well, I can crash there in the meantime at the regular room rate," said Izzy. "I'll move out if these cats show up. I just hope the gifts they bring are fit for a king."

"Gifts? You expect gifts from total strangers?"

"Listen, if these guys are real kings, traversing afar over field and fountain, moor and mountain, trust me. They'll be bearing gifts."

Yifat shook his head. "Well, mister, I gotta hand it to ya. You've pretty much monopolized all the *chutzpah* in Bethlehem. Maybe you're the one can get away with frisking kings for their goodies ... if they ever show."

Ignoring this, Izzy continued, "Now, let's us four—you and me, Joe, and the lovely ... er, what's the girl's name?

"Mary," said Mary.

"Great. Perfect name. Old-fashioned with a little bit of sex," said Izzy. "Now, why don't we all take a look at that cozy little stable?"

Before they could object, Mary and Joseph had been led around behind the inn. They beheld the boniest cow they'd ever seen, standing forlorn and ankle-deep in manure in the gloomy recesses of a cramped, filthy stable.

"Not quite ready for prime time, is it?" said Izzy. "Not that this scene don't have possibilities. But something's missing. All we've got now for props is a hangdog cow and that broken-down manger. Even if we throw in your donkey ..."

With that, Izzy disappeared. Mary and Joseph did their best to clear some of the manure, spread straw and repair the manger. An hour later, as darkness fell, Izzy was back with a group of men and one boy, all carrying musical instruments. "Hey folks, look what I found! Shepherds from the hills around Bethlehem."

"We're not shepherds," insisted one of the group.

"Actually, M&J," said Izzy in a confidential tone, "they're the band. I just hired 'em—right out from under Herod's nose. He's gonna be totally pissed off. Hey, Mac, tell 'em what you call yourselves?"

"Little Caesar and the Romans," said the leader in a resentful tone. "Listen, man, you better make this gig worth our while. We've been rehearsing this 'Seven Veils' number for two weeks."

"Don't worry. You'll get paid," Izzy replied. "Besides, you gotta think big picture, Little Caesar. This show's gonna be *huge!*"

"Yeah, we've heard that from you before, Glick."

"I kid you not, Caes, Trust me. This one's gonna go down in biblical history."

"Biblical, right," sneered Little Caesar. "Is that why we have to wear these cockamamie shepherd threads?"

"Think about it, man. This is an opening night that's gonna resonate down through the centuries, but it screams out for *authenticity*, ya dig? It ain't gonna sell if the babe in the manger's surrounded by a lot of cool cats in shades with klezmers and Stratocasters. It's gotta be shepherds, okay? With staffs."

"Well, as long as we get paid," said Little Caesar.

"Oh, don't you worry about *that*!" said Izzy, avoiding eye contact. "Hey, dig it! Here come the sheep!"

Yifat arrived, leading a half-dozen sheep and his fragrant cousin Shlomo, who looked both dubious and anxious. He said to Izzy, "Sir, my boss is going to miss these sheep. He was planning to serve them for the big Saturnalia banquet tomorrow."

"Listen, kid. This deal is way bigger than a few bowls of mutton stew," Izzy broke in. "As Marie Antoinette is eventually gonna say, 'Let 'em eat cake.' Or fish. Or escarole!"

"Marie who?" said one of the Romans.

"Escarole?" said Joseph.

As Shlomo sank into anxious conversation with Yifat, Izzy busily arranged sheep, cow, donkey and faux shepherds around the stable. He added a stray puppy to the tableau, tossed around a few pine boughs and glowed with proprietary pride. Suddenly, he turned on Mary. "So, if it's a boy—oy, what am I sayin'? It's gotta be a boy!—whaddya gonna call him?"

"We were thinking, Jesus."

"Jesus? Really? Half the kids in Israel are Jesuses. I'm thinking—liberate your minds here a little bit, kids—something a little catchier. More exotic! Like—you ready?—Elvis."

"Elvis?" said Joseph. "What the hell kind of a name—"

"Look, Joe, we're creating an image here. This baby of yours—I kid you not—could be the Christchild everybody's waiting for. He *will be,* if I have anything to do with this production. All he needs is a good promoter! A facilitator. A man with a plan!"

Izzy could tell Joseph wasn't buying it.

"Picture it. Elvis Christ! With my help, little Elvis'll have followers before he hits puberty. Followers, Joe! Elvsites. Or Eliviciples. Pretty soon, there'll be a whole movement. Elvisism. Elvisanity. Something like that."

Mary, however, stuck with "Jesus" and crept back onto a pile of straw to have her baby in relative solitude.

The child was born that night. The pseudo-shepherds got bored and asked if they could play a few numbers. Izzy agreed, but not while tiny Jesus was asleep. "And tell your little drummer boy to keep it to a low roar," said Izzy. "He's not exactly Ringo Starr, y'know."

"Ringo who?" said Little Caesar.

Joseph couldn't understand why his wife had to nurse her firstborn in a stable amongst livestock and strangers. He'd been patient with Izzy, but he decided to finally put his foot down.

"Look, Joe, my man!" Izzy retorted. "You gotta start lookin' big picture here. You think I'm in this deal for the short haul? No way, bro. I can see things ten, twenty years down the road, Joe. Picture your little Elvis—I mean, Jesus—booked at every wedding, funeral and synagogue from Tarsus to Judea. Picture him playing the main gallery at the Temple—in Jerusalem! He's talking circles around the Sadducees and ripping into the moneychangers. As clear as day, I can see this kid—your son, Joe!—leading throngs of wide-eyed believers to a mountaintop somewhere in Galilee. Holding thousands spellbound for hours, praying, preaching, hallucinating, tossing off blessings like lollipops at a Fourth of July parade! I tell ya, Joe baby. This is gonna be *huge!*"

"Fourth of what?" asked Joseph.

Izzy kept talking, but Joseph never really understood the concept. The Nativity miracle might have died there in the stable if the Magi hadn't hit Bethlehem in the nick of time. "Now here," said Izzy, rubbing his hands and arching his eyebrows, "is a team I can work with. Yo, Caesar! Strike up the Romans!"

As the band swung into a ragtime riff, Izzy huddled with Balthazar, Melchior and Caspar. "Listen, your majesties, I know you've been on the road a long time, looking for this mythical Savior. Believe me, I know what you're going through. These are hard times. The world's in sin and error pining. Rome's running the show, and the local king is a sadistic puppet who's likely any minute to pop his gourd and serve up the local prophet's head on a platter for his slutty stepdaughter's bachelorette luncheon. And then he might grab you guys and turn you into dessert! Meanwhile, you've got freelance messiahs coming out of the woodwork. How you ever gonna tell the flimflammers from the real son of God?"

"We're sure we'll know him when we see him," said Caspar. "Heaven's all-gracious King will reveal himself. He will be young and innocent, but his voice will be wondrous, his message irresistible and his faith pure."

"For your sake, pal, I hope so. But you might just be barking up the wrong cedar," said Izzy. "What you boys have to do is think younger! Think Moses in the bulrushes. Madonna and Child. Babe in a manger. Think Jesus Christ!"

"Think who?" asked Balthazar.

With that, Izzy pushed aside several sheep. The Magi beheld a destitute newborn swaddled in rags lying in a smelly stable while lounge musicians in shepherd drag sawed away at "The Girl from Ipanema."

"*Voila,* gents: the perfect Christchild. This little bundle of joy hasn't been ruined yet by rabbis and Pharisees. He isn't even circumcised! His story is a blank slate. Lucky for all of us, though, it won't be blank for long because I happen to know a young scribe who can write it all up—my cousin Irv's nephew Luke. That boy can spin a yarn that'll boggle your mind, tickle your fancy, break your heart and turn this crummy stable into the Good Lord's tabernacle. By the time he's done, my boy Luke will have angels bending near the Earth, Heaven and nature singing, hallelujahs falling like snow, giant blinding stars rolling across the night sky like Apollo's chariot."

The three kings, who were dead on their feet and ready to end their quest with the first available Savior, wavered. Izzy sealed the deal by promising the Presidential Suite at the crowded inn.

"So, you made it," said Izzy. "You've got your newborn king. Did somebody mention that you gentlemen brought gifts?"

The Magi dug into their duffles and unwrapped their stash of gold, frankincense and myrrh.

"Give Joe there the frankincense and myrrh," said Izzy. "But I'd better hold the gold. The last thing the Christchild needs, image-wise, is for word to get out that he's hip-deep in the old do-re-mi, ya dig? The kid's gotta be a man of the people. Wear sandals. Catch fish. Work with his hands. Abe Lincoln and all that, y'know?"

"Abe who?" said Balthazar.

Izzy shouted over the music. "Hey, Joe! What do you do for a living?"

"I'm a carpenter."

"Far out! Is that perfect or what? Shades of Tim Hardin!" said Izzy to the Magi. "Come on. Let me introduce you boys to Joe, Mary and the everlovin' Savior of the world. I tell ya, fellas. This show's gonna be *huge!*"

"Tim who?" said Joseph.

10 Dec. '14

Christmas Doggerel, 2015

Two thousand fifteen years have passed
Since Jesus Christ was given birth.
He came, they say, with angels singing
Hymns of hope for peace on Earth.
But now at Christmastime we wage
Religious war in Bethlehem.
We halt the Magi at the border,
Proclaiming that it's Us or Them.
Zealots rage and export murder,
Demagogues exploit our fear,
Turning victims into monsters,
Warning that they're coming here.
Beneath a star, aglow with peace,
He was God's gift to us from Heav'n.
But what we want—from Santa—now
Is an AK-47.
Embracing children, lepers, whores,
He showed his love in every way,
While now our Christmas list consists
Of those we wish would go away.
This year a host of false messiahs
Cry out that we should set aflame
Whole nations we call infidel:
A holy war in Jesus' name.
Perhaps we should postpone this feast
Until we can—somehow—recall,
On just his birthday, once a year,
His message of goodwill …
… To all.

25 Dec. '15

He's ba-a-a-ack!

MADISON, Wis. — Sirens screaming, lights throbbing, Car 54 jumped the curb, dodged several trees, skidded violently and spun in a circle before lurching to a sudden stop in a snowbank just shy of the playground. By several inches, it missed flattening a little boy in a purple snowsuit.

Officer Muldoon burst from the cruiser, slipped on a patch of ice and executed an Oliver Hardy pratfall. Officer Toody exited more cautiously, found his footing and roared, "All right, people! What's goin' on here?"

A gigantic white figure separated himself from the throng in the park and loomed above Toody.

"Everything is fine here, Officer," he said. "Isn't that right, kids?"

The two policemen saw, arrayed behind the huge white thing, dozens of children, their faces glowing with joy. On the fringes of this happy bunch, however, a ring of grownups looked angry and riot-prone.

"Oh no!" shouted one. "Nothing's fine about this, you pedophile son of a bitch!"

"Mrs. Abernathy," the great white thing chided cheerfully, "language! There are children present."

Mrs. Abernathy responded with an oath unfit for middle-grade literature.

Officer Muldoon was on his feet. "All right, everybody. Settle down." He looked into the eerie black eyes of the ivory apparition. "Who are you? What's your name? What the hell are ya, anyhow?"

"I said I'd be back again someday," was the reply. "And ta-da! Here I am."

"Get away from my daughter, you filthy sicko!" came a voice from the crowd.

An angry rumble rose from the cluster of adults, interrupted by a childish voice that shouted, "We love you, Frosty!"

And the children began to cheer, dancing in circles around the immense creature, who seemed to be wearing a puffy outer covering of pure white material. Its body reached to the ground in three orblike sections. Its feet were not visible.

"Weirdest damn thing I ever saw," Toody muttered to Muldoon. "What is he, some kind of team mascot?"

Overhearing him, the thing called "Frosty" said, "Oh no. You see, I'm a—"

"He's a pervert!" came another voice from the crowd. "What's he doing in the park with our little babies?"

"He's our friend!" cried a child. Another cheer from the kids.

"He's a jolly happy soul!" shouted a little girl. "With a corn-cob pipe!"

Ignoring all this, Toody poked Frosty. He said, "This outfit. What's it made of? Gore-Tex? Goose down? Styrofoam?"

"It's snow."

"It's no what?" asked Muldoon.

"It's snow," repeated Frosty.

"What?"

Frosty smiled mischievously. He said, "No, he's on second."

"Who's on second?"

"He's on first."

"First? What?" asked Toody.

"Second base!" roared all the kids.

Muldoon pulled his gun. "All right, I'm serious here." He pointed the gun at Frosty. "Now, who the hell are you, fella?"

"I'm Frosty. The Snowman."

"Snow? I know what 'snow' means!" came the anguished voice of Mrs. Abernathy. "He's selling cocaine! Heroin! To my little Abraham!"

"Really, Mom. Cocaine?" yelled Abraham. "Don't be an idiot."

"Don't you backtalk me, you little—"

"Everybody! Quiet!" shouted Toody.

"It's all in the song, Officer," said Frosty to Muldoon.

"Song? What song?"

"You know." Frosty sang a few verses about how he "came to life one day," his "button nose, two eyes made out of coal." Etcetera.

"He's got dead eyes!" cried a mother. "Like a shark!"

"Take the pipe away from him, dammit!" shouted another. "This is a smoke-free park!"

"Snowmen don't smoke," replied one canny kid. "Their faces would melt."

"Yeah," said Abraham. "It's a prop."

Muldoon broke in.

"You say you're Frosty? The Snowman? In that stupid song?"

Frosty took offense. "Stupid? *Au contraire,* Officer. It's accurate. It's detailed. It's good journalism. Notice the old silk hat? Here, watch me dance around."

As Frosty did just that, a parent pushed forward. "What's he doing with that broomstick, huh?" he demanded. "Do you know what child molesters *do* with long, rigid, cylindrical objects?"

Frosty intervened, "The broom's part of the outfit. Standard snowman issue. Straight out of the manual," he said. "Just like all this laughing, playing and dancing around. It's what snowmen do."

"No, they don't!" shouted Mrs. Abernathy. "They never move. They just stand there with carrots in their face. And then they melt, thank God. You're no snowman. You're … you're … well, I don't know what you are. But I want you thrown in jail."

"But I'd melt in jail."

"Make America cold again!" cried the canny kid. The others cheered.

"Look, big guy," said Toody. "These parents are worried. I want you to tell us straight. What're you up to, hangin' around the park with all these little children? Whatever you're doin', it ain't normal."

"I agree," said Frosty. "Normally, snowmen don't get around much. But me? I can. I'm not sure why. Maybe it's the hat. But the kids love it. They'd follow me anywhere."

The kids roared in affirmation.

Mrs. Abernathy cried. "You won't take my little Abie, you monster!"

"Lock her up!" cried the kids.

"Shoot him!" cried the parents.

"What happens," Muldoon asked Toody, "if you shoot a snowman?"

Frosty decided not to find out the answer. "Well," he said, "I think my work is done here. Sorry, kids. The heat's on!"

With that, Frosty doffed his hat and popped his great white head right off his body. He tossed it to Abie Abernathy. Frosty's bodiless head winked at the kids, and they burst into joyous laughter.

"Now what?" said Officer Muldoon as the bottom two-thirds of Frosty sprouted legs and took off, with remarkable speed and agility—*thumpety thump thump*—toward the streets of town.

"Catch me if you can!" said Frosty's head.

"Stop!" shouted Toody, not sure whether to address Frosty's head or body.

"Abie! My man!" cried Frosty. "Hit me!"

Little Abie reared back. He threw Frosty's head in a long, arcing spiral. Frosty caught it neatly, jammed it back on his neckless torso and galloped to the top of a hill, trailing several children. He paused there. "I'll be back again someday!" he exclaimed in a clear and jolly tone. "Meanwhile, for God's sake, folks, try to lighten up!"

Muldoon and Toody were tempted to slog after Frosty in hot pursuit, but a radio call came in. Muldoon dove into Car 54 and stuck his head out a moment later.

"We gotta get to the mall!" he said, panic-stricken. "There's a fat, hairy geezer in a red suit luring little girls onto his lap—with candy canes and promises!"

And away the cops flew, like the down of a thistle.

8 Dec. '16

Christmas Doggerel, 2016

Hey, who remembers Wenceslas,
And who the hell was Stephen?
'Tis the season we ignore
What we say that we believe in.
Love, compassion, charity
Are easily forgotten
In a world, our leader says,
That's crappy, cruel and rotten.
All the news we like is fake,
And Santa Claus is on the take.
In any case, Black Friday's past
And hurry now, we must apply
Our energy to retail sales,
Unholster credit cards and buy.
The television ads advise
A cheesy diamond for your wife.
A Lexus with a huge red ribbon
Will turn around your crummy life.
In church, the priests insist the spirit
Of the season is the Child
Born in Bethlehem, who brought
A star to light the world, and smiled.
But do we really give a damn
For acting as our brother's keeper,
When we prefer to fence him off
And dig the moat a little deeper?
The Christmas babe said bring to me
Your poor, your sick, your huddled masses.
But we prefer a Savior now
Who counsels us to kick their asses.

'Twas the season once for giving,
But now we call our needy "takers."
We celebrate the rise of Herod's
Heartless, sticky-fingered fakers.
We'll gather in our living rooms,
Surround ourselves with near and dear,
But this will be a Christmas when
We feast behind a wall of fear.
We'll give our gifts, profess our love,
Our hope and faith have yet to cease.
But here and far away, the guns
Are shooting at the Dove of Peace.

25 Dec. '16

Christmas Doggerel, 2017

(with apologies to Mr. Carroll)

SANTAWOCKY
'Twas yoolish and the midgen droves
Did moil and merrify in sync.
All rudolph were the vixenhooves,
The noggers had a lot to drink.

Beware the Santawock, my boy,
The twinking grile, the silv'ry bling.
Beware the red probosculus
And hark no herald-angels sing!

He gripped his wenceslas and he
Then scroogely grinched a gruelbowl.
So rested he by the Christmas tree,
And fraughtly donnered up the hole.

A mousely stirring made him feel
A chill of regem angelorum.
He thought of Mom and falala'd
A pfeffernusse froosted for 'im.

But then a blitzen-footed din
Announced the Santawock was near.
Aslither, sooty, blunging in,
It said, "I'm parched, pal. Gotta beer?"

He swung the wenceslas around
And laid the jollosaurus down.
He snooked the bag from off the ground,
And then parumpummed back to town.

And hast thou brained the Santawock?
And glommed his trove of walmartloot,
And left the reinmoose on the roof?
I drink to you, my thievenpoof!
'Twas yoolish and the midgen droves
Did moil and merrify in sync.
All rudolph were the vixenhooves,
The noggers had a lot to drink.

"... Darkness is cheap, and Scrooge liked it ..."

PARIS — The "spirit of Christmas" isn't just a needlepoint sampler or a seasonal blurb. It's a philosophy of life. This dawned on me when I was still a kid, discovering on TV the 1938 Reginald Owen version of *A Christmas Carol*. The words of Ebenezer Scrooge's nephew Fred capture that philosophy.

"I have always thought of Christmastime, when it has come round—apart from the veneration due to its sacred name and origin, if anything belonging to it can be apart from that—as a good time; a kind, forgiving, charitable, pleasant time; the only time I know of, in the long calendar of the year, when men and women seem by one consent to open their shut-up hearts freely and to think of people below them as if they really were fellow passengers to the grave and not another race of creatures bound on other journeys ..."

This burst of oratory comes before Scrooge's haunted journey through Christmas Past and Christmas Yet to Come, on route to emergence from his cocoon of callous and miserly greed. Dickens' story implies the salvation for all mankind promised in the Nativity of the holiday's namesake, but the subtlety of that theme—Dickens never once drops the name of Jesus—lends to *A Christmas Carol* a sense of the universal. Dickens fashions from Luke's lyric a secular parable and a moral creed.

Watching the film version at an impressionable age turned me into a maven of Christmas stories and movies. I came to prefer Alastair Sim's 1951 portrayal of Scrooge over Reginald Owen's, partly because it hews closer to the Dickens script and partly because—also true to Dickens—Sim's character is darker, meaner and bitterer than any other Scrooge, before and after.

Fear, you see, is the secret ingredient. Inept Christmas

stories—they're everywhere this time of year—drip with sentimentality and sicken with treacle. Dickens' *Carol* is barely more sentimental than a Raymond Chandler novel. He drags Ebenezer Scrooge—and us with him—through the choleric London slums and holds up the skull faces of Want and Ignorance. He takes us straight to the doors of Death before giving Scrooge a break. The Dickens Rule is that you can't do Christmas without suspense. You need an air of menace.

Fear, greed and suspense are, for example, the elements that lurk within *A Christmas Story*, the now classic Bob Clark film based on the BB-gun saga in Jean Shepherd's anthology, *In God We Trust: All Others Pay Cash*. Shepherd's screenplay achieves the Dickensian balance of dark night—the terrifying department store Santa Claus snarling, "You'll shoot your eye out, kid!"—and morning light essential to a Christmas tale that doesn't cloy.

Of course, the best Christmas flick of all is Frank Capra's *It's a Wonderful Life*. The scenes in which George Bailey staggers through a Hobbesian hell with Clarence the angel are a chilling exercise in black-and-white bleakness. In the same alternate reality, Donna Reed gives one of the scariest Christmas movie performances ever filmed. Stripped of makeup and bereft of her soft-focus lens, fleeing in terror from her other-life husband, she becomes the stark, staring epitome of barren spinsterhood. Without the counterpoint of George Bailey's lifelong discontent, culminating in Clarence's horror show, the tearful, cheerful climax of Capra's film would collapse beneath a crushing load of feel-too-good shmaltz and Zuzu's petals.

In *It's a Wonderful Life*, echoing Dickens, there is more than message. There is an ideal for a human community that amends the golden rule. The spirit of Christmas, as expressed by Dickens and embodied by Scrooge, who, in the end, was "as good a friend, as good a master, and as good a man as the good old city knew," is a sort of golden rule 2.0:

"Do unto others more and better than you would ever expect anyone else to do unto you."

Dickens' fable reflects the higher standard of love, compassion and selflessness that the infant Christchild would eventually preach when he set forth on his grim journey to the ultimate sacrifice.

However, there's a rub here. The fatal—or perhaps merely tragic—flaw in all of our best-loved Christmas fiction, from Dickens to the Grinch, is the problem of probability. Scrooge, after all, is not moved to mend his rotten ways by the slightest measure of self-examination, nor by the supplications of his loving nephew Fred, nor by any living person. He only sees his malignancy after being visited, frightened, berated, browbeaten and transported through the Wayback Machine by a triumvirate of pushy ghosts.

Likewise, George Bailey only escapes despair and death through an angel's intercession.

In real life, with ghosts and angels hard to come by, the mere prospect of December 25 does little to melt the gilded hearts of the incorrigible. We need only regard the Oval Office, where now resides the closest facsimile of Ebenezer Scrooge we've ever encountered—greedy and cheap, selfish and suspicious, incurious, uncouth and seething with anger. Holed up against the world, he counts his coin and stuffs his purse. He shouts "Humbug!" at every word that does not please. He perceives no people below him. Squint though he might, he sees no "vacant seat in the poor chimney-corner, and a crutch without an owner, carefully preserved."

Our contemporary Scrooge bellows his defiant "Merry Christmas" without merriment or meaning. He raises it, rather, as a battle cry against a nebulous army of fancied foes and faithless mongrels who blaspheme against his name. He won't be enlightened and redeemed, either by Clarence or a King of the Jews in swaddling clothes. He is a Scrooge without self-examination, without doubt, without remorse or repentance, without a Marley to fear or Tiny Tim to save, without even the prize turkey in the poulterer's window.

In a nonfiction world, absent humility and generosity, without wisdom or wit, without grace and the hope of redemption, Christmas isn't much better than a BB in the eye.

7 Dec. '18

Christmas Doggerel, 2018
A Christmas miracle

The troops are strung like Christmas lights
along the Rio Grande.
A few are wearing Santa hats, but they are lined with Kevlar.
Razor wire and guns are not a holiday they'd planned,
And eating MREs in pup tents lacks a certain yuletide flavor.

Not far away, the migrants huddle, hungry and heartbroken,
Stranded at the river's edge in tragic, teeming mass.
They'd fled from terror to a land where freedom is outspoken
Only to encounter rifles, hatred, yellow clouds of gas.

One soldier sees a little girl who turns an empty box
With straw and colored rags into a makeshift manger.
Her sheep and shepherds, make-believe,
are merely sticks and rocks.
She tends her creche beneath the wire,
forgetful of the danger.

The soldier leaves his gun behind. He ventures softly near.
He leans across the deadly wire and looks into her eyes.
But even though his sign is peace, her face is taut with fear.
The soldier's smile—he thought it kind and friendly—dies.

Finally surrendering, the soldier draws away.
He hurries down a dusty road with hope that he can find
Perhaps a token that, if there at all, might possibly allay
The girl's abiding fear and grant him, maybe, peace of mind.

The sun has set, the evening's chill has
gripped the border while
The soldier hurries back to camp, his humble gift to share.
Digging deep and dirty, he had pulled it from a roadside pile.
It lacks an eye, its hair is sparse and it has not a stitch to wear.

The tiny girl has barely moved.
She turns and looks up, terrified,
And there she sees, in dying light,
the guilty soldier reach across
The cruel rolls of razor wire, stretching to the other side:
A plastic, naked baby doll, delivered with a gentle toss.

A GI's red bandanna then, he takes it off his head.
She knows exactly what to do and swiftly wraps
the grubby doll.
She lays her newborn Christchild gently
in a homely cardboard bed,
Then gazes up into the night, as though to
hear the angels call.

But hark the herald though she does,
no Christmas carols fill the night.
The soldiers' senses mimic her, but they
can hear no angels sing.
Still, the fear has left the girl, and on her
face there shines a light
That flows, it seems, directly from her tiny plastic King.

The light begins to grow, and finally it reveals a throng
Of refugees around the girl, tempest toss'd and yearning.
She lifts the Babe and carries him, the others
meekly come along.
The GIs snip and part the wire, their
fingers gashed and burning.

But then, their wounds—struck by the light—
miraculously healed.
A crowd of poor, still frightened folk,
as far as any eye can see,
Led safely by a glowing Child across an angry wall unsealed
Begins to do what once they barely dared to dream:
Breathe free.

DAVID BENJAMIN

Variations on a Nativity theme (#7)
The skeptical shepherd

I

A long time ago, on a cold winter's night that was so deep, a certain poor shepherd was keeping his sheep and trying to catch forty winks. But it wasn't easy. He was haunted, almost every time he nodded off, by visions he didn't understand.

The shepherd's friends kept telling him not to drink the cheap hooch that the bootleggers in Capernaum made from figs and fish liver. But it was the only brew that put him to sleep, although it always woke him later with nightmares and apparitions.

Tonight, the shepherd's problem wasn't the usual hallucinations. Beneath his eyelids, he perceived a brilliant light and, on a hillside usually as quiet as the grave, the noise was almost deafening. He opened one eye to peek and saw an angel bending near the Earth to touch his harp of gold. Worse, the angel wasn't just touching the harp. He was whaling away like Bruce Springsteen.

Of course, the shepherd had no idea who this Springsteen dude was going to be. He had merely seen him in an especially frightening vision one night after too much fig lightning. Hence, the angel's licks struck the shepherd as more ghastly than danceable.

"Hey, fella, listen," he said (well, he actually had to shout). "Could you practice that thing someplace else? I'm trying to get a little shut-eye."

"I'm not practicing, shepherd. I'm harking the herald!"

Realizing that he was dealing with a lunatic, the shepherd rolled over.

The angel paused in mid-riff and spoke. "Hey, I'm an angel. Didn't you notice the star? It's really bright—to guide our way. I'm harking the herald for the king of Israel, who is born this very night."

The shepherd recognized the type. He'd met them in taverns. This harp-twanger was not going to quiet down. Reluctantly, the shepherd sat up and rubbed his eyes. The lunatic was easy to see because, like the lunatic said, the sky was as bright as daytime, lit by a humongous star the shepherd had never before beheld.

"Why me?" he muttered to himself. He unsquinted his eyes and tried to focus. Somehow, the lunatic was hovering above the ground, flapping his wings. *Wings?* thought the shepherd. "Nu, maybe this really is an angel," he said under his breath. "What do I know from angels?"

But, no, he decided. This was just another one of his visions, and the freak with the wings would soon flit off over the hill, like a big-ass butterfly.

But he stayed. This was becoming the shepherd's longest nightmare ever, the worst part being whatever slightly off-key song the maniac was trying to play. The "angel's" instrument was the biggest harp the shepherd had ever laid eyes on. The apparition strung out a treble-boosted scream with his wah-wah pedal, and the shepherd winced.

"Ouch," said the shepherd. Thankfully, the guy in the sky took a break and started talking.

"Blessings to you from Our Lord on High. How are you called, humble shepherd?"

The shepherd didn't regard himself as all that humble. But he answered. "Amram. What's yours?"

"Noël," said the apparent angel.

"Hm, odd name," said Amram, who was growing curious about this floating maniac. "You're the first Noël I've ever met."

The angel's eyes lit up. "Hey, that's catchy! The first Noël! You mind if I use that?"

"Use it? For what?"

"Well, my main gig is playing my ax here. But, on the side, I do a little songwriting."

The shepherd sensed the conversation wandering. He said, "Sure, it's all yours. But please. What the hell are you doing here on my hill (if you're actually here at all), stirring up my sheep?"

"I told ya. Us angels are here to greet with anthems sweet the coming of the King of Kings, who salvation brings," said Noël. "And you guys are supposed to come along."

"Which guys?"

"The shepherds! Look around."

Amram peered across the hills. In the light from the star, he saw all of his fellow shepherds standing and hip-swaying dreamily to the music while Noël's backup band of angels harped away in deafening dissonance.

"Have you … um, angels considered the possibility of hiring an arranger?"

"So," said Noël, "rise and shine. Time's a wastin'!"

Amram, who took pride in his education—he had memorized several passages from the Torah—bridled. He shook his head. "I should go along with those shmucks. They're just ignorant shepherds."

"You think you're not an ignorant shepherd?" replied Noël, astutely.

This stung. Amram sighed but stood his ground. "Where am I supposed to be going?"

"Come to Bethlehem and see him, whose birth we angels sing," said Noël. "See him in a manger laid."

"Wait a minute. All the way to Bethlehem? In the dark?"

"It's not dark," said the angel. "We'll be following yonder star."

"Right. Well, I can't leave my sheep behind, especially to take a look at a baby in a manger. Who puts babies in mangers?"

The angel was stumped. All the other shepherds were swinging to the beat and ready to hump it to Bethlehem, except Amram. But Noël had orders from God. "Listen, we can't leave without you, Amram. We're running late."

"No, you listen to me, angel-puss, or whoever you are," said Amram. "I don't even know if you're real. I drink too much, y'know—and my stomach? Oy! You could be an indigested bit of beef, a blot of mustard, a crumb of cheese, a fragment of an underdone potato."

"Do I look like a potato?"

"Honestly, with the wings, you look like a fruit."

The angel puzzled over this. Clearly, he had not expected any flak from shepherds.

Amram went on. "Give me one reason, besides all of this singing, twanging and razzle-dazzle, why I should lose a good night's sleep and get blisters hiking to Bethlehem?"

"Well, because," stammered Noël, "because he's the Savior."

"Yeah? Whose Savior?"

"Your Savior! Everyone's Savior!"

"This baby over in Bethlehem. He's gonna save me from this?"

Noël, for the first time, studied Amram, who was grimy, wearing a ragged robe that was probably his only piece of clothing. He was old beyond his years, with streaks of gray in his dirty beard and scabs on his scalp. His feet, in straw sandals, were blue from the cold.

Amram straightened up and thrust out his chest defiantly. "I know what you mean, angel. I'm no fool. You're talking about saving us, all of mankind, from the sin and folly of our lives, hauling us up to Heaven and gathering us at the throne of God, right?"

Noël uttered a low whistle. He realized he wasn't dealing here with a run-of-the-mill wool-wrangler. "Well, that's the plan, more or less," he said.

Amram snorted. "C'mon, man. That's not what's gonna happen," he said. "Not the way you think it will. I know."

"You know?" asked the angel. A few other angels had drawn near, amused by Noël's argument with the ignorant shepherd. "What? How?"

"I have visions, man. I wish I didn't."

"Visions?"

"Yeah, you guys have Heaven and your friggin' harps. I got visions."

"Visions? Where does an ignorant shepherd get visions?"

"Beats the hell outa me," said Amram. "Maybe from God? Maybe he feels sorry for this rotten existence he's stuck me with. You know I haven't had a bath for four months. I've got balky sheep, my dog Morris hates my guts and my whole scrawny flock is surrounded by marauding wolves who'd just as soon kill me as piss on me. Take a whiff, Noël. I've got B.O. that would gag a camel, I got crabs in my crotch and lice building an entire civilization in my hair, and my clothes stink permanently of sheep shit. And there won't be a decent laundry detergent on Earth for at least eighteen centuries."

Noël interrupted Amram's bellyaching. "Laundry detergent? What's that?"

"Search me," said Amram. "I saw it in one of my stupid visions. I never get explanations. It's like a goddamn silent movie."

"What's a silent movie?" asked Noël.

"Hey, if I knew, I'd tell ya," said Amram, spreading his arms in exasperation.

"You get these ... visions often?"

"Seems like every other night," said Amram. "I think it's the future, but who knows? But if it is the future, that kid over in Bethlehem, well, trust me. He ain't gonna make this vale of tears any drier."

"But he's supposed to," said Noël. "He will."

"All better?" asked Amram pointedly.

The question perplexed the angel. "What do you mean?" he asked.

"Okay, I keep seeing this symbol in my nightmares—a cross. First time I saw it, this guy was hanging on it with nails through his hands. Nails! Through his *hands!* The poor sumbitch is all cut up, with a crown of thorns, blood running down his face and then—dear God!—this soldier goes up and rams a spear into the poor guy. And that's when I woke up."

"Well, that's awful," Noël said. He was so distressed that he put down his harp.

"Yeah, well, it gets worse," snapped Amram. "This cross keeps popping up every time I drink too much fig juice or fall asleep. I see this great wave of men in shining armor, on horses, with crosses on their chests. They're armed with spears and swords, and they're killing brown people, burning cities, pillaging the countryside. And the brown people are fighting back. The Earth is flowing with blood! But then, I see people—peaceful ones—gathering under the same cross, falling to their knees. I can hear them praising God. I want to understand, but before I can figure it out, I see a couple more armies. They're both waving banners with big fat crosses on 'em. They're charging one another and killing, killing. Again, the Earth is red with blood. Then I see a city, magnificent buildings with roofs of gold and great gold crosses piercing the sky. There are priests bedecked in gold and silk and vast crowds kneeling before them, singing, praying. And the priests are feeding the hungry, healing the sick, consoling the bereft and teaching everyone to read the word of God. And I think finally, after all that horror, a sort of Heaven on Earth …"

"Okay then! This is what I'm talkin' about," said Noël.

"Oh yeah?" said Amram. "Well, then explain this vision. I see a man, naked. I'm close enough that I can see that he's circumcised, like me. He's a Jew, poor deluded bastard. I see him in a great mass of people, all naked, being herded by men in uniforms with helmets. And on their collars, I can see skulls. Above this great mass of soldiers and naked Jews, a black cloud that smells of burning meat. And through the greasy cloud, I see it—the cross, again. It's black on a blood-red flag. But all its members are bent over, as though to break the arms and legs of those it crucifies."

"But this is just a dream," Noël protests. "It's not real."

"Right. You go ahead and believe that, up in Heaven, with the clouds and the harp and three squares a day."

Noël was perplexed by Amram's skepticism, an attitude unknown among angels.

"So," Amram continued, "you wanna hear last night's dream?"

"Probably not," replied Noël, looking mildly nauseous.

"Well, there's another cross. It's burning, set on fire by a figure in a white robe who's in the middle of a great crowd. They're all drinking and celebrating. And above them, hanging from a tree, another naked man. This one is black, twitching in the throes of death. He's all cut up, with a crown of barbed wire, blood running down his face, and then—dear God!—this robed figure goes up and rams a spear into the poor guy. His entrails spill out. And that's when I woke up, thank God."

Noël was silent.

"What does this mean, angel baby?" asked Amram. "Have I got the D.T.s, or is this some sort of prophecy? Is your Savior going to save us from all that?"

Noël picked up his harp. He fluttered away from Amram and signaled to the other angels. "I guess it'll be okay to go on to Bethlehem without you, Amram. Sorry I woke you."

"Yeah, well," replied Amram. "Sorry to be a party pooper."

And the angels floated down the road, followed by all the shepherds but one.

2

Of course, after all the ruckus, Amram couldn't sleep, and he was fresh out of fig lightning. He might have eventually drifted off, but then along came the kid with the drum.

He stopped beside Amram, who opened an eye and talked to himself. "First the harps, now the drums?"

"Shalom," said the boy, who rattled off a rim shot.

"Hey! Enough with the drum, fella," said Amram. "It's after midnight."

The kid played a neat little tattoo but finally stopped. "Aren't you going to Bethlehem?" he asked.

Amram sighed. "Why should I?"

"A newborn King to see," said the drummer boy.

"Yeah, I've heard. A Savior, right?"

"Yes. Which road do I take?"

Amram stood up. He was wide awake, and he knew he wouldn't get any rest that night. Besides, his sheep were all sound asleep, as though the angels had slipped every one of them a mickey.

Besides, despite himself, Amram was getting curious about this newborn King.

"C'mon. I'll show you the way, son. What's your name?"

"Krupa," said the boy.

"Odd name," said Amram.

"Tell me about it," said the kid, executing a languid rim shot.

As they walked toward Bethlehem, Amram offered a word of advice: "When we get to this stable where the babe's supposed to be, I'd cool the drum if I were you."

"But I'm a poor boy, too. I have no gift to give."

"I'm just as poor as you, Krupa. But I've been around the track a few times," said Amram. "I've never met a mother, especially one who's just gone through childbirth, who's gonna appreciate someone whacking his bongos while she's trying to get her baby to sleep."

"Gosh, I never thought of that," said Krupa.

"Well, don't blame yourself. You're just an ignorant shepherd."

"Shepherd? Me? No, I'm not an ignorant shepherd."

"Look around, son," said Amram, wearily. "We're all ignorant shepherds."

The drummer boy pondered this.

"Look, you want to help?" said Amram. "Forget the drum. Or use the brushes instead of sticks. Think lullaby. Some nice regular rhythm that lulls the brat to sleep. Something, like, let's see ..."

"How about," said Krupa, working out a silent beat in the air with his drumsticks, "*pa rum pum* something?"

"Hm, not bad. But it's a little short."

"Okay, then. How 'bout this," said the boy. "*Pa rum pum pum pum, pa rum pum pum pum, rum pum pum pum, rum pum pum pum.*"

"Not bad at all. Good beat, easy to dance to," said Amram. "You could put a whole nursery to sleep with that one."

The drummer boy beamed. Amram raised his open palm. He said, "High five."

The boy looked puzzled. "High five? What's that?"

"No idea. I saw it in a vision."

As the ragged twosome crossed into the outskirts of metropolitan Bethlehem, the shepherd could be heard mumbling to himself, "Harps, kids with drums, two hundred angels hallelujahing away at the top of their lungs. What's a guy have to do to get a silent night around here?"

3

The crowd at the stable in Bethlehem was almost impenetrable. Krupa, who was young and thin and could use his drumsticks to beat his way through the mob, worked his way toward the manger. Amram, tired after the long walk, stayed on the fringe and leaned on a donkey.

"Hey, get offa me," said the donkey.

Amram had never before encountered a talking donkey. "Sorry," he said, choosing to lean on a hitching post. "I didn't know donkeys could talk."

"We can't," replied the beast. "It's a miracle."

Amram's curiosity overcame his fatigue. He said, "Oh yeah. When did this miracle happen?"

"Just this minute," said the donkey. "I think he wants me to talk to you."

"Who?" asked Amram. There was suspicion in his voice.

"Who else? The Savior."

"You mean that baby in the manger? C'mon, donkey. The kid was just born."

"Call me Dave," said the donkey.

"Dave," said Amram, who felt uncomfortable addressing an ass by name.

"I didn't used to have a name. That's another miracle," said the donkey. "The kid's gonna be famous for miracles."

Suddenly, it hit Amram. "Wait a minute! Miracles!" he said. "I think I've seen that. There's this tall thin guy with a clean beard, right? He wears a pure white linen robe, and he never has food stains. Yeah! And he's walking on water. Turning water to wine! Healing lepers! Making blind men see. Multiplying loaves and fishes like a house afire. Could that happen, Dave—what I saw while I was drunk? Could it be true?"

"Hey, don't ask me. I may be talkin', but I'm just a donkey."

"I think—no couldn't be. But I'd swear I saw this character raise someone from the dead," said Amram.

The donkey nodded. "These are visions, right? You get visions?"

Amram nodded.

Dave said, "I think that's why he wanted me to talk to you."

"To me? What for? I'm an ignorant shepherd."

"And I'm a talking donkey. Does any of this conversation make sense?"

Amram had to think about that.

The donkey said, "Look, all I can figure is your visions were another miracle. You were chosen."

"Chosen for what? Why? What's the point? What did he want to tell me?"

The donkey snorted once, softly, and lost the power of

speech.

Amram tried to get Dave to answer again. He got nothing but a malevolent glare from the donkey's jockey.

"I knew this was a waste of time," said the shepherd.

Just then, the crowd around the manger stirred. Slowly, the throng of shepherds and villagers, cows, goats, sheep, Oriental kings, vagabonds and rabbis parted, creating a path into the stable for Amram. He felt a nudge on his shoulder and turned.

Noël, the angel, was hovering there like an overweight moth. "G'head. He wants to see you."

"Who wants?"

"The Christchild."

"What's a Christchild?"

"Just go, will ya? Everybody's waiting."

"For what?"

"For you, shlemiel," said Noël. "Get moving."

Amram, reluctantly, shuffled into the stable. He saw the baby's mother, who was wearing a spotless blue gown and matching veil. Her eyes were dark and gentle. She didn't look as though she'd just been through labor on a bed of dirty straw. She looked more like she was on her way to the junior prom.

Junior prom? Amram asked himself. *What the hell is that?*

"Goddamn visions," he muttered.

Approaching the Christchild's mother, Amram felt ashamed. His sandals were worn paper thin. He had blisters on his feet and sores on his face. He was unwashed and unshaven, infested with parasites. He knew that he smelled like a burning sheepflop. Worst of all, he didn't believe any of this Savior crap. He couldn't tell if the babe's mother—or the old guy beside her, probably the husband—believed it, either. But he didn't want to get into an argument. The lady looked too nice to fight with, and she must be exhausted.

But the crowd urged him forward. An Oriental guy in silk robes patted Amram on the shoulder. He felt his feet moving to the rhythm of Krupa, the little drummer boy, who was going "*pa rum pum pum*" like crazy and getting everyone to join in.

"Yo, shepherd," said Krupa, waving a drumstick.

Amram finally—"*pa rum pum pum*"—reached the manger. He stood awkwardly before the mother. A cow whispered to Amram that her name was Mary. Amram gave the talking cow a sidelong look. The cow shrugged, sheepishly. Mary reached up and took Amram's hand. She seemed untroubled by the big scab there, where Amram's vicious, disloyal sheepdog, Morris, had bitten him. She coaxed Amram to kneel, and she placed his hand gently on the breast of the sleeping infant, tender and mild.

They stayed in that pose for just a moment. The stable was silent. All was calm. All was bright. Just as Amram was starting to feel awkward and out of place, Mary smiled and released his hand. He stood and politely bowed toward Mary, who nodded to him. An old guy, apparently Mary's husband, spoke the only three words Amram heard in the stable (except for the talking cow): "Go with God."

It wasn't 'til he had turned to go that Amram noticed the scab on his hand. It was gone. So were two liver spots and a persistent film of filth. Both of his hands were clean: no dirt under his nails, no grime in the cracks, no cracks in the skin. Outside the stable, clear of the murmuring crowd, Amram examined himself with growing wonder.

His robe, ripped and threadbare, streaked with dirt, had somehow cleaned itself, become heavier and warm against his body. He ran his fingers through his hair and beard, now silky and untangled. As hard as he dug through his scalp, he couldn't find any of the lice who had nested there, feasting and copulating, most of his life. He reached 'neath his robe. Not only were his crabs gone—no itch, no sting, no tickle of tiny legs along his skin—but he was wearing underwear for the first time in thirty years. It was snug and warm, and he suddenly felt like dancing in his sandals of new leather with arch supports. And when he danced, he heard a tinkling. He plunged a hand into his pocket—he'd never had a pocket—and drew out a handful of shekels.

He counted it. "Enough to buy a new dog," he said to himself.

A voice startled Amram. "You won't have to," said Noël. "Morris loves you now."

"Well," said Amram, "*that* would be a miracle."

"It is," said Dave. The donkey was talking again.

Noting the transformation in the shepherd's appearance and fortunes and— allegedly—in his dog, Noël said, "I hope you see now."

Amram said, "Actually, I've seen this before, in my visions. He does miracles. He cleans my clothes. He feeds the hungry, heals the sick, succors the dying, raises the dead. But he's helpless against the biggest problem of all. The problem that God put on the Earth and no Savior can fix."

"What problem?" asked Noël.

"People, angel," said Amram, who noticed a new scarf around his neck. "People are the problem."

"You got that right," said the donkey.

"He knows this," said Noël. "The Christchild came neither to save all men nor to wipe them righteously from the face of the Earth."

"That's too bad," said the donkey.

Noël turned. "Thanks, Dave. I'll take it from here."

With that, the donkey went speechless again, forever.

"He came," said Noël, "with a message of love, hope and fellowship for men and women to heed and follow. Or to choose otherwise, to go on hating and killing, crucifying and lynching, building barriers and making war."

"Which is what I saw in those godawful nightmares," said Amram. "It keeps me up at night."

"You'll see no more visions," said Noël, "save what you choose to see. Darkness or light. Hope or despair."

"Well, that would be a miracle," said Amram.

Noël began strumming his harp, Krupa joined in, softly matching his rhythm. The angels broke out into song again. Amram double-timed it back toward his field, looking for a little peace and quiet.

He found his sheep undisturbed. As he sat on the hillside, cozier in his new clothing than he had felt for months, he shuddered at the sight of his dog bounding toward him, his teeth shining in the moonlight. Amram reached out for his staff, which always served to beat off Morris' frequent attacks.

But the staff was out of reach. Amram raised an arm to protect his face.

A moment later, he had to peer past his defenses. Morris was licking, not gnawing, his hand. The dog was wagging his tail. He wiggled his way into Amram's lap and started lapping at his face. Irresistibly, Amram started petting Morris for the first time since he was a puppy.

Amram couldn't help but smile as he scratched the dog's belly, and Morris crooned happily. He remembered Noël's promise.

"Now *this,*" he said to himself as he spotted the Christmas star, "is a miracle."

24 Dec. '18

An American Christmas, 2019

'Twas a chilly night on the southern border
When a sprightly figure alit at its portal.
Vigilant Vern, the guard, barked an order.
But his fierce "Who goes there?!" drew only a chortle.
"I'm merely here," said the fat man in red,
"With presents to give to the children in cages.
Please don't let it get into your head
That Christmas succumbs to political rages."
"Just one stinkin' minute," said Vern with a leer,
"I'm taking my cues from a super-tough boss.
Unless you're from Sweden, you ain't welcome here.
You'll be shot like a dog before you can cross!"
The bolt of Vern's rifle rang out in the night,
Erasing the smile from the intruder's visage.
A dozen armed ICEmen stepped into the light,
Conveying to Santa the new, revised message
That this land's no refuge for teeming brown masses.
"We're the tempest," said Vern, "that will toss them aside
And drive them away with barbed wire and gases.
Who said you'd be safe here? Forget it. They lied!"
The fat man in red refused to be frightened.
"I'm here for the children," he said with a grin.
"At Christmas, the saddest lives need to be brightened.
Relax, men, and cool it. Just please let me in.
My bounty will take away some of the pain
That you have inflicted on these girls and boys.
When I'm gone, you can abuse them all over again.
You can steal all their candy, destroy all their toys.
Christmastide is but a moment in time.
It cannot crush tyrants. It won't change the world.

The moment it ends, then all of the crime
You strive to commit with banners unfurled
Will smother the hopes bestowed from a manger,
And I will retreat to my frozen North Pole."
Alarmed by these words, Vern cried out, "Whoa, stranger,
We keep out the riffraff. It's our only goal,
Which makes me worry, Mac, frankly, 'bout you.
This North Pole you mention, what state is it in?
Let's see your ID and your photograph, too!"
Santa's eyes twinkled, he lowered his chin.
"I've never belonged," he said, "to a state.
I've never joined up with a party or creed.
I belong to humanity, and I share its fate.
I give—when I reach them—to those most in need."
"Well, fella," said Vern, entirely unmoved,
"If you got no papers, then we got your ass.
You're an illegal alien until you have proved
That Homeland Security has issued your pass."
Santa had nary a green card nor visa,
And so, he was handcuffed and taken in tow.
His beard and "disguise" convinced ICE that he was a
Persian assassin from Querétaro.
Santa was shipped to Guantánamo Bay,
And Christmas was placed on indefinite stay.
All the toys disappeared, I'm sorry to say,
And North Pole largesse went under embargo.
But all was not lost, for Santa's reindeer
Were rescued and flown off to Mar-a-Lago.
Could they now be grazing untethered, released,
And never again have to pull Santa's sleigh?
Or, instead, have they ended as part of the feast,
Their livers impersonating foie gras pâté?

Variations on a Nativity theme (#8)
The stranger in the stable

BETHLEHEM, 0000 A.D. — He had been there, in the haystack, long before the young couple arrived. But no one had noticed. He slept through the young girl's labor and barely stirred from his hibernation at the sound of the infant's first reedy cry.

He only awoke when a shepherd, eager to see the newborn babe, stumbled over his scuffed black boots.

"Hey!" roared the bedraggled figure in the far corner of the stable, "Get offa my dogs, you wool-gathering clodhopper!"

"Oh, sorry," said the shepherd. "I was just trying to see the Savior."

This statement plunged the awakening vagabond into thought. "Oh, right," he muttered. "Stable, manger, Savior. I'd almost forgotten. Well, it's about time."

"Forgotten what?" asked the shepherd.

"You wouldn't understand," said the stranger as he sat up and brushed crumbs off his bodice. "Listen, hayseed. Tell the husband to come over here."

"The father of the Lord?"

"Well, technically, he's not the father. But what the heck? Send him over."

This bizarre command from an unwashed bum alarmed several listeners, who began discussing how to dispatch this unwelcome character. Meanwhile, the stranger drank noisily from a goat bladder flask. A thirsty shepherd took notice.

"Whaddya got there?" he asked.

The stranger, his cheeks now glowing, grinned crookedly. "This?" he said. "It's a local brew called Bethlehem Blindness. Wanna blast?"

The shepherd accepted the offer, quaffed deep from the bladder and almost passed out on the spot. The stranger, laughing mightily, passed the spirits among the gathering of shepherds, farmers, fishermen and a couple of overdressed swells who claimed to be kings from the Orient. The mounting air of festivity in the deepest corner of the stable inevitably stirred the interest of the infant's (step)father.

He was perhaps sixty years old. Tall, straight and dignified, he approached. The throng gave way. The stranger offered a libation. The older man declined.

"You," said the stranger, "must be Joseph."

"Yes, I am."

"I know all about ya," said the odd little man.

Joseph suppressed his puzzlement over this intruder's familiarity. He said, "And who are you?"

"Well, you might call me the Ghost of Christmas Yet to Fa la la."

"Christmas? What is that?"

"It's your kid's birthday, Joe. It's gonna be celebrated everywhere but the Ottoman Empire. But you'll be long gone by then. Too bad. You'd love it. Lights, jingle bells, presents, joy to the world, Good King Wenceslas, midnight Mass, fruitcake and wassail."

Joseph was further confused, so he decided to change the subject. "What's with the red suit?" he asked.

The stranger finally stood up. He was shorter than Joseph and much rounder, with a greasy white beard that was thick with food scraps and apparently home to a colony of insects. "This is all part of my look," he said. "The boots, the whiskers, the big belly. I'm gonna be famous, thanks to your little boy over there."

"Famous? You? But you're just—"

"A drunk, a slob, a homeless derelict," said the stranger. "That's right. But it's been a long wait, and I didn't have much to do but sleep and drink 'til the kid came along. But now, I'm cleaning up my act. This'll probably be my last blast from the bladder for two thousand years—except for maybe a little egg nog by the tree."

"Egg what?" said Joseph. "Tree?"

"Hey, Joe, come on. Chill. Call me Nick. You sure you don't want a sip? It's good stuff. Local! Turnips and flax roots with a nice fish head for that extra kick."

"Maybe I will."

Joseph gulped down a swig of Bethlehem Blindness and coughed for a while. When he could finally catch his breath, he said, "Jesus!"

"Right. That's it. That's what you're gonna call 'im."

"Call who?" asked Joseph.

"Your son, the babe in swaddling clothes. The Light of the World. The King of the Jews. The everlovin' son of God! That's our little Jesus, man! Right over there in the manger, next to the cow."

Joseph could make scant sense of Nick's rambling oratory. He replied, "No. We've already decided to call him Benjamin after my great uncle, who co-signed my business loan."

"*Benjy Christ*?" said Nick. "You gotta be kiddin', dude."

Joseph recoiled. "Dude?" he said.

"Trust me," said Nick. "Go with Jesus."

"Go with Jesus," said several shepherds in reprise. "We will go with Jesus."

They began to chant, "*Go with Jesus. Go with Jesus. Go with Jesus, son of God.*"

"That's the spirit!" said Nick. "You see? These guys get it already, Joe. And wait 'til they spread the word to the fishermen and the lepers. Not to mention dead people and whores. I tell ya, this kid's gonna be big time. I mean, *epic*! Loaves and fishes, sermons and parables, miracles, crucifixions, resurrections! Your little boy's gonna have enough groupies to fill the Colosseum—right up 'til the moment that bastard centurion shoves the spear into his heart."

"Spear?!"

"Ah, don't worry, Joe," said Nick. "You'll be ashes to ashes by then."

Joseph sighed. He was exhausted from the journey to Bethlehem and a sleepless night during the birth of the babe. This crazy fat man in a filthy red suit was the last straw. He was being assailed by mysteries—Christmas, egg nog, miracles and spears. Joseph waved a hand dismissively and said, "You're not making any sense. You have no idea what we've—"

"Oh no, Joe. I know what you and Mary've been up to. Trust me, man. I've done the reading. I even know you're not the kid's real father."

Joseph blanched. "But that's a secret."

"Don't worry, Joe. Ain't nobody gonna know about all that 'til Luke dredges up the story about Elisabeth getting pregnant and Mary being highly favored by the Lord, Gabriel dropping in all of a sudden and the Holy Ghost 'coming upon' Mary. That's the sort of yarn nobody can keep secret forever, Joe, except it doesn't make you look exactly ... well, manly. Sorry. But trust me. By the time anybody finds out what really happened between your virgin wife and the horny angel, hey! You'll be long gone and on your way to becoming a saint."

Joseph's head was spinning. "A saint? What's a saint?"

"Hey, and here's the crazy thing. I'm gonna be one, too. Saint Nick! Can you believe it? Me, the smelly wino in the stable with the cockamamie red pajamas? I mean, really, those voters at the Vatican? Man, they'd canonize a ham sandwich if it showed up on the table at the Last Supper."

"Last Supper?"

"Let's not get into that, Joe. It ain't gonna be a good weekend for your stepson," said Nick. "Anyway, this blabbermouth Luke is gonna write up all this mishigoss about how you were espoused to Mary and then, before the wedding, she got boinked by the angel."

"Boinked? Angel?"

"Hey, come to think of it—that would make a great Sunday night TV series on CBS." Nick made a frame with his hands. "*Boinked by an Angel*. All new episode! Right after *Sixty*

Minutes!"

Joseph looked faint. The shepherds held him up. He shook his head and stiffened his spine. He looked into Nick's eyes. "Look here," he said. "This might only be a humble stable, but it's the birthplace of my son. You're making a disturbance and you'll have to leave. You're drunk—"

"Of course I'm drunk. But I'm happy-drunk. Joe. Now that your kid's finally born, I'm immortal. I mean, you're gonna die. Even little Jesus is gonna die eventually—for a few days, anyway. But me? I'm forever now."

"Nonsense. No one is immortal," insisted Joseph.

Nick smiled knowingly. "Actually, some of us are, Joe," he said. "Me. Napoleon. The Easter Bunny. John Wayne. The second gunman on the grassy knoll."

Joseph ignored this. "I'm sorry, but I rented this stable, and I really wish you would leave. You're bothering my wife and little Benjamin."

"The kid's name is Jesus, dude," said Nick. "It's in the Bible. You could look it up. Luke 1:31."

"Goddammit. Who the hell is Luke?"

A large, helpful king came to Joseph's aid. He took Nick by the scruff of his neck. "Time to go, fella," he said.

"That's right. Hit the road, fatso," said Joseph. "And take that crippled camel with you."

"She's not a camel," said Nick." She's a reindeer named Vixen."

"Vixen?" said a shepherd. "I have a ewe named Vixen."

"You?" asked a king.

"No, ewe," said the shepherd.

"Wait a minute!" cried Joseph, pointing at Nick. "You! What's a reindeer?"

"Oh, that's right. They don't grow around here," said Nick. "Well, a reindeer is a nomadic ruminant, native to the regions in and around the North Pole. It's sort of a moose, actually."

Joseph couldn't help himself. "Moose?" he asked. "North Pole?"

Nick was being hustled out of the stable by a delegation of kings and herdsmen. "The Earth is a globe," he shouted over his shoulder. "It's round. Right on top, that's the North Pole. I'll be moving there soon to set up a toyshop, hire some elves, rustle up a few more reindeer, build an aerodynamic sleigh—"

"Wait a minute," shouted Joseph. "A globe? You said the Earth is *round?*"

"Yeah! And I'm gonna fly all the way 'round it every Christmas Eve!"

"Well, that tears it," said Joseph to the others with a shrug of relief. "That loudmouth tub of lard isn't just drunk. He's crazy!"

"Obviously," said one of the kings. "But I still think you should go with 'Jesus.'"

17 Dec. '19

Christmas Doggerel, 2020
What color the child?

The stable was cluttered with men of all sorts,
With brown men and darker and tones in between.
What color the Christchild—for he was not white?
His mother a Jewess, her pigment unknown
No story revealing the shape of her face,
No hint of her eyes or glimpse of her hair,
No word in the Bible to capture her beauty.
But there, then? No blue eyes nor ivory blondes.
What shade was the babe? Could not have been white.
Turned back from the inn, but not for their faith,
Among throngs full of heathens, nomads and Jews,
They found in a hovel a place for his birth—
A stable, a manger, a patch of bare earth.
Surrounded by strangers, a donkey and cows,
By shepherds and nomads, by heathens and beggars.
A Christmas bereft of both bounty and feast,
When no one was Christian, not even the Christ.
It's said that they called him the King of the Jews,
But Jews had no kingdom, erected no throne.
They honored no princes nor clashed over crowns.
They fished and they wandered, they bought and they sold,
They bowed and they chafed 'neath the power of Rome.
When Caesar said "Go," they did as were told.
This Jesus of Nazareth, he did not belong.
His Bethlehem origin was forced and unwelcome,
An immigrant mishap in alien straw,
But he came as a wonder lit bright by a star
That glowed on his face in tones pink and gold
And prompted the shepherds to call him the Lord—
Perhaps because they had sensed his glory?
But maybe because they just liked the word.

Like all of his people, this baby was poor
In a land, it seemed, that had never been free.
He would answer at last to a higher power
For whom he would be expected to die,
To perish for others, too young and in pain,
As do we all, united in our final gasp,
No longer special, light or dark,
Our creeds and politics in ashes,
Our righteousness a silent whine.
What color this Christchild?—for he is not black,
Nor Asian, Caucasian, not boy and not girl.
He is what we make him and what we should not.
His message a Babel, distorted by time
And tortured by prophets who parrot his name
To buy and to sell and to husband their fame.
What color was he? What race was his mother?
What difference if we can't even love one another?

2 Dec. '20

The fourth ghost

"So now Della's beautiful hair fell about her, shining like a falling stream of brown water. It reached below her knee. It almost made itself into a dress for her."
—O. Henry, *The Gift of the Magi*

Ebenezer Scrooge awoke in a daze from a fitful sleep. Rubbing his face and recalling his trio of disturbing dreams, he said, "Damn, what a night!"

He swept aside his bed curtains and saw rays of morning sun seeping through the window drapes. "What's happening? What day is this?" he mumbled. "Oh, yes, Christmas Day! Wait. I wonder if it's still Christmas."

"Of course, it is, Ebby," came a disembodied voice from inside Scrooge's spacious but disorderly bedchamber.

Having spent the night seeing ghosts, Scrooge took this unearthly utterance in stride. He reached down for his slippers and headed toward the window in hopes of spotting a passerby who might confirm the date. He was brought up short, bumping into an immense form that began to take corporeal shape as Scrooge groped to find a way around it.

As the strange barrier solidified before Scrooge's sleep-crusty eyes, he realized what he was looking at.

"Oh, for Pete's sake," he said. "Another ghost. I thought the mute creep in the black robe was the last one."

"Not quite, Ebby," said the apparition, now fully materialized and nearly opaque. "I'm the Ghost of the Stuff That Was Left Out by the Other Three Ghosts. But you can call me Howie."

"Howie?" said Scrooge, thinking this a queer name for a spook. This ghost was enormous. He was dressed in little boy clothes, with knickers and buckled shoes, a broad-brimmed hat with a bow on the hatband. He had apple cheeks and was licking an all-day sucker.

"In life, they called me Huge Howie."

"Who? Who called you Huge Howie?" asked Scrooge, staggering back and gazing up at the gigantic juvenile.

"My mom and dad," said the ghost. "Bob and Hermione Cratchit."

"Cratchit?" exclaimed Scrooge. "You're the son of Bob Cratchit?"

Huge Howie crouched down so that he could speak face-to-face. Scrooge backed up and plumped onto a chair. "You bet your bippy, Ebby. I was their very first child. And their fattest. I had a runaway glandular problem. I just kept getting bigger and bigger. Couldn't help it, which was a big, big problem because, unfortunately, we were living upstairs from my father's offices. Bob Cratchit wasn't always an impoverished clerk, you know. He had a successful shipping business near the West India docks. You remember?"

"Vaguely," said Scrooge uneasily.

"Well, to make a long story short," said the Ghost of the Stuff That Was Left Out by the Other Three Ghosts, "I just kept getting bigger and bigger 'til one day, when I was about six and weighed twenty-five stone, the timbers couldn't take it anymore. The floor began to creak and moan, the boards commenced to splinter and then, *kaboom*! Down I went, straight through the floor. I landed on a shipment of hand-smithed carbon-steel scimitars from Persia. I was cut to shreds and died in a heap. Blood everywhere! My young mother, who was pregnant at the time with my sister Martha, screamed and passed out. She almost miscarried."

Scrooge was speechless.

Waving his all-day sucker, Huge Howie went on.

"After that, my dad had to take out a loan to rebuild everything. But what with my funeral and the midwife for Martha—and then Dad's customers bailing on him—the firm of Cratchit & Son (I was going to be the "Son") went down the tubes. Toward the end, Dad was begging on his knees for an extension from his lender. You know who that was?"

Scrooge shrank a little. "Scrooge and Marley?"

"Jacob Marley, to be exact," said Huge Howie. "Of course, Marley refused, foreclosed on my father, seized the family's assets and sent us all to the debtor's prison in Southwark. Dad and Mom and little Martha would have languished there for years if not for Mom's hair."

"Her hair?" asked Scrooge.

"Yes, it was long and lovely, and Marley coveted it fiendishly. So he sent an unscrupulous hair wholesaler over to the prison and bought Mom's hair—cut it right off in front of Dad—snipping and giggling and piling silken tresses into a basket."

"But your family got out of prison?"

"Yes, but that wasn't the whole deal. My dad had to agree to work as a lowly clerk at half-salary for Scrooge and Marley. He was indentured for life."

"I always wondered," said Scrooge, "how Cratchit ended up as our clerk."

"Ebby, you are a squeezing, wrenching, grasping, scraping, clutching, covetous, old sinner! No question about that. But you had a few good influences in your life—your poor sister Fan, for instance, and your nephew Fred. But Marley? Man, he had nothing and nobody. He was raised by wolves, rotten to the core and seething with malice. Watching Bob Cratchit slave away in a dead-end job was Marley's daily dose of sadistic pleasure."

"I remember," said Scrooge. "But I guess death must have changed Marley for the good. When his spirit visited me last night, he took pity and gave me a chance to redeem myself."

"Actually, that wasn't his idea. Me and the other ghosts—we got together and told Marley if he didn't talk to you, we'd gang up and load the nasty old skinflint down with a ton of chains."

"But he was wearing chains," said Scrooge. "I saw!"

Huge Howie shook his head over Scrooge's gullibility. "Fake chains," he said. "They looked real, but they were just plastic."

"Plastic? What's plastic?"

"Never mind, Ebby," said Huge Howie. "Let's move on."

"Okay, so after you died," said Scrooge, "you became a ghost?"

"Hey, it's not like I had a lot of career choices," said Huge Howie. "But enough about me. Let's deal with your reclamation."

Scrooge objected. "But I've been reclaimed. I'm fine now. I learned my lesson from the Ghost of Christmas Past, the Ghost of—"

"Really?" said Huge Howie, his interruption dripping with skepticism. "Tell me something, Scrooge. What's your plan?"

"Plan? Right. Well, okay, I guess I'm gonna do a lot of good deeds."

"Like what?"

Scrooge scratched his bristly jaw and groped in his mind. He came up empty.

Howie pounced. "When's the last time you did a good deed? Ever?" he asked. "Would you recognize a good deed if it came up and bit you on the ass?"

"Well, I was thinking," said Scrooge meekly, "of maybe reducing my debtors' interest rate by, like, a half a point."

"Half a point?" Howie was visibly disgusted. "Why am I

talkin' to this piker?"

"No, no," cried Scrooge. "Don't give up on me!"

Huge Howie stamped on the floor, resoundingly. "All right, cheapskate. Let me show you something."

Howie reached out and said, "Bear but a touch of my hand *there*," and—as Scrooge had done with the previous three ghosts, they passed through the wall. Scrooge found himself in a dim and cluttered bedroom, where Jacob Marley lay dead. Scrooge shuddered at the sight.

"This is one of the parts the other ghosts left out," said Howie. "Look here, dude." He lifted the corpse's left eyelid.

"What?" said Scrooge, frightened and suddenly guilty.

"There's petechial hemorrhaging in the pupils, Sherlock. You know what that means?" asked Howie.

Scrooge had no answer. Howie waved his lollipop, magically. Together, he and Scrooge scrolled backward in time exactly one hour.

"And here we are," said Huge Howie. "The turning point in your life. The night that you decided—well, let's watch."

And they watched as a slightly younger Ebenezer Scrooge, seated beside his ailing partner, whispered, "You look terrible, Jacob. But the doctor says you've rallied. You're cheating death, you money-grubbing scoundrel."

Marley, asleep, made no response.

The Scrooge of the past spoke softly. "I can't let that happen, Jacob. I want to be rid of you. The world wants to be rid of you, and no one will ever know what I've done tonight."

With that judgment, Scrooge straddled his vile and insufferable business partner, snatched a pillow from beneath Marley's head, pressed it onto his face and smothered him to death. It took but a moment.

Impassively, the present-day Scrooge watched his bygone self suffocate Marley. He said nothing and felt less.

Huge Howie spoke. "As you predicted, nobody missed Jacob Marley. Hundreds celebrated. The stock market went up. No one asked questions. You got twice as rich overnight, and—by God—you got away with murder."

Howie waited a beat.

"Or did you?"

Scrooge trembled. "Did I? What do you mean, did I? Didn't I?"

"Look here," said Huge Howie.

The scene expanded to show Marley's entire house. There, in the doorway of the bedroom, a gaunt and timorous figure stared aghast as he watched Ebenezer Scrooge coolly smother the heartless miser beside whom he had worked for thirty years.

"Cratchit saw?" said Scrooge astounded.

"Not only that," said Howie, "he went home and told his wife. And I overheard. I happened to be haunting my dad's house at the time."

"But, but," said Scrooge, "why didn't Cratchit turn me in?"

Howie chuckled genially. "Oh, lots of reasons. Remember, my dad was probably the only person on Earth who hated Marley more than you. He was thrilled to be shed of the greedy bastard. Besides, who would believe Bob Cratchit? He was a mere clerk, disgruntled in his crummy job. You were rich, scary and influential."

"I still am," said Scrooge.

Huge Howie waved his sucker again. "Here, let's listen."

Suddenly, Scrooge and the ghost were back in the past, peeking into the humble Cratchit parlor, where Bob and Hermione conspired in whispers.

"If I report Mr. Scrooge to the police," Bob was saying, "they probably won't believe me. But if they do believe me, think of it. Scrooge and Marley's goes bankrupt. I lose my job."

"Oh dear, Bob," replied Mrs. Cratchit. "If that happens, we'll be broke. Tiny Tim will wither and die. His sad little crutch will lean on the hearth."

She broke into tears. "Dear, dear, don't fret," said Bob

Cratchit. "What I'm going to do is bide my time. Someday, I might be able to use my knowledge of Mr. Scrooge's dastardly deed to seek some boon from him. If he refuses, then I'll turn him over to the constabulary."

"Oh, Bob, yes. Keep that terrible secret clutched to your bosom," said Mrs. Cratchit. "Jacob Marley will be our insurance policy."

"Why, those sneaky Cratchits! They were gonna blackmail me?" expostulated Scrooge, standing up and fuming with indignation.

"Well, gee whiz, Ebby," said Huge Howie. "You are a murderer."

"C'mon, Ghost! I only killed Marley. No jury in the world—"

"You're missing the point here, Ebby," said Howie.

"Point? Point? What point?"

"Okay, let's review," said Howie. "Tell me what happened yesterday. On your way home from work?"

"Um, lemme think," said Scrooge. "Oh, right. The snowball thing."

"The snowball thing?"

"Yeah. That idiot Cratchit threw a snowball at me and knocked off my hat."

"He knocked off your hat?"

"Yeah. With a snowball. A grown man, throwing snowballs. I mean, really—"

"And then you fired him?"

"Oh," said Scrooge, somewhat chastened, "that's right. I did."

"You fired from his only job the only witness to the night you throttled Jacob Marley to death in his own canopied bed."

Scrooge sank into a suddenly self-aware reverie.

"Scrooge, my man," Howie went on, "if ever there were an occasion for Bob Cratchit to spill the beans about Marley or *threaten* to spill the beans ..."

"Okay, okay, I get the point. I'll give Cratchit his job back," said Scrooge. "I'll give him a raise. Two percent. Three! Three percent."

"You could do that," said Huge Howie, "but even if you went up to four percent, it wouldn't actually qualify as a good deed."

"But it's a job," protested Scrooge, "with a big raise."

"Look. If Bob Cratchit threatens you with exposure, and you pay him off for his silence, nobody comes away clean. You stay rotten and some of that rot rubs off on Bob, his sweet wife, even Tiny Tim."

"I see." Confused and irresolute, Scrooge sank back down. "What can I do?"

Huge Howie stood up, towering over Scrooge, and started to disappear. He licked his sucker. "Well, Ebby, if you can't figure that out for yourself ..."

The rest was inaudible as Huge Howie, the Ghost of the Stuff That Was Left Out by the Other Three Ghosts, faded into filmy oblivion.

Tired and bewildered, Scrooge stumbled toward the window. Opening it, he heard the bells of Christmas tolling and felt the sunlight warming his face. "Golden sunlight, heavenly sky, sweet fresh air, merry bells. Oh, glorious! Glorious!" He looked down and—as though on cue—a remarkably intelligent boy happened to be passing by. The sight of the boy, somehow, reminded Scrooge of the poulterer in the next street but one at the corner, and the prize turkey that hung in the window.

In a burst of ghostly inspiration, Scrooge knew exactly what he must do. Regardless of Bob's guilty knowledge about him, he would begin his atonement willingly and immediately. Even if Cratchit had already gone to the police and ratted him out, Scrooge knew he must still—at last—bestow on the good Cratchit family the rewards for which Bob had toiled and which Scrooge and Marley had long denied him.

So, of course, Scrooge bought the prize turkey for Bob and Hermione. He heaped a toy store full of presents on the

Cratchit kids and delivered the loot in a carriage. He went to church, apologized to his nephew Fred and danced the night away with Fred's fiancée. The next day, he gave Bob Cratchit a whopping raise. The day after that, he said, "What the hell!" and made Cratchit his partner in the business. He started a university scholarship for poor children and made Bob's son Peter its first recipient.

Tiny Tim, of course, did not die. As Dickens recalls, Ebenezer Scrooge "became as good a friend, as good a master, and as good a man, as the good old city knew, or any other good old city, town, or borough, in the good old world."

And once a week, on a table beside his fireplace, Scrooge played cribbage all night long with a see-through partner so huge that he filled half the room.

4 Dec. '20

Christmas: It's not all shmaltz and treacle

"If I could work my will, every idiot who goes about with 'Merry Christmas' on his lips should be boiled with his own pudding and buried with a stake of holly through his heart."

—Ebenezer Scrooge, *A Christmas Carol*

MADISON, Wis. — As I was scrolling the channel guide last night, I grudgingly faced the great annual quandary of the holidays: Why does just about every Christmas movie ever made suck?

The simple answer, brilliantly circumvented by Charles Dickens in 1843, is that Christmas poses few surprises. Whether you're attempting a variation on the biblical Nativity or depicting a secular Christmas in modern times, you're stuck with a pat story. Any scenario that deviates too far beyond the cozy and familiar ends up falling flat or strikes the audience as rude and vaguely blasphemous.

When Dickens wrote *A Christmas Carol*, he set the standard for storytellers trying to work a new wrinkle on this delicate theme. The Dickens Rule requires that a credible, satisfying Christmas story must chronicle a journey from darkness (the death of Marley and the embitterment of Scrooge) into light (Scrooge's rehab and the rescue of Tiny Tim). Also inherent in any such story is an intimation of how fragile and ephemeral the warmth of that light.

Indeed, the Star of David shone over Bethlehem for but a single night, and we are relentlessly reminded that "Christmas comes but once a year," after which it's a dog-eat-Tiny Tim world for the next 364 days.

Dickens' story has been filmed—and adapted for the stage both dramatically and musically—more than any other holiday premise. In my imposture as a theater critic in Boston, for example, I was compelled for consecutive years to sit through *A Christmas Carol* facsimile (with music, I think) by playwright Israel Horovitz. Every year, after the ordeal, I warned parents among my readership to avoid the Charles Playhouse and spare their children because the Horovitz *Carol* was an insult to Ebenezer Scrooge and a blot on the map of Massachusetts. I advised readers instead to simply wait for Alastair Sim's version of Scrooge to come around free on TV, where it has shown up faithfully every year since 1951.

There is an eternal debate among cineastes about who played the best movie Scrooge. The first I saw in my childhood (on TV) was Reginald Owen's portrayal, produced in 1938 by Joe Mankiewicz with half the Lockhart family among the Cratchits. Owen was my favorite for a while. But I ended up siding with Alastair Sim, whose face, seemingly without effort, traveled a range of feeling from seething hatred and sneering contempt to shattering remorse and boyish joy. Other actors have attempted Scrooge, from Seymour Hicks to George C. Scott and (God help us) Kelsey Grammer, but Sim lifted the bar, and no grasping skinflint since has gone so high.

I'll watch almost any variation of *A Christmas Carol* when it comes around, reciting lines by memory. I'm fond of the little-seen Albert Finney version because it features one of the great Scrooge moments. During the visit of the third ghost, all of London rises up and throngs the snowy streets merrily singing Uncle Ebenezer's macabre casket-dancing death carol, "Thank You Very Much."

It's the darkness in this sarcastic tableau that makes Dickens' original tale effective, over and over, in a dozen versions. We think of *A Christmas Carol* as a sentimental journey, but it never descends to the hackneyed shmaltz and toxic treacle with which lesser talents have polluted our holidays.

The modern pinnacle of Dickens' formula is, of course, Frank Capra's *It's a Wonderful Life*. George Bailey is not, indeed, as despicable as Scrooge. Capra dropped that burden onto Mr. Potter. But a Dickensian shadow creeps over George when his father dies. It darkens when the Depression cancels his honeymoon. Uncle Billy's blunder at Potter's bank on Christmas Eve is the equivalent of a visit to George Bailey by Marley's ghost. And Clarence, the wingless angel, standing in for Dickens' three transformative spirits, serves as George's savior.

Even in the film's tearfully happy ending, a reflective viewer might well ponder how close to death and utter despair, for all his family, George Bailey stumbled. And like Scrooge, George wasn't rescued by his own strength of character but by the agency of a magical wraith to whom none of us, in real life, has access.

There is, after all, no Santa Claus.

Speaking of Santa, the preeminent film on this theme—with shades of Dickens—is *Miracle on 34th Street* (the original 1947 non-colorized version, not the 1994 imitation). Like its forebears, *Miracle* is rooted in disbelief. Doris and daughter Susan are doubters. The film's vessels of Scroogian villainy are a corporate drone named Granville Sawyer and a heartless

Manhattan district attorney. True to Dickens and Capra, the movie's halting progress toward comfort and joy requires intervention by a figment of our Christmas imagination—Kris Kringle. Without ghosts, angels and Saint Nick flying through the sky, where would any of our heroes land?

Although *Miracle on 34th Street* might be the cheeriest of our Christmas classics, it never sinks into the sentimental quagmire that drowns most of the boilerplate holiday movies that defile our every December. As with Scrooge and George Bailey, Capra's Manhattan is shadowed by menace and infused with fear. It begins, after all, with a drunken, degenerate Santa. It proceeds to the near incarceration of the "real" Santa Claus in Bedlam. In the end, it leaves Kris Kringle resident of an old folks' home with no family of his own, where his inevitable prospects are confinement, senility and a lonely death.

Meanwhile, Doris, Susan and Fred (named after Scrooge's nephew) drive off to live happily ever after in suburbia.

Often, to decide whether a Christmas flick is worth your attention, you need but read the title. Any title, for example, that begins with *A Christmas in [Location]* is probably a waste of time, as is *A Christmas With (or Without) [Something or Other]*. Smartass Christmas comedies stuffed with frathouse humor (*Bad Santa*, *Scrooged*, anything with Chevy Chase) are rarely funny, and they age poorly.

In the right hands, however, Christmas is a rich lode of comedy. *A Christmas Story*, blessed with the writing—and voice—of Jean Shepherd, deserves classic status, as does Macaulay Culkin's insouciant performance in *Home Alone* (the first one, not the sequel). My holiday guilty pleasure is *Die Hard*, not only because of John McClane's steady flow of crisp one-liners (screenwriter Jeb Stuart) but also because of its cleverly chosen musical bookends. Run-DMC's "Christmas in Hollis" accompanies McClane to Nakatomi Plaza, and Vaughn Monroe croons "Let It Snow" as the closing credits roll—with Beethoven's "Ode to Joy" in between.

The essential measure of movie love is how often you're willing to watch. Among Christmas movies that I'd merrily re-run for days at a time (with egg nog and a plate of ginger snaps), my first choice is Alastair Sim's *Scrooge*. Add to this the Reginald Owen and Albert Finney versions of same. The rest—barely enough for a Top Ten—in no particular order: *It's a Wonderful Life*, *Miracle on 34th Street* (1947, black and white), *A Christmas Story*, *Comfort and Joy* (directed by Bill Forsyth), *Home Alone*, *The Shop Around the Corner*, *Die Hard* and—maybe—*Holiday Inn* (but not *White Christmas*) and *How the Grinch Stole Christmas* (thanks to Boris Karloff).

All the rest are humbug.

22 Dec. '20

A Murray Christmas to all

I

It all started when Maureen O'Hara threw Murray off the Macy's parade float for being drunk as a skunk.

Still in his soiled Santa suit, Murray Lefkowitz staggered into an alley off West 45th and polished off the last drops in his bottle of Old Polecat. He plopped down beside a dumpster and considered his options. The top choice was the same as it had been for the last six years. He sighed in surrender to his destiny. From a pocket, he drew the knife that served to protect him from his fellow bums. He did his best to sharpen it on a chunk of cinder block.

Murray pushed up a sleeve, muttered a brief prayer in memory of himself and pressed the nicked blade to his left wrist. As he was looking down, contemplating the end of a wasted life, he saw a stained and filthy flyer on the greasy pavement. He peered more closely.

Help Wanted

No experience necessary.
Room and board, low pay, long hours, no benefits, crappy weather
Apply K. Kringle, North Pole

A phone number with a strange country code followed the ad.

Murray Lefkowitz reconsidered his situation. He was an unemployable derelict with no talent, a squandered education, no marketable skills, an aborted job history, no resumé, no cash or credit, no future. He was on the verge of killing himself, an endeavor which, if previous experience was any guide, would fail. He envisioned himself bandaged up on a lumpy bed in the charity ward—surrounded by sick and dying old dipsos like himself—of the most infectious hospital in New York City.

Murray took another look at the flyer.

He grabbed the paper and struggled to his feet. What the hell? He was ready to call the number, but he didn't have a phone.

Murray stumbled out of the alley, feeling ominous pangs of sobriety. He bumped into a girl. Well, possibly a girl. The creature had a moth-eaten stocking cap covering its head, tufts of yellowish-brown hair sticking out of several holes. Most of its face was hidden. Murray discerned a button nose and cracked lips. The possible girl was wrapped in a ragged baby-blue blanket which, judging by its range of stains, splotches and odors, had been salvaged from the lower depths of a dumpster. Below the fringe of the abominable duvet, there were dirty blue jeans with torn knees and two mismatched shoes, one a seam-spring Chuck Taylor sneaker, the other a fatally scuffed men's wingtip without laces and evidently three or four sizes too large for the sockless foot inside.

"Er," said Murray. "'Scuse me."

"Oh no," came a voice—almost certainly female—from the mouth. "My fault, Steve."

"Don' mention it," replied Murray. "And it's Murray."

Murray was moving on, but the blanketed mound stopped in his path. "What's Murray?" it asked.

"Me," said Murray. "I'm Murray."

Irrelevantly, for reasons he could not grasp, he added, "Lefkowitz."

"Joy," said the other.

"Well," said Murray politely, "It's a pleasure t'meet you, too."

"No," said the cracked lips.

Murray wrinkled a brow. "No, what?"

"That's my name, not my attitude."

"What's your name?"

"Joy," said Joy. "Tuddah."

"Tuddah?"

"That's my last name."

Murray understood. He nodded. "Well," he said, looking around, ready to depart this curious dialog, "so long."

They began on their separate ways when Murray was hit by a wild conjecture. "Hey," he said.

Joy paused along her uncertain way. "Huh?"

"You wouldn't, by any chance," said Murray, "have a phone?"

Joy turned, shoved the stocking cap up to her forehead, revealing deep blue eyes and an even coat of grime on every inch of her face. "Yup," she said, "'til the mark cancels the contract."

Joy half-smiled at Murray, who looked harmless to her—and to pretty much everybody—because he was skinny and drunk with a permanently goofy look on his fuzzy old kisser.

"Mark?"

Joy said. "Yeah, I swiped it off a guy I gave a blow job over in the park. When he figures out it's gone, well …"

Murray understood.

"I don't suppose I could borrow it," he asked, "just for one call."

Joy shrank away but didn't flee. "I dunno," she muttered.

"I won't take it," said Murray. "I promise. Y'see, there's a job."

"A job?" Joy's blue eyes gave off a flicker of curiosity.

"Yeah," said Murray. He waved the crumpled flyer.

"What kinda job?"

"Crummy, from what I can tell," said Murray. "But it's, y'know, better'n nothin'."

Murray handed over the flyer. Joy studied it for a while. "Hm," she said.

"So?" said Murray.

"Y'can't use the phone," said Joy.

"Oh."

"Don' know ya. Can't trust ya."

"I hear ya, Joy," Murray conceded.

"But I'll call for ya."

"Okay."

Laboriously, with cold fingers, Joy punched out the number on the flyer.

After several rings, there was an answer. "North Pole, Bippy speaking."

"Bippy?" asked Joy.

"Yeah," came the voice. "I'm an elf. We all have cute names."

Joy nodded.

"So," said Bippy. "Who's calling?"

"Joy. Joy Tuddah."

"World?" asked Bippy with a snicker.

"Huh?" said Joy.

"Forget it," said Bippy. "So, what's shakin', Joy Tuddah?"

"I wanna talk to K. Kringle. About the job."

"What job?"

Joy sighed impatiently. "Look, Bippy. I got this piece of paper from this drunken bum here (excuse me, Murray) that says you got a job, no experience necessary, room and board—"

"Wait a minute," said Bippy. "You found that flyer?"

"Sort of," said Joy.

"You want *that* job?"

"Well, no. I'm calling for ..." She paused to think, "a friend."

"Aw," said Murray.

"Far out!" exclaimed Bippy. "Hang on, kid. Lemme get the boss."

While they waited, Joy stared at the phone. It could go dead any second.

"This is Nick," said a deep, jolly voice suddenly. Joy put the phone on speaker so Murray could hear. "You're calling about the want ad I put out?"

"Yeah, it's right here. I'm lookin' at it."

"Ho ho ho," said Nick.

"Whaddya mean by that?" asked Joy suspiciously.

"Well, nobody has ever answered one of those things," said Nick. "It's sort of a running joke around here."

"What?" Murray broke in. "You mean there's no job? The ad's a joke. You're just kiddin'?"

There was a moment of silence.

"No job?" said Joy, joylessly.

"Er ..." said Nick.

"Well, that's just plain mean," said Joy. "A fake job offer at Christmastime?"

"Wait a minute," said Nick. "I gotta think about this."

More silence.

Finally, Nick said, "Y'know, actually, I could use another sleigh team."

"Slay team," asked Murray. "What? Like a murder squad?"

"No, no! Sleigh." Nick spelled it out. "You know, like in 'Jingle Bells.' A one-horse open sleigh?"

"Uh huh," said Murray, dubiously.

"Do you think," asked Nick, "you could round up, say, five more folks? That's the usual elf complement on a sleigh."

"Elf complement?"

"Yes," said Nick. "Me, your basic eight-reindeer team and

five elves to do the chimney work. I'm way too fat to fit down your typical chimney."

Murray and Joy were both puzzled.

"Elves? Chimneys? Reindeer?" said Joy. "What the hell are you, mister—Santa Claus?"

"Jesus," muttered Nick. "It took you this long to figure it out?"

"Sorry, Kris ... Nick, whatever," said Joy apologetically. "But this guy with me here is a falling-down drunk and I'm a junkie whore comin' down from a high. We ain't neither of us real sharp at the moment."

"Uh huh," said Nick. "Well, nice talkin' to ya. Merry Christmas."

"Wait," said Joy. "What if we could do it? Put together a sleigh team? I mean, this town is crawlin' with people like us, need a job, need a place to sleep, need—Hullo? Hullo?"

The phone was silent. Joy stared at a blank screen. "Shit," she said. "The cheap bastard canceled his phone service."

"Like you figured," said Murray.

"Yeah," said Joy morosely.

They stood together in a chill wind blowing up 45th Street. Joy flung the dead phone away. She shuffled her mismatched feet as though to continue her aimless progress.

"You got money?" asked Murray.

Joy looked suspicious.

"I mean," said Murray, holding up his hands in a gesture of harmlessness, "the mark. He paid you, right? For ... you know ..."

"Yeah, he better pay, or I'd bite off his—"

"Well, look," said Murray, preferring not to hear the end of that sentence, "if you could afford to buy me a cup of coffee, we could maybe come up with a plan."

Joy sneered. "What kind of plan?"

Murray pointed toward a food truck on a distant corner. "I could use a cup of joe. Helps me sober up."

Silently, Joy followed Murray to the food vendor. She bought two cups of black coffee and splurged on a couple of doughnuts, paying with a crumpled sawbuck and squirreling the change somewhere deep beneath her aromatic comforter.

They huddled against a building, sheltered from the November wind.

After a while, Joy said, "There's this kid I know. Named Fingers."

"Fingers?"

"Yeah," said Joy. "He hustles these business guys who come to town, stay in the fancy hotels. He got the moniker 'cause he's, like, good with his hands."

Murray demurred a description of Fingers' technique. Joy smiled and said, "Anyway, he arranges his dates on the phone. He has, like, a regular account, with, like, Verizon."

Murray brightened. "Do you know where to find him?"

Joy said, "I know his territory."

"Let's go," said Murray, displaying more energy than he had shown in months.

Joy led Murray on a circuit of midtown luxury hotels. The quest ended at the Park Hyatt, where Joy spotted Fingers emerging, hunched against the cold in a thin, satin jacket. He was bareheaded, his hair a mixture of lank brown locks and blue-dyed braids. His face was smooth, pale and almost pretty, with alert, gray eyes and plucked eyebrows.

"Hey, Fingers," called Joy.

The young man, perhaps eighteen, probably younger, halted and glared. "Don't call me that," he said. "That's my professional name."

Murray almost laughed. "What's your amateur name?"

Fingers scowled as he moved in and glared down at Joy. "Who's this?" he asked, nodding toward Murray without looking at him.

"Murray," said Murray. "Lefkowitz. We wanna use your phone, Fingers."

Fingers turned menacingly. "Don't call me that."

"So, whaddya want me t'call ya, dipshit?"

Murray and Fingers closed in, face-to-face, clenching their fists.

"Oh, c'mon, guys," said Joy, shoving her way between them. "Murray, call 'im Rafael."

"Okay, then, Rafael," said Murray, backing down, "we know you have a phone, and we need the use of it. Borrow it. For one little call. Please."

Murray went on to explain to Fingers that he had the chance to get a straight job, off the streets. There might be, he said, a job for Joy and even for Rafael, if Fingers might choose to graduate from selling hotel-room hand jobs to transient junior executives. Rafael seemed doubtful about altering his career path but slipped the phone to Joy, who re-dialed the North Pole and got Nick on the line.

"Y'know, sweetheart," said Nick, "this is my busy season."

"Yeah, well, that's why we're callin', fatso," said Joy. "You said you want a team. I'm the girl who can get you a team. But we're gonna need a little seed money, ya feel me? And how the hell we gonna get up there t'the fashlugginer North Pole."

Nick was quiet for a while.

Finally, he said, "Okay, here."

"Okay, what?" asked Joy.

"Look in your pocket."

Joy handed the phone to Murray and rummaged around under the blanket. She re-surfaced holding a plastic gift card bearing the logo of the First Avenue Army Navy Surplus Emporium.

Needless to say, the three street scavengers were surprised by Santa's magical solicitude.

"How'd he do that?" said Fingers.

Ignoring this, Nick said, "So, Joy, how many volunteers ya got?"

"Two, so far—me and Murray," said Joy. She peered at

Rafael, who was visibly impressed by the appearance of the gift card. "Maybe three."

"There's enough money on the card," said Nick, "to outfit five sleigh pilots with warm clothes, thermal long johns, galoshes, earlappers and mittens. But the card expires at noon tomorrow. So, you need to find two more volunteers, and you don't have time to dick around. Ya got that, sweetie?"

"Yeah, lardass. I hear ya."

"Yo, Murray!" said Santa.

Murray said, "What?"

"You've got to go cold turkey. There's no drinking on my watch."

"Yeah, okay," Murray muttered.

"And Joy," said Nick.

"Huh?"

"You think you need a fix," said Nick, "eat a brownie."

Joy looked crestfallen and a little twitchy.

"I'll help the girl," said Murray.

"The blind leading the blind," said Nick. "Get to work. I'll call you tomorrow. Noon sharp."

Murray and Joy's first challenge was talking Rafael into sticking with them for the next twenty-four hours. They needed his phone. Joy noticed that Rafael's lips were turning blue, and she won him over with the promise that Santa's card was his ticket to a winter coat.

Next up: Finding two more apprentice elves among the burned-out dregs of the Big Apple demimonde. Their first candidate was Joy's ex-boyfriend Muhammad, a former glue sniffer whose previous professional niche was mugging tour bus golden-agers. After a second stretch in Sing Sing, Muhammad had switched his livelihood to gathering cans and bottles on the fringes of the city with a shopping cart and a hunting knife (for protection from poachers). Joy, Murray and Fingers tracked down Muhammad as he was scavenging the alleys in Hell's Kitchen. They followed him along his route, then stood outside in the wind blowing off the Hudson while Muhammad redeemed 4,879 bottles and cans at a recycling center off the West Side Highway. Finally, Muhammad, who still carried a torch for Joy, said okay, for old times' sake, he'd join the "team"—at least 'til their trip to the Army Navy store. Prodded by Joy, Muhammad agreed to dip into his can-redemption stash and stand everyone to burgers and fries at the McDonald's on Fulton Street.

By then, it was past seven o'clock, and Murray was sober as a night-court bailiff. Headachey and sick to his stomach, he almost upchucked his Big Mac.

"You gonna be all right, old-timer?" asked Muhammad.

"Don't call me that," said Murray, using a phrase that had become almost a motto for the motley crew.

Joy and Murray had sort of assembled a team of four, although Rafael and Muhammad might bolt any second. Finding a fifth volunteer seemed like an elf too far. The circles in which the Don't Call Me That Gang traveled were disinclined toward entrepreneurial initiative and goodwill toward men, women or children. Approach the average street-dweller and they were prone to scurry into a shadow, assume a defensive crouch and brandish a box cutter.

When the unwashed foursome entered the First Avenue Army Navy Surplus Emporium at opening time next morning, they were still short one sleigh jockey. Joy reminded the others not to even think about shoplifting because—if the song was true—Santa knew where they'd been sleeping, knew that they were awake and knew if they'd been bad or good.

"If he's watching, he knows there's only four of us," said Joy. "He could cancel the card right at the cash register. That happens, we get nothin'. I got no job, and I'm back in the park, on my knees."

Aware of this likelihood, Joy, Murray, Rafael and Muhammad roamed the store's vast selection of surplus dry goods in search of clothes heavy enough to shield the North Pole's wintry blast. Murray was digging through a stack of flannel-lined blue jeans looking for a 34 waist with a 32 inseam, when he bumped into a tall, craggy stranger struggling to separate one set of pants from another. The man had only one arm.

"Can I help?" asked Murray.

The response was a curse, directed not at Murray. He recognized it as an indictment of the state of things in general. Murray had often expressed similar sentiments since the day—drunk, violent and out of control—he had lost his job, alienated his wife, Sandra and abandoned his two kids, Elvira and Chadwick.

"I know where you're comin' from, brother," said Murray. "What happened to the arm?"

"Fuckin' Iraq," replied the man tersely, pronouncing the word "eye-rack."

Murray was a little surprised. "You mean, you don't have cover—"

"Fuckin' VA," growled the other, interrupting Murray. "I had a goddamn prosthesis. I lost it."

"How?"

"Shit. How do ya lose a goddamn plastic arm? I'm at the bar at McSorley's, and all of a sudden I get one of my post-traumatic flashbacks, and I think the guy next to me is Osama bin Fuckin' Laden. I rip off my arm and start beating on the A-rab bastard's head. Next thing y'know, ten, twelve guys jump me. And well, after that, I don't remember a thing 'til I wake up the next day in a toilet stall at the Port Authority, and I got no fuckin' arm."

"And you can't get a new one?"

"Fuckin' VA!"

It came to Murray, in a sober epiphany, that this guy was just the sort of bitter dead-ender who could fill out their starting five.

"Murray," he said. "Lefkowitz."

"Jewish?" asked the man.

"Sort of," said Murray.

The man nodded, looked Murray up and down, took in his besmirched Santa suit and grinned grimly. "Santa the Jew," he said. "Fuckin' A."

They shook hands. "I'm Stan," said the down-and-out veteran. "Seasons."

Murray found his fellow aspiring elves among the aisles of military surplus and introduced Stan Seasons.

"Greetings," said Stan, cheerlessly.

In a half-hour, the team had finished outfitting their wardrobes. They piled their selections on the counter.

Joy asked the cashier, a grizzled harridan with a blue-rinse coiffeur, "Is there a dressing room?"

The cashier snorted once and growled, "Does this joint look like Bloomingdale's, dearie?"

The crew changed in the alley, consigning most of their old clothes and Joy's abominable blanket to the nearest dumpster. Out of sentiment that he didn't think he had left in his heart, Murray decided to hold onto his Santa suit, stuffing it into the Army Navy bag. The five derelicts hit the street in new duds.

They were shivering on a stone wall in Washington Square Park when, at the crack of noon, Fingers' phone rang. Joy grabbed it. "We got your team," she said. As she spoke, she stared sharply at Rafael and Muhammad, issuing an implicit warning that if they even thought of backing out at this point, she would sauté their balls in motor oil.

Nick insisted on taking a look at Murray's new circle of friends. Joy engaged Facetime and scanned the group.

"Sweet Jesus on toast!" said Nick. "I knew printing that flyer was a mistake."

Joy was instantly indignant. "You mean we're not hired?"

Nick said, "Hey, look, if this bunch of losers think you can stand the cold and put in fourteen hours a day, wrapping your fingers to the bone (no offense, Rafael), I'll take you on. Frankly, I don't think any of you'll last through your first day."

Joy calmed. "Okay, how do we get there?"

"Just a minute," said Nick.

In exactly one minute, a sleigh, twenty feet long, manned by apple-cheeked midgets wearing green doublets and curled-up shoes, drawn by eight somewhat scruffy ruminants with huge antlers, swept out of the leaden November sky.

"Hi," shouted the shrimp with the reins. "I'm Bubbles. Climb on, folks. Time's a-wastin'!"

True to their heritage, fifty other New Yorkers in the park paid little heed to the sight of five people dressed in military garb climbing onto a sleigh led by eight reindeer, lifting off from Lower Manhattan and flying north.

Murray, Joy and the others were shocked by the speed of the reindeer. The group had to scrunch down to keep from freezing their noses, and they saw little of the scenery below as they dashed, danced and pranced across Canada to frozen wastes beyond.

Suddenly, there it was—Santa's Christmas complex, a hundred corrugated spec buildings painted red and green, stretching along the ice and snow like an immense military encampment.

"This all goes up in three days every year," said Bubbles with a hint of pride. "And we take it down on the 26th of December, lock, stock and tinsel."

"Really? Where does it go then?" asked Murray.

"We have a warehouse in the Brooklyn Navy Yard," said Bubbles. "Everybody there thinks we're in there secretly developing a new generation of nuclear submarines."

"Where do the ... er, elves, go?" asked Joy.

"Where else? Fort Myers."

2

Nick had been right. Their first day in Santa's workshop nearly killed the five refugees from the mean streets of Gotham. Stan Seasons tried assembling bicycles with one arm and fell so far behind the elves that he was pulled off the production line. He ended up in the robotics lab, where Handy Andy, one of Santa's elfin machinists, proceeded to fashion Stan a new prosthetic arm.

Meanwhile, after several hours in the Barbie Department, Joy went into heroin withdrawal and had to be padlocked in a plastic playhouse with a case of the screaming meemies. Murray had similar troubles with alcoholic heebie-jeebies, which sent him into a violent rampage in the Sports Wing, wielding a Louisville Slugger in one hand and a bowling ball in the other. Before he could be tackled by a dozen burly elves and wrapped into a badminton net, he had smashed a half-dozen foosball tables, reduced a hundred video tennis games to smithereens and set back skateboard production by forty-eight hours.

Meanwhile, Rafael collapsed from exhaustion and had to be wheeled to the infirmary. Muhammad tried—and failed—to hide himself in the kitchen behind Mrs. Santa's colossal cast-iron wood stove. He ended up with second-degree burns.

Despite their rocky start, however, Murray's Don't Call Me That Gang were all back on the line within the first week, earning their room in the elf barracks (where their feet tended to hang off the ends of the beds), their three squares a day and their wages of twenty Santacoins a day.

In the second week, they began a crash course in sleigh navigation. Murray, whom Nick chose as the pilot, studied high-altitude topography and weather patterns under the tutelage of Howdy Cloudy, the aeronautical elf. Joy was taught reindeer wrangling by a pixie named, predictably, Bambi. She learned how to feed, clean, curry and hot-walk the five spavined steeds assigned to their sleigh, led by Adolf the Cleft-Palate Reindeer, with Vomet and Stupid, Numbnuts and Nixon.

"Only five?" Joy asked Bambi on the first day.

"Originally, besides Adolf, there were eight," said Bambi,

sadly, "but the others, poor little Flasher and Cancer, Yonder and Blitzkrieg, well, they caught Chronic Wasting Disease, and all just sort of shriveled away."

"Gross," said Joy.

"By the way, honey, watch out for Numbnuts," said Bambi. "He bites."

"Oh."

"And Nixon's a leg-humper."

Together, Murray, Joy, Rafael, Muhammad and Stan Seasons hurriedly learned the craft of steering an unstable, top-heavy sleigh, loaded with goodies, through an ice-cold stratosphere against gale-force headwinds. Taught by a brilliant young elfette named Poodgy, Muhammad proved especially good at managing simulated sleigh flights.

Christmas Eve came faster than anyone expected. Or wanted.

"I've always hated Christmas," muttered Stan.

When Murray's team arrived in the sleigh barn to begin their night's work, they discovered that Snarky, the sarcastic elf, had named their sleigh "Titanic." He painted the title on the sleigh's fuselage, along with a cartoon effigy of Joy, nude, drowning in the ocean.

The Titanic's crew, with Murray Lefkowitz in the driver's seat and Joy at his side soothing the reindeer and gently patting Numbnuts on the rump, included Muhammad in the elevated observation seat handling the pontoons and rudder. Rafael worked the radar set and Stan Seasons was in charge of a stack of Santa bags fifteen feet long and twenty feet high.

Poodgy was there, too, in a strictly advisory role. She snuggled in beside Muhammad, holding his hand. Another elf, a teenage intern named Twinkly-Dinkly, was along for the ride.

Looking at the pile of gifts and goodies towering above him, Stan turned and said, "Christ, Murray. This fucker's never gonna get off the ground."

With that, Murray raised his whip and flicked the rear end of Adolf, the Cleft-Palate Reindeer, who—lacking a nose that glows—had a miner's helmet strapped between his antlers. Adolf shook his horns, kicked his feet, turned on his halogen headlight and flew upward into the frigid North Pole night, followed dutifully by Vomet and Stupid, Numbnuts and Nixon, and a sleigh crew consisting of a suicidal drunk, a junkie hooker, a professional onanist, a mugger of the elderly and a one-armed, hair-trigger ex-Marine with PTSD.

Not to mention Poodgy and Twinkly-Dinkly.

"Holy shit," said Stan. "We're in the air."

"Until we crash," mumbled Fingers.

Their route carried Murray's crew into regions where, most every Christmas Eve, children expected little more than rat turds in their stockings. To these bleak and desperate regions they delivered not Cabbage Patch Kids, tricycles and Xboxes, but shoes and socks, loaves of mold-free bread, eyeglasses, flak jackets, cornmeal, lentils, dried fish, fresh fruit, Spam, clean underwear, tampons, pickaxes, second-hand t-shirts, soap, salt, mosquito nets, insecticide, hydrogen peroxide, quinine, iodine, antivenin, sunglasses, scissors, tweezers, cigarettes, cellphones, wind-up radios, Swiss Army knives and a hundred other glamourless items necessary for day-to-day, hour-to-hour survival in the underbelly of the world.

On several stops, they found themselves dodging anti-aircraft fire. They stopped jingling their bells after a sniper in Syria clipped two points off one of Vomet's antlers. Vomet retaliated fragrantly by unloading nine pounds of deer apples. As they descended toward a dwelling in Yemen, they were overtaken by a Saudi drone that blew up the house before they could deliver their yuletide bounty.

Their sleigh ride sent them through Haiti, El Salvador and Nicaragua, to Afghanistan, Azerbaijan, Iraq, Tajikistan, Bangladesh, Xinjiang and East Timor. They ventured into Somalia and the war-torn Congo, then on to an impoverished village in Mali, where, as she handed out candy canes and Legos to little kids, Joy was kidnapped by Touareg guerrillas. They dragged her into a windowless room, where she was stripped down, spread out and about to be raped to death. In the nick of time, Murray, along with Muhammad, Rafael, Stan Seasons and Twinkly-Dinkly, burst into the hovel, each wearing a Darth Vader helmet and brandishing Star Wars light swords. The Touaregs were so dazzled and bewildered by this display of powerless force that Joy was able to slip from captivity, after which the whole crew cheezed it for the sleigh, which escaped potential disaster with only a few dozen bullet holes on its fuselage and a flesh wound on the tuchis of Adolf the Cleft-Palate Reindeer.

At their stop in South Sudan, the parents of a darling little girl took one look at Muhammad and decided that he belonged to a tribe they hated. Muhammad was bound and gagged, marched into the village square and set atop a heap of oil-soaked garbage to be burned alive as a sacrifice to a local deity named Adu Jamaja the Conqueror.

But Joy cried, "No, you don't!" To save her old boyfriend, she literally hypnotized the bloodthirsty villagers by improvising, sinuously, with talent she never knew she had, the Dance of the Seven Used Goodwill Store T-Shirts, stripping away each layer with excruciating grace and alluring languor. As Joy tripped the sedative fantastic, Murray circulated on the fringes of the mob, handing out Twix bars and mini-Oreo cookies while reciting the mind-numbing text of *Good Night, Moon*, a story that had put him to sleep every night of his infancy.

After forty-five minutes, Joy was down to a camisole and a pair of hand-me-down lollipops. The villagers were propped up, dozing, against one another. It took but a moment for Rafael and Stan to untie Muhammad and spirit him back to the sleigh, which then silently soared into a starless African night.

They flew next to Gaza, where—from the sleigh—they saw a small boy hugging a mound of dirt in a ravaged cityscape. When they landed, they discovered that below the mound was the child's dead mother, killed on the street by a spray of bullets from unknown guns. By then, the sleigh had been emptied of everything but two bags. One held no gifts, just a lot of empty bags, a half-gross of Saltine crackers and a hundred pounds of candy corn. The other bag was sealed and mysterious.

Haltingly, the boy told Murray that his father was also dead, vaporized by a stray missile. Rafael, who saw something familiar in the little boy's plight, said, "Let's take him with us."

Murray almost said no. But then, seeing tears in Rafael's usually stony eyes as he cradled the little boy's dusty head, Murray said, "Nu, what the hell. It's Christmas."

"Fine," said Stan, "but frisk the kid first."

They wrapped the boy, whose name was Oz, into a blanket and flew away before the Holy Land could pump him full of shrapnel.

Their last scheduled stop was Washington, D.C., where the mystery of the last bag was solved. It was a huge load, tightly sealed, with Stan's name stenciled on it. Following Stan's directions, Murray steered the sleigh to the Veterans Administration building and hovered over its chimney.

Stan untied the last bag, which was the biggest of all, and began dropping its contents down the chimney. Murray, Joy and the Don't Call Me That Gang watched as hundreds of attachable, detachable, interchangeable electronic prosthetic arms and legs, hands, hips and electronic knees—all designed by Handy Andy—poured down pell-mell into the VA. When all had been unloaded, and Stan had shaken the bag to make sure it was empty, he removed a note from his pocket and added it to the strange cargo he had just delivered.

No one else saw the note, but here's how it read:

To all the luckless, loyal guys—and brave women—who've been shot, blasted, burned, broken, maimed, amputated, crippled, fucked over and sacrificed on the altar of freedom, democracy, Big Oil and the chicken brass at the Pentagon ...

Season's Greetings
Stan

As the sleigh lifted off from Washington, Murray then took out an envelope given to him by Nick and not to be opened 'til all the loot had been delivered. He smiled as he read and directed the reindeer toward a small town in upstate New York. When the sleigh landed on the snowy lawn, Joy looked around in alarm.

"This is—" she began.

"Home," said Murray. "Your mom and dad have been looking for you, crying and praying ever since you took off."

Joy said, "I can't go back there."

"You're here," said Murray.

"Kid, you're gettin' a second chance here," said Stan. "Don't fuck it up."

"I don't know," said Joy. "They won't ..."

"Oh no," said Twinkly-Dinkly, "they will. I read their letter to Santa."

"Whose letter?" asked Joy suspiciously.

"Your mom and dad," said the elf. "Actually, there were, like, twenty letters."

"They sent letters to Santa?" said Joy. "They're grownups. They don't believe in Santa Claus."

"Any port in a blizzard, kid," said Murray. "Your folks were desperate."

"All they want for Christmas," said Twinkly-Dinkly, "is you, honeybunch."

"But," said Joy, "they always hated me."

"Did they?" asked Murray. "Really? Hate you?"

"Okay, maybe not hate," said Joy. "But they didn't understand me."

"Jeez," said Muhammad, "you're a teenage girl. Who understands teenage girls?"

Murray took Joy's chin in his hand. "Joy?"

"What?"

"Do *you* understand you?"

A light went on in the house. The front door opened, and a head popped out. Then another head. Joy stood up hesitantly. A gasp of recognition from the doorway, followed by slippered feet trampling through the snow. The rest of the scene is too saccharine and sentimental to record here. Suffice to note that the sleigh departed bereft of Joy.

3

Thin shafts of a frozen pink dawn were caressing the ice pack as Adolf guided the brave and battered Titanic back into its slip in the reindeer barn. It was only then that Murray's team turned to notice that Poodgy and Muhammad were making out passionately in the back seat of the sleigh. Subsequently, they were married and they lived more or less happily ever after, shuttling seasonally between Fort Myers and the North Pole. Poodgy and Muhammad also adopted Oz, the orphan from Gaza, and got him inducted as an honorary elf. His elf name was Ozzie.

On Christmas Day, Saint Nick gathered Murray, Muhammad and Fingers in his office.

"Where's Stan?" asked Murray.

Nick just shrugged. Then he said, "Muhammad, you've already gotten a gift I would have been powerless to bestow. You have a family."

Next, Nick said to Rafael, "You've been wasting your talent, Fingers. Take this."

He handed Rafael a compact disc. On the cover, it read, "Flying Fingers: The Piano Stylings of Rafael Rodriguez."

"That's me," he said.

"Yes, it is," said Nick.

"What's goin' on here?" protested Rafael. "I didn't record this!"

"You will," said Santa, "as soon as you start playing the piano again."

"This shlemiel plays the piano?" said Murray.

"Like an angel," said Nick, "until the terrible day he was molested by his piano teacher."

"This shlemiel was molested by a piano teacher?" said Murray.

"Don't call me that," said Rafael.

Nick ignored this exchange. "The CD comes with a piano," he said to Rafael. "Yo, Kookie!"

At this, Kookie, the head elf, snapped his fingers. Four other elves rolled a Steinway into the room. "Play us a little ragtime, Fingers," said Kookie.

At first, Rafael hesitated. But the lure of the keyboard was too powerful. He sat down at the piano, tinkling away at first with a Scott Joplin tune, then moving on to snatches of Chopin, passages from Mozart and a thundering blast of Beethoven. The elves went wild. Nick wept openly. Rafael hugged Murray and whispered in his ear, "Thank you, thank you."

"Hey," said Murray, "all I did was pick up a want ad in the alley. I thought it was porn."

Santa offered Murray nothing that day. But, the following morning, Santa gave Murray a coupon good for three months of boot camp rehab at a maximum security health spa in California. When he got his release from the spa one day in early spring, Murray found a sleigh waiting for him in the driveway. Kookie was at the reins. Murray recognized Santa's first-team reindeer, Dasher, Dancer, Prancer and Vixen, Comet, Cupid, Donner and Blitzen.

"Climb on, ace," said Kookie.

Hesitantly, Murray took a seat beside Kookie. "Where are

we going?"

"Where else?" said Kookie. "Fort Myers."

"I'm not sure I want to—"

Before Murray could finish the sentence, the sleigh was aloft, soaring upward and eastward at dizzying speed.

A few hours later, an elfette named Dearie led Murray out to poolside at Santa's summer compound. Nick was under an umbrella, dressed in a bright red terry robe, silk ascot and sequined flip-flops, sipping a piña colada. Directing Murray to a chair, Nick said, "Something to drink?"

"Club soda," said Murray,

"Attaboy," said Nick.

Murray settled in and looked around. He'd never seen elves in bathing suits and aloha shirts before. But there they were, lounging by the pool, drinking cocktails and playing croquet on the lawn.

"How'd it go?" asked Nick.

"It was rehab hell. I just about died the first week," said Murray. "Y'know, I wasn't strictly sober when I was up there at the Pole."

"Oh, I knew that," said Nick.

"You're everywhere," said Murray.

"You better watch out!"

They were both chuckling as Dearie arrived with Murray's fizzy water. She also delivered a gift box.

"What's this?" asked Murray.

"Sort of a belated Christmas present," said Nick. "Go ahead. Open it."

Murray tore off the bright paper and lifted the lid. Inside was a velvet Santa suit with patent leather boots, a meerschaum pipe and a tasseled red hat. Murray was bewildered.

"You'll have to put on a little weight," said Nick, "and let your beard grow out. You can't get away without whiskers, you know."

"You mean, I'm getting another shot at the Macy's

Thanksgiving Day parade?"

Nick laughed. "Sorry, Murray. By Thanksgiving, you're gonna be four months at the North Pole, wrangling elves and working your jolly red ass off."

"Say what?"

"Look, Murray, I'm a tough old dog, with emphasis on the 'old.' I've had my day in the midnight sun. Last Christmas was my 233rd. I can't stand the cold anymore. And frankly, this new generation of elves? I don't like their music and I can't speak their language anymore."

Murray didn't understand.

"Murray," said Nick, "unless you decide to go back to the streets, climb back into the bottle and piss away the rest of your life, you are officially—as of right now—Santa Claus Number Seven, the latest in a noble line."

"Me, Santa? I can't," said Murray. "Nick, I don't deserve—"

Nick waved Murray to silence. "Murray, do you have any idea where I was before old Santa Number Five tricked me into taking over his job?"

"Well, no," said Murray. "But you haven't exactly confided in me."

Nick nodded ruefully. "I know. I'm sorry. I tend to be a little closed-off."

"Okay, so, open up," said Murray. "You had a career before you became Santa?"

"A career? Hardly," said Nick. "I was a pirate on a stinking, broken-down square rigger out of Port Royal. I raided, raped, burned, fought, plundered and spent half my life so wasted that I couldn't tell a featherbed from a stack of cannonballs. My predecessor was worse. For ten years before he moved up to the Pole, old Number Five was captain of a slave ship."

Murray was astonished. "So, you were—"

"Damn right, Mur. I was just like you. The scum of the earth," said Nick. "Only worse. Number Five and I were downright evil. Slavery and piracy, pillage and plunder. Which is exactly the reason why we got stuck with this job."

"For being evil?"

"No," said Nick. "For being evil and knowing we were evil—and hating ourselves. We had no idea how to escape our own rottenness, no way to make up for all the pain, death and misery we had caused."

"So, being Santa Claus is ..."

"Atonement, Murray. The North Pole was my last chance, and it's your last chance to do good, to make up for wrecking your life and a whole lot of other lives. Murray, you've got at least a hundred years of penance to pay, and every one of those years you'll be spending five or six months freezing your nuts at Santa's workshop with no cable TV. And no women."

Murray shook his head. "But I don't deserve the chance, Nick."

"You think I did?" said Nick. "I should've died with a dagger in my guts, drowning in my own blood. But then, one fine day, when the chance fell into my lap, to atone, Murray, I sure hadn't earned it. But I grabbed it, anyhow."

Murray stared at Nick but couldn't see a hint of his past wickedness. Santa's face was a living portrait of kindness and generosity. Murray scanned the scene, studying the diminutive figures on the lawn, pool and near the house. He didn't see what he was looking for. He said, "Wait a second, Nick. You said 'no women.' But isn't there supposed to be a Mrs. Claus?"

Nick smiled. "Now that you mention it." He waved again.

A familiar figure appeared, strolling across the patio in a green elf suit, wearing an apron and a toque blanche. "Introducing," said Nick, "the new Mrs. Claus."

"Stan?" said Murray, recognizing his one-armed sleighmate.

"Greetings," said Stan, whose new, improved prosthesis was tattooed intricately with a Currier and Ives Christmas scene.

Murray looked toward Nick. "Mrs. Claus?" he said. "Nick, have you noticed? Stan's not a girl."

"Maybe not, but I can cook," said Stan. "Learned in the

Army. Six months in cook school, and then they shoved me into the fuckin' infantry."

Murray leapt from his chair to shake his old friend's hand but ended up hugging him. He was surprised at how glad he was to see the old sourpuss.

"So, Mur," said Nick. "You want the job or not?"

Murray looked again at Nick. The famous "jolly old elf" now looked more weary than merry. Murray turned then to Stan and realized that—just like that day in the Army Navy store—he held another man's fragile fate in his hands. Stan Seasons, a lost and bitter castoff from society, had been offered the unlikeliest opportunity—as the wife of Santa Claus—to arrest his downward spiral and restore his self-respect.

Murray, for that matter, faced prospects no better than Stan's. His thirst still nagged at the back of his throat. He was one bottle away from sinking into a pit of guilt, self-reproach and surrender. The gutter, with its comforting promise of oblivion unto death, still tugged at him.

Murray Lefkowitz hesitated to answer Nick. One more thought troubled him.

"Y'know," he said, "I'm Jewish."

Nick's eyes—how they twinkled! His dimples, how merry!

Chuckling softly, he replied, "So was Jesus."

Murray ran his hand over the luxuriant fabric of a Santa suit that was, for the moment, too big for him.

"Well then," he said. "Ho ho ho."

22 Nov. '21

Christmas Doggerel, 2021
It was a dark and stormy Christmas

Until he reached the border somewhere south of Thunder Bay,
Santa's sleigh soared high and swift, with nothing in the way.
But then, an eerie darkness seemed to sweep across the sky.
A roaring wind blew bitter cold and made it hard to fly.
Santa couldn't see below. The Earth had gone entirely black.
He cast his wary eyes about. He looked behind his back.
Santa saw, through gloom that seemed to mimic an eclipse,
Mounted, grinning horribly, the Horsemen called "Apocalypse."
As they pursued him, they unleashed a fusillade of lightning
That even Santa, used to storms, found a little frightening.
The Horsemen quickly drew abreast. They shouted a command:
"Stop, go back! There is no 'joy' in that benighted land!
"There's no goodwill and no one there who'd lend a helping hand.
"We've won, we've taken over. We are that tragic nation's fate!
"Our names are Doom, Despair, Division—and our captain's name is Hate.
"We're riding high and mighty on a wave of popularity.
"Twixt races, strangers, even families, there's nothing but disparity!
"They're at each other's throats today. They live in constant fear.
"If you fly low, best watch your ass. They'll shoot if you come near!"
Santa smiled. He wasn't stopped. He'd merely been delayed.
He plumbed his heart, where glowed the inspiration that had made

DAVID BENJAMIN

This holy night so meaningful. It wasn't toys and sugarplums.
"Tonight's the night," said Santa Claus, "when newborn hope to all men comes,
"December twenty-fifth—my day!—has always been a magic date
"When peace and love, however brief, have power over Hate.
"The child was born in Bethlehem, although there was no room,
"When all the angels sang on high and drowned the voice of Doom.
"Despair, Division have, for just a breath, no place, no force—
"And look beneath you, oops! For all of you have lost your horse!"
Looking upward, Santa laughed as all four Horsemen plunged to Earth,
Undone, and banished from our hearts, by mem'ry of an infant's birth.

25 Dec. '21

Have Yourself an Analog Christmas

"He sees you when you're sleeping
"And he knows when you're awake.
"He knows if you've been bad ..."
—J. Fred Coots and Haven Gillespie

NORTH POLE — Santa Claus punched his intercom for the fourth time, a moment of frustration that had reduced his jollity to the point of wiping the dimples off his face. Even when Humpty, head elf of the North Pole, stepped into his office, the exasperated Santa could barely crack a smile.

"Where on earth is Boopsy," said Santa, referring to his

elfin assistant. Boopsy was normally the epitome of efficiency (besides being cute as a bug's ear).

"Gone," said Humpty, "where all the good elves go."

Santa scowled. "What the hell do you mean by that?"

Humpty showed a glimmer of perplexity. "Santa, you didn't get the email?"

Santa sighed. "Humpty, c'mon! Santa Claus doesn't do email."

"Right, I keep forgetting," said the elf, with a note of pity. "You're totally analog."

"I'm what?"

Humpty pressed on. "I thought you knew, Santa."

"Knew what?"

"They're gone."

"What are gone?"

"Your elves. They're gone, all of them, except for me, of course. I'm serving in a sort of interim caretaker—"

"GONE?" No jollity remained in Santa's disposition. A glint in his eye and a twist of his head gave Humpty to know he had something to dread. Saint Nick held the stump of a pipe so tight in his teeth that it snapped in two. He stood up and bashed his desktop. Humpty could not remember Santa being angry.

"Where the hell did the little slackers go?" he bellowed.

Biding for time, Humpty took out his iPhone 14 and tapped the screen several times. "Ah, here," he said, keeping his eyes lowered. "Tucson. A place called Tinytoon Village."

"Tucson?" Santa roared. "What in God's name are my elves doing in Ariz—"

"Redundant, sir."

"Redundant?"

"Downsized."

"Downsized? We're talkin' elves, for Pete's sake! Weren't they short enough already?"

"I mean fired, Santa."

"Fired? You fired my elves? Without asking me? Why? How?"

"Well, sir. They all received a gold monogrammed cigarette lighter and a very nice severance—"

"You sent my elves to the desert? With Zippos?"

"Well, yes, we did, Santa. But it's a lovely facility—Tinytoon Village—designed uniquely to accommodate the, er … height challenged. Dwarfs, elves, fairies, midgets, pygmies. I have the brochure right here."

Santa turned with a jerk and took Humpty by the throat. "Dammit, it's Christmas! Get 'em back. We've got work to do here!"

"Oh no, sir. Forget it. They're gone. There's no bringing them back, not at this late date."

"Late date? You're damn right it's a late date. Christmas is twenty goddamn days from now!"

"Yes, but the elves, y'see, had to go. We did studies. They were, well, inefficient."

"Studies? You did studies?!" Santa was livid. He pushed Humpty away. "You're an elf, Humpty. Are you *inefficient*?"

"Well, Santa, I never thought—"

Humpty was interrupted by Santa's deafening *cri de coeur*. "I WANT MY ELVES!"

"I'm afraid that's impossible, sir. Sorry. Bringing them back, my goodness, the logistics? Besides, that would be a huge breach in policy."

"Policy? What policy? Firing my elves? Bibbsy and Goo-goo? Fancy-Pants and Squinchy? I love those little guys. They love me! Who made this stupid policy?"

"Well, sir, that would be the director of IT."

Santa growled. "You keep talking in riddles, Humpty. What the hell is eye tea."

"Information technology."

"Yeah, whatever that is. Another riddle," said Santa, impatiently. "All right, Hump, next dumb question: Who's this director of Inflammation Technology?"

"Information," Humpty corrected, cautiously. "That would be your brother, sir."

"My brother?!" roared Santa. "Bruno did this? That shiftless idiot? He's the one who up and fired all my elves?"

"No, no, Santa. Not fired. Replaced. Upgraded, sir."

"Reindeer manure!" said Santa. "Get out of my sight, you feather-hatted twit. And send Bruno up here. Now!"

Gladly, Humpty slunk from the room. Santa fumed and paced for ten minutes before his kid brother, Bruno, who had been—until just before Halloween—selling turquoise tie clips and rebuilt slot machines out of a strip mall in Henderson, Nevada.

Instead of the standard Claus family uniform of red velvet with fur trim and shiny black boots, Bruno came in spiffed out in black pinstriped Armani with a red shirt, white tie, a paisley hankie in his breast pocket, and two-tone wingtips.

Santa stared. "Bruno, you look like a pimp."

Bruno ignored the crack, saying only, "Mornin', Nick. How's it hangin'?"

"Hanging? It's hanging by the neck until dead. Christmas is coming, and my elves are in the wind," said Santa. "Apparently, thanks to you, moron!"

Bruno shook his head. "Elves, really, Nick? In this day and age?" said Bruno condescendingly. He pulled up a chair, took a seat and spent a minute lighting a panatela with a monogrammed cigarette lighter.

Santa grew red with rage. His cheeks were like roses, his nose like a cherry.

Finally, Bruno blew out a smoke ring and said, "Nick, this is the twenty-first century. Look around. Nobody's using manual labor anymore except to pick tomatoes and flip burgers. You gotta think silicon, robotics, AI! Algorithms, brother. *Algorithms*!"

Santa staggered to his desk and slumped in his chair, his

little round belly shaking like a bowlful of jelly. "Algo ..."

"Rithms," said Bruno, leaning forward and flicking an ash. "Lemme show ya!"

With that, Bruno tapped his Apple watch. Santa's door flew open, and a dozen shrouded figures marched—in perfect unison—into the office, crisply dressing right, snapping their heels and forming a straight line. They were all exactly three feet in height, covered in charcoal-gray robes with peaked hoods. If they had faces, they were not visible. Each wore rope sandals, from which protruded waxy toes that looked more plastic than flesh. They emitted a low hum, like an air conditioner fan.

"What in God's name?"

"Algorithms, Nick," said Bruno, proudly. "An army of 'em at your service. Every one seemingly identical, but you'd be wrong! Each of these little beauties is embedded with a different code—one doing erector sets, another Cocomelons or Madden NFL '23, another doing Mario Brothers, another Squishmallows. Y'see that one on the end? All it does is Crazy Aaron's Amazing Prediction Putty, and I have no idea what that means. And action figures! G.I. Joe, Wonder Woman, Stormy Daniels, you name it."

"I knew it was a mistake to hire you, Bruno," said Santa, trying to peer into the eyes of an algorithm. "But Mrs. Claus kept saying, Nick, he's gambling all night, he's drinking. My wife, your sister-in-law, bless her heart, said you were consorting with loose women. 'You could get VD,' she said. 'Bring Bruno up here,' she said. 'How could he screw up in the North Pole? There's nowhere to go, nothin' to do, nobody to talk to, except you, me, eight tiny reindeer—well, Rudolph makes nine—and a lot of elves.'"

Bruno wasn't listening. He said, "Cookies! Do ya know about the cookies, Nick? That's somethin' else I've started here."

"Cookies? You think *you* started cookies? Gimme a break,

Bruno!" said Santa. "Every Christmas Eve, I'm up to here in cookies and milk. Oreos, snickerdoodles, Toll Houses, pfeffernusse, gingerbread. Oh, and y'know what I love? Those sugar cookies with the Hershey's kisses sitting right on top."

"Wait, no, you don't get it," said Bruno, waxing technological. "I'm talkin' digital here—HTTP cookies, Nick. I'm talkin' about the text files we're using everywhere to monitor little kids' website use."

"Monitor little kids? Why would we want to—"

"C'mon, Nick. What's our motto here? 'Naughty or nice,' right? And cookies are the answer—way better than whatever half-ass ad hoc system you've been using all these holidays to keep tabs on the sneaky brats," Bruno enthused. "We can watch every move made by every computer-literate, game-playing, porn-seeking moznik on the face of the Earth. We've got twenty-four-hour surveillance, just waiting for kids to cry, pout, shout, bully, sext or deny the Holocaust. The little snots can't get away from us. Best thing? They don't know we're there, peeking over their shoulder, waiting for 'em to trip up and blow their Christmas morning."

Santa went white.

Bruno went on. "In just two weeks, Nick, we've already upped our Naughty Demographic by 19.5 percent. Do you have any idea how this impacts our gross sleighload numbers? We're gonna be hauling, lemme see here ..."

Bruno clicked away on his digital tablet. "Look at this!"

Bruno showed Santa his screen, on which the spreadsheet was too small for him to read without his wire-rimmed spectacles. "We'll be cutting back on rooftop Christmas Eve deliveries by at least 143 metric tons. For you, Nick, that comes to 1,439 fewer slides down the chimney."

"Cut back?" said Santa, bewildered. "Why would we want to cut back? I'm Santa Claus. This is the season of giving. The more, the better. I *like* sliding down chimneys!"

"Oh, c'mon," said Bruno." All that soot and creosote. It's

gonna kill ya, Nick!"

Santa leaned forward. "Bruno, listen. I don't really give a shit whether a kid behaved or not. It's Christmas! All is forgiven."

"Hey, nice attitude, Nick, but that's twentieth-century thinking! We can't afford to just fling out presents to every Tom, Dick and Mary with an Advent calendar and a Christmas tree. Besides, we've already launched the program. It's in the system, baked in. Cookies rule! Any kid who pouts, shouts, cries or sets fire to the kitty, well, that's tough titty. He ain't gettin' nuttin' for Christmas."

"Nuttin'?" asked Santa, looking distressed.

But Bruno was out the door, his herd of little algorithms tagging along behind him.

Problems began to show up the next day.

For the first time in his career, Santa Claus switched on his personal computer and started reading the daily production numbers and inventory tallies. He noticed glitches. Instead of getting a Malibu Barbie, a little girl in St. Paul was slated to receive a marble rye and a roll of galvanized barbed wire. There was a kid in Atlanta named Stevie who wanted a toy fire truck but he was going to get, instead, a nine-liter, foam-loaded, high-power fire extinguisher. A toddler in Tulsa who asked for a tricycle was going to receive, instead, a replica triptych of Hieronymus Bosch's *Garden of Earthly Delights*. Bobby Shaftoe, a ten-year-old in Indiana who had asked Santa for a Red Ryder BB gun, was going to find, under the tree, a .45 caliber semiautomatic Ruger handgun, accompanied by a stocking full of hollow point ammo. Fourteen thousand boys and girls who scribbled "Legos" on their wish lists were going to get L'eggs pantyhose in egg-shaped packages in various sizes and shades.

Santa called Bruno to his office and showed him a printout revealing all these algorithmic anomalies.

Bruno, flanked by two of his spooky little algo-gnomes, waved off Santa's concerns. "Hey, Nick, yo, no system is perfect.

Ya see what I'm talkin' about?" he said. "A bit flip here, an overload there. No big deal. Right now, on our maiden digital voyage here, we're lookin' at a right-gift/right-kid ratio that's better than seven-to-three."

"You mean," said Santa, "that a third of my friends in Little Girl and Boy Land are gonna get Christmas presents they don't want?"

"C'mon, man. That's Christmas!" said Bruno. "Remember that bunny suit that Ralphie got from Aunt Clara? Remember what Mick Jagger said: 'You can't always get what you want.'"

Maybe it was the invocation of Mick Jagger that shattered Santa's poise. He dug through a pile of Christmas gifts, found Bobby Shaftoe's Ruger .45 and pumped three rounds into the nearest algorithm. Instead of bleeding, the little freak disintegrated into a clutter of ones, zeros and plastic toes.

"Oh my God!" cried Bruno. "The humanity."

"You're next," said Santa, fitting the gun barrel up Bruno's left nostril, "unless you can fix every one of these screwed-up Christmas wishes!"

"Now?" said Bruno, somewhat nasally.

"Yeah," said Santa. "Today."

"Jeez, Nick, I don' know," replied Bruno, sucking his teeth. "Sure, I can send our faulty units to the shop—"

"What shop?"

"The shop. Where they re-code bad algorithms."

"*Naughty* algo-somethings?"

"Naughty? Yeah, nice one, Nick."

"Where's this shop?"

"Sunnyvale."

"California?"

"Yeah, Nick, but listen," said Bruno, staring cross-eyed at Santa's gun. "Trouble is, y'know, chances are, what with the backload, the holidays and all? These suckers ain't gonna be outa the shop 'til, like, April."

"April? Christmas in *April*?"

DAVID BENJAMIN

"Better late than never, Nick."

"That does it! Bruno, you're fired!" said Santa. For good measure, he sprayed his good-for-nothing brother in the face with the full nine-liter load from Stevie's fire extinguisher.

Five minutes later, Santa had Humpty back on the carpet and Boopsy on the phone.

"Hey, sweetie. How are things in Arizona?"

"Hot, man. Hot!" said Boopsy. "And everybody here is *old*!"

"Well then, come on home!"

"Really?"

Within forty-eight hours, Santa had rounded up an entire herd of flying reindeer, plus a few caribou and one aerodynamic team of musk oxen. He dispatched more than a hundred sleighs to Tinytoon Village, where Humpty happily liberated every one of Santa's exiled elves. Along the way, Humpty dropped Bruno off in the desert and told him to find his own goddamn way back to Vegas.

Three days later, Boopsy was making Santa's list and checking it twice—by hand. Santa's toy shop was humming. Led by Squinchy, the elves were singing "Joy to the World" and "Frosty the Snowman" in four-part harmony. Vixen, Blitzen and the rest of the reindeer were fortifying themselves with carbs and Reese's Peanut Butter Cups. Rudolph, who was secretly tech-savvy, was fitting himself with an LED nose and plugging his septum into a charger.

As for the algorithms, they were tossed out into the snow until their synapses froze and their little red lights ceased to blink. After that, the elves stripped them down, fluffed them up in the dryer, added a hint of fragrance and used them to stuff teddy bears and toboggan cushions.

6 Dec. '22

A definition of winter

"Winter is icummen in, Lhude sing Goddamm. Raineth drop and staineth slop, And how the wind doth ramm! Sing: Goddamm."

—Ezra Pound, "Ancient Music"

MADISON, Wis. — When does winter start?

Although I've seen a hell of a lot of winter by now, I hesitate to pin down the exact moment that it settles down across the land and exerts its icy grip on mind, body and spirit. The onset of winter, of course, has its official *kyrie eleison* at the solstice. But the turn of a season doesn't punch a clock, nor is the shortest day of the year usually the coldest or most wintry.

In search of winter's certainty, I can step outside and stroll the frigid streets, spotting the signs: shriveled jack-o'-lanterns rotting on doorsteps, the death of the last geranium in a window box, a ragged V of tardy geese honking down the flyway, naked trees and snowy sidewalks with trampled ice patches, Christmas lights and Salvation Army Santas. I could likewise mark the season's transition with my change of clothes, from flannels and sweaters to a muffler, gloves and a serious overcoat. Or I could look around one morning to recognize—and surrender to—winter's invasion of my body, as Jack Frost creeps into my blood, scours my skin, seeps to my bones, chills my innards, numbs my nose and ices my beard.

None of this sensory data, however, means to me that winter has come in, really, truly and irreversibly. Its harbinger is, rather, a feeling that occurs randomly, a moment when a fleeting impression—sent perhaps by a biting gust or a hot sip of coffee—triggers emotions and summons memories of winters past, when the air, the cold and the darkness whisper to me, "Bundle up, pal. This is it."

Or, maybe, it's all about a girl.

Paris, where I was 'til mid-December, was colder than usual, but it was not winter. Instead, the city presented a persistent—and familiar—gray autumn. The sun crouched behind shrouds of clouds, its angular light streams now and then pushing through briefly to illuminate brilliant gold and orange treescapes that blur on the eye as though rendered by Sisley or Monet. There were leaves. There were café-goers still dining on the *terrasse*. This is not winter.

On the morning I departed, Paris attempted a wintry tease, with a thin dusting of snow on cartops and grassy patches. This was hardly convincing. Nor was the snow that fell in Madison the night I landed here, after three flights and seventeen weary hours on route. It looked wintry, but it wasn't yet. I wasn't ready. Something was missing.

In the back of my mind, faintly, there was a girl.

The next morning, I awoke to snow on everything, but wet and sloppy, melting, dripping, slushing. Sweater weather still, not winter.

That night, driving back to the airport to collect my wife, I watched through the windshield a fresh snowfall barely visible in the air but swirling and dancing, ghostly against black pavement. I knew the feel of this snow, which was not soft and flaky. These were tiny ballistic specks that pelt your eyelids and make you blink. Each one bounced off your skin, leaving behind an icy pinprick a millisecond in duration, like an acupuncture ambush.

Even inside the car, I knew this feeling. As we inched home

on suddenly treacherous streets, I tried to describe to Junko the pleasure of walking toward the wind on just such a night, wincing at the attack of the driven pellets, moving in a cocoon of white-streaked blackness as my skin tingled and my ears froze. In the cold, in the hard snow, in the night, beside a lake just beginning to freeze, there's a solitude that leaves you feeling like the last living soul on the first day of an eternal Ice Age.

Here, then, was winter—almost.

If I could just remember that girl.

The next morning, a woman passed me, leading an embarrassed dog decked out in a Fair Isle sweater and four tiny pooch booties. A DPW worker, spreading salt, nodded a chilled hello. I came across Jason, a hobo friend whose stall is the doorway of Walgreens, with his stoic, human-tolerant dog, Alabama. I gave Jason the usual offering and told him, "Don't stay out here too long."

"Don't worry. I won't."

But he would. There were people to see and, with each, a conversation.

That night, as it snowed again, I remembered the girl. Her name was Toni. We had met at religion class, ironically because both of us were drifting from the Church. She was in ninth grade, I in tenth. But, in some ways, she was old beyond her fourteen years. So I was surprised when I proposed a date and she, glowing and flirtatious, said, "Okay, great."

"Really?"

"Why not?"

We were both too young to drive, so we took the bus downtown to the movies. It's too long ago now. I don't remember the film, or even the theater, or whether, afterward, we went to the soda fountain at Rennebohm Rexall. I have no idea what we talked about. But I remember the snow. It started before we caught the bus back to Toni's neighborhood. We had to brush it off our coats when we boarded. As it fell, we watched it through the bus window. As I walked her home, it covered us. She was—I remember this, too—heartbreakingly lovely in the snow. The cold had turned her cheeks gently pink. A wisp of her hair had escaped her hat and rested on her forehead, dusted with snowflakes.

When we stopped in front of her house to say goodbye, the snow was several inches deep around us, and the world was deathly silent. We'd been drawn into the cocoon. There were just two of us on earth, and Toni—I know this now, did not then—wanted me, expected me, to kiss her. She'd been kissed already. Of this, I was sure. But I had never kissed a girl and knew no tactics to accomplish the feat. Kissing Toni, that sweet, perfect face—even if I'd done it badly, even if Toni had to correct my technique until we got it right—would have made us both happy. It would have made that night, despite the bus and the weather, the best date we'd ever had. We would have fallen, as much as possible and perhaps not for very long, in love.

I said good night. I left her on her doorstep—unkissed—and trudged home in the snow.

Here, then, was winter.

Just a few days later, on the phone, I said something wrong. Suddenly, we were finished. I never saw her again. Of course, having lost Toni, I was finally in love with her. I've felt the same ever since. Lately, I've come to see that night in the snow, when I fumbled away the most innocent and thrilling kiss of my life, as the perfect romance. It's like a dragonfly trapped in amber, forever the same. Toni will always be soft-focus beautiful. I'll always be clueless. It began with a surprise, lived out its entire lifespan in one snowy evening, and ended with the kiss that should have been but wasn't. It was my first lesson in love and in love's regret. It left me with a dream girl for life and a definition of winter.

In the snow, I'm always walking away from Toni.

22 Dec. '22

Yuletide blowback

"My road of good intentions led where such roads always lead. No good deed goes unpunished."

—Idina Menzel, from *Wicked*

THE NORTH POLE — For a few days after Christmas Eve, Santa Claus is dead to the world, sleeping off his whirlwind journey, soothing the bruises from squeezing his ample and aging hindquarters down a million chimneys.

When he finally revives, he settles beside the fire with a spreadsheet, a bottle of Bushmills and Mrs. Claus. Together, they assess the emotional damage and bitter recrimination wreaked by another season of love, giving and goodwill toward men.

Blurry from his long winter's nap, Santa scanned a scroll of holiday blunders, disappointments, complaints and ingratitude that stretched across the floor, more than twenty feet long. "Look at this," he growled, pointing to the first item.

Mrs. Claus had been studying the list for two days. "You mean tiny Tommy Tilden from Tulsa?"

"Judas priest!" exclaimed Santa, struggling to curb his language. "He's bitching because the scooter I delivered to the little snot wasn't motorized? He's six years old. Give him a motor and he'll run it into a tree. He'd kill himself."

"Would that be such a loss?" asked Mrs. Claus. She pulled Tommy's naughty/nice rap sheet from a folder.

"My God!" said Santa. "He put the cat into the microwave?"

Mrs. Claus smiled mirthlessly. "Blew the door right off. His mom is still scraping fur off the ceiling."

"Why didn't we just give the sadistic brat a stocking full of coal?"

"Nick!" said his wife. "You know we don't do that anymore. The litigation costs were killing us. Not to mention the time Greenpeace sank our coal barge."

Santa fought the urge to toss the scroll into the fire. "Do we have any issues here that won't give me a migraine?"

"Hardly," said Mrs. Claus, handing Santa a brimming mug of hot whiskey. "Let's start with little Billy Bumpus."

Santa inhaled the steam curling from his mug. "Billy? What's his beef? I got him what he wanted, didn't I?"

"Well, sort of. He asked you for a radio-controlled firetruck."

"And that's what he got, dammit!" Santa drank half his glass in one gulp, burning his palate and barking in pain.

"Yes, but the thing is," said Mrs. Claus, "that was before the Apple people flooded his social media account with propaganda for the new iPhone 14, leaving Bobby terrified that he would be the laughingstock of third grade—using an out-of-date device—when he got back to school after New Year's."

"So, you're telling me little Billy wanted a phone instead of a toy truck?"

"At the last minute, yes," said Mrs. Claus. "That's how kids are."

"Well, how the hell was I supposed to know?"

"We texted your sleigh, Nick. You were … let's see …" Mrs. Claus riffled through Santa's delivery manifest. "Probably somewhere over Schenectady."

Santa shook his head. "You know how phone batteries freeze up and die in the cold, over New York, in December. By then, I wasn't getting any reception."

"Well, maybe if you were using an iPhone 14?"

Santa scowled. "I can't solve Billy's phone issues tonight. Too bad for him. What next?"

"Well, Billy's sister, Britney?"

"What about her?"

"She wanted to switch gifts, too," said Mrs. Claus, tapping the next item. "She didn't get the new set of skis and a round-trip ticket to St. Moritz that she wanted."

"Well, of course, she didn't get skis and a trip! She didn't ask for that. Last time I knew, she was begging me for a fully furnished three-story, gabled Victorian dollhouse with silk wallpaper—which is exactly what I left under her tree. How could I forget? It took at least fifty elf hours to put the damn monstrosity together!"

"I know, Santa baby. But two days before Christmas, Britney found out that her BFF, Ashley, was getting a trip to the Swiss Alps with her new skis."

"I knew what Ashley wanted. And she got her skis. I almost killed myself getting them down the chimney."

"Only, well …" Mrs. Claus sighed and poured more steaming Bushmills. "I know you tried, dear. But I'm afraid Britney changed her mind about the skis and about going to St. Moritz."

"What the hell for? That's expensive stuff. The kid is spoiled rotten."

"Well, she is spoiled. That's part of the problem," said Mrs. Claus. "But the main thing was Buzz."

"Buzz?"

"Ashley's new boyfriend. She wanted to stay home so she could ride behind Buzz on the new Harley Davidson motorcycle he was getting for Christmas."

"Just a goddamn minute," said Santa. "I distinctly remember NOT delivering any Harley to any kid named Buzz."

"Right again. No bike for Buzz," said Mrs. Claus. "However, according to your final—revised—flight plan, you were supposed to give Ashley the Harley so she could re-gift it to Buzz. There's another message you missed, honey."

"Ashley? I wouldn't give that kid a motorcycle even if I knew she wanted one. She's fourteen! You don't give a 150-horsepower hog to an eighth-grade girl!"

"Ninth, actually," said Mrs. Claus. "And you know darn well you can't do anything about her parents. They give her anything she wants. Remember the pet baby elephant you had to smuggle out of Zimbabwe?"

DAVID BENJAMIN

"Oh, Christ," said Santa, "do I remember! I was bailing elephant shit out of the sleigh all night long."

As Santa and Mrs. Claus began to cope with hundreds of thousands of rejected, unwanted and misdirected Christmas presents, Santa had a brainstorm. "Wait. If Ashley's not using the skis and the ticket to the Alps, why can't Britney take her place?"

Mrs. Claus laughed, succumbing to sarcasm. "Fuggedaboudit, Nick," she said. "Ashley's and Britney's parents haven't spoken to one another for two years."

"But they live right next door."

"Yes," said Mrs. Claus. "On opposite sides of the twelve-foot spite fence that Ashley's dad built after Britney's dad ripped up his lawn and replaced all that manicured grass with wildflowers, dandelions, prairie grasses and beehives."

"Oh, that's right. The Bumpuses went green," Santa nodded. "I remember. And then Ashley's dad sicced the Homeowners Association on Britney's dad for violating community streetscape standards."

"Yes, but then Britney's dad took the Homeowners Association to court."

"Right," said Santa. "And when the Homeowners Association lost the case, Ashley's dad was so pissed off he set fire to Britney's dad's prairie."

"Which backfired," said Mrs. Claus, "because the fire fed fresh nutrients into the soil, which stimulated the weeds to grow back bigger and healthier than ever and spread their seeds onto Ashley's dad's lawn."

"Which sent Ashley's dad totally around the bend."

"And he started lobbing cantaloupes, eggplants and rotten tomatoes over the fence."

"After which," said Santa, smiling nostalgically, "Britney's dad bought three goats, who ate the fruits and veggies as soon as they cleared the fence."

"Which brought the Homeowners Association back into

the battle because they were shocked—shocked!—at the presence of omnivorous livestock in a gated community."

"Except," Santa recalled, "for the loophole. There's no mention of goats in the Homeowners Association bylaws. Just cows, pigs and horses. Yahtzee!"

"So, last holiday season, Ashley's dad walked next door with his Christmas present (remember, Nick?)—a pump-action twelve-gauge over-and-under Remington shotgun—and blew all three goats to kingdom come."

"I remember the bloodstains on the siding," said Santa wistfully.

"Oh, goodness!" said Mrs. Claus, standing up. "That reminds me."

She toddled over to the magnificent North Pole Christmas tree and came back with a big, gaily-wrapped package. "Merry Christmas, Nicky," she cooed.

"For me?" said Santa.

"Open it, sweetie."

As he beheld his gift, Santa's eyes, how they twinkled, his dimples how merry! It was bright red with white fur trim, size XXXL (to accommodate his not-so-little round belly).

"Oh, you darling girl! Just what I wanted," he said, kissing Mrs. Claus. "A bulletproof vest!"

29 Dec. '22

How George wrecked Christmas

George was accident-prone.

For example, the first time he met Jody's mother, he boldly leapt into her lap. She was drinking tea at the time, but she only spilled a few drops because George, despite his tendency toward minor, forgivable mishaps, had a knack for soft landings.

Jody's mom, who was known to friends, family and officialdom as June Noel, however, was sorely surprised. She didn't expect an encounter with a strange cat. Indeed, in more than one respect, George was a strange cat. Mom had never seen this black-backed, white-bottom, pink-nosed creature before. He didn't belong. As far as she knew, he had no name. She had no idea where he came from or how he got into the house. She could only guess that he had climbed the ridge from one of the bungalows nestled among the pines along the lake below.

Mom said, "Eek," softly when the cat landed. She didn't stand lest she spill tea on her sweater, a cherished family heirloom. The garment had been knitted of midnight-blue yarn by Mom's grandmother in the last few months of her long life. Of all Mom's keepsakes, the sweater was her most precious because, when she wore it, she felt as though she had snuggled into Nana's arms.

This is why Mom was alarmed when George, while luxuriantly stretching his long, lithe body across her startled lap, caught a claw in one strand of Nana's sweater. Mom dropped her teacup and cried out in distress.

It was George's turn to be sorely surprised.

Now, of course, any attempt to read the mind of a cat is unwise and inevitably fruitless. However, measured by George's reaction, it seems likely that he expected to be welcome in any lap he chose to grace with his presence. Hence, when Mom greeted George's condescension with the crash of china on the floor, hot tea sprinkling his fur and a squeal of alarm, George had ample reason to panic and flee.

Flight, alas, posed difficulties. George's right front paw refused to unhook from the discourteous human's fuzzy garment. George couldn't turn around. He looked up to Mom's face but perceived no empathy. It was red and growing redder. Her eyes bulged out unattractively. Her mouth, full of teeth, kept repeating, louder and louder, one word: "No, no, no, NO!"

Instinct told George to escape. This imperative left him no choice but to back up hurriedly, as fast as his hind legs and one free front leg could carry him. His other paw remained stubbornly connected to the raving biped's lumpy sweater.

Fortunately for George, even as he tried to run awkwardly backward, the garment—to which his errant claw continued to cling—stretched. As George pulled away, the sturdy strand of midnight-blue wool grew longer and longer ... two feet, then three.

Mom watched in horror. This cat, yanking and tugging a loop of yarn from her sweater, was threatening to unravel the last beloved product of Nana's ancient, blue-veined, arthritic fingers. Mom had no choice. To keep this intruder from stretching her sweater, by a single thread, to a point beyond repair, she had to lunge from her chair and follow the cat like a dog on a leash.

But she couldn't simply follow the panicky, backscrabbling cat to wherever it wanted to go. She had to stop the cat. She had to seize the feline fiend, hold it down and unhook its talon from her keepsake.

When George saw that the woman had left her feet in what he could only interpret as a flying tackle aimed at him, he redoubled his backward scramble. His trapped claw twisted and turned but would not let go the tenacious strand. George's blind retreat stopped suddenly when his rear parts thumped into a solid object—one of the end tables near the family fireplace. George was trapped. The woman might have crushed him if not for the end table, which she struck with her face. The impact caused her to lurch sideways, delivering a mere glancing blow to the cowering cat.

Mom dropped to the floor, dizzied by the punch to the bridge of her nose and gasping with pain. On the bright side, her sweater went slack. The strand of yarn fell limp, and George regained his claw. He wasted no time savoring his liberation. He found his feet, skittered a moment on the hardwood floor and lit out, up the ladder and out through the gap from whence he had come into the house.

Jody's sister, Gabrielle—known informally as Gaby—had heard the ruckus faintly from her back bedroom. She found her mother prostrate on the floor, bleeding from a crease between her eyes and woozily struggling to tuck a yard of yarn back into the bodice of Nana's woolen masterpiece.

After that incident, relations between Mom and George remained irredeemably cool. Nothing Jody said or did on George's behalf had any effect. Although Jody made an excellent case that the entire episode had been an accident, Mom wasn't swayed.

The Champagne Incident

Matters worsened that year on Thanksgiving. The Noels were hosting a feast for colleagues of Jody's dad, Carl, who worked as an architect in the big city forty miles away. In preparation for the guests' arrival, Mom had carefully washed twelve crystal champagne flutes, setting them along the length of the breakfast bar that marked the border of the kitchen.

The kitchen was broad and equipped with every appliance necessary for gourmet cookery. Stretched across the back wall were a double oven and gas range, microwave oven, a great silver refrigerator, a butcher block and a long counter punctuated by a toaster, blender, rice cooker and other culinary gadgets. Cabinets were above. Jody's dad, who had designed the house, had situated an island in mid-kitchen with a double sink and more counter space. Beneath were the dishwasher and cabinets. Above the kitchen was a mezzanine, accessed by a sturdy oak ladder. This was Jody's room.

Jody slept on a mattress laid on a frame a few inches off the floor and tucked toward one of the mezzanine's slanting walls. In the middle of his A-frame room, Jody could stand up straight with more than a foot of headroom. But the closer he got to either wall, the more he had to crouch. If he woke up on the wrong side of the bed, he was prone to bang his head. So, he was always careful about which way to roll in the morning, especially in winter when there was no sunshine through his skylight.

It was the skylight that had served as George's portal. Because heat rises, Jody's mezzanine tended to be the warmest room in the house. To cool his face and waft him with fresh air, Jody kept the skylight open at least a few inches, even on winter days. For Jody, this pane set into the sharp slant of the roof was his window on the universe. Framed by the skylights, the stars were countless brilliant holes in a black dome. From night to night, he could follow the quarters and course of the moon. When a full moon inched into his square of sky, the light was bright enough to read by. On moonless nights, Jody was enveloped in a blue-gray aura, tinged with fear, that he could almost feel on his skin. He would pull his blankets up to his nose and fall asleep among harmless hauntings. One morning in early autumn, on one of those ghostly nights without moonlight, Jody woke to the feel of footsteps, small paws crossing his body.

Jody's first thought was of a giant rat. The woods were full of squirrels and curious raccoons, but Jody thought of rats because of a movie scene that had stuck in his mind for months. This memorable episode took place in an underground tunnel lined with rotting dead bodies and skeletons draped with spiderwebs, where a million rats were crawling all over Indiana Jones and a waxy-faced blonde who later turned out to be a Nazi and then ended up dead from falling through a crevasse in another tunnel. Awakened by footsteps and haunted by vermin, skulls and Nazi blondes, Jody came terribly awake, feeling as though he was in a spider-infested sewer where rats trampled his blankets.

This moment of terror lasted as long as it took Jody's eyes to adjust to the dark and he could see the white parts of George's fur and the white muzzle beneath his black burglar's eye mask. "Oh, it's a cat," said Jody, softly. "Hi, cat." George then immediately came over to Jody and rubbed his head against the boy's face. Jody responded by deciding that the cat's name was George.

For a while, no one else in the family knew about George.

Rather like Indiana Jones, George was an explorer, and he was thorough. After his typically soft landing on the bed and making Jody's acquaintance, George commenced an exhaustive examination of Jody's mezzanine. When he returned a few nights later, he repeated the search as though he had never set foot in the room before. This exploration was clearly tiring because George would then join Jody in bed, snugging his face against Jody's cheek and dozing for a while, working up a powerful purr.

Then, *boing*! Up to the skylight in a single bound and gone.

The sweater incident, as it came to be known, was George's first foray down Jody's ladder and into the "main" house. Of course, it wasn't his last. But George maintained no discernible schedule. For a while, he would drop in every day—even twice—but then go a week without visiting. There were times when George was so furtive and silent that no one, not even Jody, knew that the transient cat had come and gone. Only later would evidence emerge. A lampshade might be slightly askew, a throw rug rumpled, a hairball upchucked onto the seat of a chair, and a remark tinged with exasperation. "Hm, looks like George was here."

Anyone in the family could have checked with Dozer, the plod-footed, good-natured English sheepdog who had been Jody's Christmas puppy when he was five years old. Dozer could sniff out fresh cat scent as soon as George slipped through the skylight. If so inclined, the dog could show the family exactly where George was hiding or creeping, sleeping or puking. But Dozer was a *laissez-faire* sort of mutt. He had no strong feelings about cats, he was loath to be seen as a tattletale, and he only barked in a dire emergency, such as when his dinner was late.

Dozer's misgivings about George only developed after what became known as the champagne incident. This title is somewhat of a misnomer because no actual champagne was involved.

Nor could there have been after George leapt, with catlike grace, onto the shiny tile breakfast bar where a dozen crystal flutes waited for Dad to uncork a bottle or two of Laurent-Perrier and fill them. It was the popping of the first bottle that surprised George. The sudden noise sent him scurrying along the breakfast bar, nudging all in a row—as he ran—the exquisite cut-glass vessels just enough to set them spinning in a terpsichorean spiral until each lost its balance.

Dozer, who had been napping beneath the breakfast bar, was rattled into wakefulness by the crash of one champagne flute inches from his tender nose, and then another champagne flute, and another, and seven, eight, nine—holy Saint Bernard!—how many more? Dozer found himself sprinkled and bewildered by a shower of exploding flutes and surrounded by glistening shards of shattered crystal. His confusion only grew when the roar of his master and the soprano shriek of his mistress followed the tempest.

Dozer was not so dumbfounded, however, that he didn't notice the black and white blur of the burglar cat as it climbed the ladder to the mezzanine in two Olympian leaps and vanished.

"Wow," said Jody, staring at a jagged expanse of broken Baccarat.

Holding the bottle, which had overflowed and soaked his sleeve, Dad said, "That goddamn cat. Where'd it come from?"

Mom, tears on her cheeks, replied, "Hell."

Gaby had a theory, which she unspooled during that Thanksgiving dinner. George, she had deduced, was a French cat.

"French?" asked Mom.

"Why French?" asked one of the guests, who was drinking champagne from a Dixie Cup.

"Oh, well, you have to listen to him," said Gaby, who was in her first year of middle school French. "He doesn't say, 'Meow,' in English. He says, 'Miaou.'"

This quieted everyone but Jody, who said. "That's the same."

Gaby shook her head piteously. "Jody, you doofus, it's not the same. You have no ear for *la belle française*."

Jody sneered at his big sister. "But George does?"

"In French, his name is *Georges*—with an 's.'"

Mom broke in. "Gaby, his name isn't George or Georg-*es*. We don't know his name. He's not our cat." Then she added, "Damn it," and blushed.

Gaby, however, stuck to her theory, pointing out that the occupants of the nearest bungalow down the ridge and beside the lake were two young French women named Anne-Françoise and Alienor. She had met them once.

"They're really nice," said Gaby. "Besides, *Georges* must be theirs 'cause the other bungalows were all closed for the winter.

"Well, why didn't they close down, too? And go away?" asked Dad.

"Because they love the winter, Daddy. They're ... um ... *sportive*!" said Gaby. "They ski, they skate, they snowshoe."

"Yeah, well," asked Jody, "do they have a cat? Did you see them with a cat?"

"Well, no," said Gaby. "But I can tell. *Georges* is French."

"Well, French or not," said Mom, "as soon as I get my hands on the little pest, I'm going to crate him up, ship him to Paris and tell him '*Bon voyage!*'"

"Oh, Mom, no!" cried Gaby.

"Gaby's right," said Dad. "That's too much work. It's easier to just pitch him off the deck."

Now, it's true that cats always land on their feet. However, tossed from the Noels' deck, George might not survive the flight regardless of where he pointed his feet. Jody's dad had built his dream house into a hill that overlooked a steep gorge. A rocky incline stretched downward a hundred yards, below which a dense forest of pine and oak concealed a stream that was only visible fleetingly on days when it reflected the noonday sun. If flung far enough out from the deck that overhung that precipitous valley, George would plummet a hundred feet before touching down and tumbling down a treeless jumble of granite and gravel.

"Oh, Daddy," cried Gaby.

Jody didn't join the argument. He knew that his parents didn't have the heart to kill any living thing. His mother had once rescued a yellowjacket from drowning in a glass of iced tea at a picnic. She blew on it gently until its wings dried, and it was able to fly away.

That Thanksgiving night, unrepentant, George slipped into Jody's bed and purred a feline lullaby.

The Shower Curtain Incident

Jody's dad preferred to maintain the impression that he stood aloof—and above the fray—in most domestic tussles. He was, after all, the breadwinner. He strove to preserve a certain air of sangfroid. In the ongoing controversy over George, therefore, Dad expressed his neutrality by repeating, tediously, the platitude, "Cats will be cats."

This would draw from his daughter a juicy razzberry, which Dad paternally overlooked.

He was able to cling to this pose until what became known as the shower curtain incident.

The Noels' dream house had two bathrooms. The large main bathroom was set into the hillside, between the master bedroom and Gaby's smaller, cozier boudoir. Dad had a separate bathroom in the cellar, a space only large enough for a modest office and "man cave." Dad had installed a desk, a drawing board, a few bookshelves, a television and a billiard table. Family members were discouraged from entering Dad's domain. But they were not forbidden, nor was the door to the cellar staircase ever locked. Often it stood open, allowing access to, for example, any curious cat who happened to pass by and notice how dark and inviting was this unexplored netherworld.

And so it came to pass one night, perhaps a week after Thanksgiving, that Mom had undertaken a lengthy occupation of the upstairs bath, coloring her hair. At the same time, Dad wanted to take a shower.

"No problem, honey," said Dad. "I'll go downstairs."

Downstairs, in his "private" bath, Dad was in store for a shock, which did not occur 'til he had stripped down to his briefs and reached inside the shower curtain to turn on the hot water.

One of the peculiarities of certain cats is the pleasure they derive from curling up and sleeping on a cool, smooth stretch of porcelain, the sort of unnatural surface that's rarely available except, of course, in a bathtub. George happened to be one such porcelain-prone cat. Weeks before, on his exploration of the cellar, George had reconnoitered Dad's bathroom, discovered the irresistible tub and had enjoyed several sensual and undisturbed catnaps there. George was, in fact, indulging himself in another forty winks in the tub when Dad reached in and turned the spigot.

As any cat lover can attest, cats hate getting wet. Water suddenly turns the tranquilest tabby into an airborne banshee. So, when the first cold gush hit George and woke him from a mouse dream slumber, he was as though lightning-struck. To escape the flood, he flung himself upward as high and as fast as he could fly. This bound threw him violently into the shower curtain, a plastic drape adorned with a pattern of bright-hued polka dots.

Stepping innocently away from the faucet, Dad did not expect his shower curtain to move or make noise. It had never done so in the past. This time, it uttered a piercing wail that was half shriek and part growl. And it came at him, suddenly and violently, bulging outward, striking his naked shoulder and—although this seemed incongruous—sinking its claws into his skin.

In reflexive self-defense, Dad tried to fend off the attack of the rampant shower curtain, clutching at it and raising a fist to fight it off. Before he could land a blow, one of the rungs holding the shower to the rail gave way, then another. Dad felt himself tipping backward. He tried to stay upright by grabbing hold of the curtain, a foolish move that only guaranteed Dad would tumble to the floor, which he did, with the smack of bare skin on cold tile. While Dad struggled in the clinging grip of the plastic shroud and began to cry out for help, the seemingly possessed curtain continued to writhe and claw at him, its voice a constant, ululating falsetto snarl.

Raked and punctured by the monster from the bathtub, Dad contrived to creep toward the door, pulling himself partly out of the shower curtain's death grip. Just as his head emerged and he was able to breathe, he felt feet pounding for barely a second along his back and saw, in the corner of his vision, an unmistakable black and white streak emerge from the bathroom, skid on the floor and vanish up the steps.

Dad remained where he was, breathing heavily, picturing the ravenous clawed monsters in *Aliens*, the giant cockroach of *Men in Black*, the mutant bathtub slugs in *Slither*. When he saw two feet in front of him, he recoiled in terror.

"Dad," said Jody. "What are you doing on the floor? And why are you wearing the shower curtain?"

It took a moment for Dad to find his voice and utter the syllable that explained it all.

"George."

The Paper Bag Incident

Over breakfast the next day, everyone, even Dad, agreed that the shower curtain incident was hardly George's fault. It was natural, after all, for cats to lounge around in enameled dissipation. Cats, after all, will be cats. And how was George to know that Dad was out there, on the other side of the curtain, turning on the water? And how was George to react other than in a state of frantic feline hysteria? Besides, all of Dad's wounds were so superficial that he didn't even need the dozen-odd Band-Aids suggested by Mom, just a few dabs of mercurochrome on the worst traces of George.

Dad even conceded that holding a grudge against George was beneath his dignity. Still, Dad's equability toward the surreptitious cat was shaken. He occasionally entertained thoughts of how he might be able to cat-proof his dream house, just in case.

Soon, though, he would stop and reproach himself for entertaining exaggerated anxieties. *Just in case what?* he would ask himself. *It's only a cat.*

However, the mishap that came to be known as the paper bag incident suggested an answer to Dad's "just in case" quandary. It definitely proved a wake-up call for Dozer.

The mishap probably would not have happened if the Noel family had not revived their tradition of marking Mom's birthday by gathering 'round a blazing fire and toasting the beginning of the Christmas season with hot, spiced apple cider. This took place in one of the front corners of the house, where Dad had designed a family den with a semicircle of easy chairs and end tables that faced the fireplace. In the middle of this oasis was a broad table close to the floor, where the family often set out food, played games or worked on jigsaw puzzles. On this occasion, however, according to tradition, the table featured Mom's birthday gift from her loving husband, two dozen red roses, surrounded by baby's breath and fern fronds, in a blue butterfly cloisonné vase. As usual, the party was grand, with more presents for Mom, cake and ice cream and Christmas music on Dad's surround-sound stereo system.

The morning after the party, George entered the quiet house. He was in safari mode, hunting for fresh stimuli. George was a cat who, above all, could not stand to be bored. In his every waking moment, he kept out an eagle eye for anything even slightly out of the ordinary.

And there it was! The Noels were neat, middle-class people, and Mom was a fastidious housekeeper. But, as Bob Cratchit might phrase it, they had been "making rather merry" the night before. Proof of this lapse in discipline were several cider cups left unwashed on the breakfast bar and, lying on the floor of the house's central atrium, a paper bag. Its mouth was open, and from its dark interior wafted the vague redolence of mulling spices.

Cats have no willpower against empty boxes and open bags. There was certainly a time in prehistory when Cenozoic cats, prowling for prey, saw a dark hole in the earth or the hollow in a tree and entertained visions of juicy marmots and delectable chipmunks. So, there they went. This urge to plumb the darkness is an instinct that has never perished, which meant that George could not help himself in the presence of the gaping sack on the floor in the atrium.

So, there he went. George burrowed all the way into the dark recess and then even further. There was, to his amusement and soon dismay, a hole in what should have been the bottom of the bag. So, as he squirmed through, he found himself suddenly popping out into the light.

But not quite.

George managed to push his head and front feet through the hole. That was all. The rest of George stayed in the bag. His front feet managed some traction on the polished floor but they could not pull him free from the bag. His hind legs churned busily, then frantically against the smooth paper surface, but took him nowhere. George was puzzled. He paused a while in jellicle thought. He looked around for a helpful human. The children had gone to school. Dad and Mom were working somewhere. His only companion, Dozer, the dog, was not only useless, he was nowhere to be seen.

Dozer, however, was roused by the noises George made while scrabbling on the smooth hardwood floor and struggling to break free of the clinging bag. So, Dozer, curious as a cat, emerged from hiding and clicked over to George. As is the wont of virtually every dog, his first gesture toward any puzzling situation was to sniff. He extended his muzzle toward George.

Normally, George maintained a diffident truce with the languid hound. But George, half-immobilized, was in no mood for canine inquisitiveness. And both his front paws were operative. So, bracing himself on his left paw, he swung the other, talons extended, toward that intrusive nose.

Raked across his most delicate organ, Dozer yelped and leapt backward. Sensing his advantage, George swiftly scrabbled two-footed toward Dozer, forcing him backward.

Dozer, of course, had no idea where he was going. His nose was bleeding, and this scissor-handed feline, clawing his way across the floor like a deranged hermit crab, seemed determined to rip it right off his face. So, Dozer kept backing away. His tail led him toward the circle of chairs ranged around the fireplace. Driven by terror and propelled by the substantial muscles in his haunches, Dozer rammed through a narrow gap between a chair and a table, on which stood a lamp, which toppled to the floor, smashing its lightbulb with an alarming pop.

The noise increased Dozer's panic and, inexplicably, redoubled George's two-legged attack. Dozer spun desperately on his heels and bounded blindly away from the crawling, hissing cat. The family's game table—and a cloisonné vase—blocked Dozer's escape. Halfway across the table, he flopped onto its surface and slid toward the fireplace. His lacerated nose hit the floor as the beautiful Chinese amphora—top heavy with roses, fronds and baby's breath—teetered once, then twice, then tipped over, smashing decisively and covering the startled Dozer in a rush of cold water.

Soaked, shocked and terrified, Dozer found enough of his feet to plant one or two on the floor and another somewhere atop the suddenly wet-slippery table and lunged …

into the fireplace. Suddenly, Dozer was wallowing in a bed of warm ashes and surrounded by brick walls. The ashes flew into his face, filled his mouth and clogged his nose. He was suffocating. He spun in circles, unable to see, coating his wet fur with fine, adhesive powder. He spluttered and whimpered 'til, finally, there! He saw light. Dozer got his feet under him. With a leap that carried him over the table and past George, Dozer flew from his breathless cave and scampered, each step a muddy footprint, across the house, up the ladder—where he had never gone before—and onto Jody's bed, where he lay cowering and soiling the counterpane for the next three hours.

George, on the other hand, had a stroke of luck. Beneath the fireplace table was a rug. Once on the rug, the paper bag no longer slip-slid along the floor. George's hind paws got traction at last. With a mighty, mehitabelic yowl, he sank his claws into the clinging paper, shredding it 'til he was able to roll free from its grip and restore all four feet under his body. Without looking back (cats never look back), George strolled away from the scene of the incident with leonine dignity.

George passed Dozer, tucked into a muddy ball on Jody's bed, as he departed by way of the handy skylight.

Of course, when the family got home, they found wreckage. Dad had to carry a still traumatized Dozer down the ladder. Mom nearly wept over the shards of her vase and the trampled roses. Jody helped clean up the fireplace and the trail of Dozer's pawprints. Jody's bedding went into the laundry. Save for a suspiciously shredded paper bag, there was no evidence that George had been there that day.

Gaby's theory of the crime, to which no one else subscribed, involved a squirrel entering through the chimney and searching for acorns in the paper bag. Furious after finding no nuts, the squirrel attacked Dozer, who retaliated by chasing the squirrel into the fireplace. There, after a flurry of paw-to-paw combat, the squirrel escaped up the chimney like Santa Claus, leaving Dozer, bloody, muddy and blameless, as the fall dog.

For a week, there was no sign of George, an absence that allowed the paper bag conundrum to fade in the family's memory.

The Bronze Angel Incident

Carl Noel was a yuletide fanatic. He loved the season. He had actually designed his dream house with Christmas in mind. On one side of the front door opposite the fireplace, a floor-to-ceiling window, fifteen feet tall, dominated the house's facade. Every year since the family moved in, Dad had hauled into the house a gigantic fir or balsam that he decorated with a thousand colored lights blinking and winking away. He had become a voracious collector of Christmas ornaments, Santa Clauses, elves and gnomes and snowmen, reindeer, moose and cardinals, stars and snowflakes, bunnies, teddy bears, owls and mice, cherubs, Magi and nutcrackers, balloons, half-moons and sunbursts, drums, violins, harps and horns, clowns and cuties, Virgin Marys and Christchildren, even frogs and vegetables. His crowning glory was an angel, custom-molded in polished bronze after the abstract style of Constantin Brancusi. This, his *pièce de résistance*, went on the very top of the tree every year, and every year Mom trembled with anxiety as Dad climbed fifteen feet up the ladder to laboriously affix the glistening angel just below the ceiling.

Dad even installed a revolving tricolor lamp on the wall opposite the treetop to spotlight his bronze angel. Every year, after descending the ladder, he would stand staring upward, studying the angel's position, asking Mom if it was straight, judging whether the light was showing it to best advantage, pondering whether he should climb back up and make adjustments, to which Mom always said, "Oh no, honey. It's perfect. I wouldn't touch it. It's fine, really. Please don't go back up there."

Carl Noel was also an ecumenical guy. He loved all the year-end holidays. So, besides an elaborate papier mâché Christmas creche beneath his mighty tree, he also installed a menorah to honor Chanukah. He was never actually sure when Chanukah fell during any December, so—to play it safe—he kept all nine candles lit throughout the season. The effect, beginning just after Mom's birthday, was an almost blinding display of Christmas tree lights along with the blazing menorah and another dozen candles fashioned in the shape of Santa Claus, Frosty the Snowman, Rudolph the Red-Nosed Reindeer, etc. Jody loved it. Mom was always relieved when the day-long project of trimming the tree had ended. Gaby, the family busybody, inevitably quibbled. She would say, "Daddy, you put this humongous tree in this big window. But we're here in the woods. There's nobody to see it!"

To which, every year, Dad would say, "We see it, sweetheart. It's a family thing."

"Yeah," Gaby would reply. "Right."

Indeed, after the tree went up and Dad turned on all those thousand dazzling lights and the whole family trooped outside to behold its glory through the towering window, it was an indisputably breathtaking sight.

"Oh, dear, it's very nice," Mom would tell Dad.

"Pretty cool," Jody usually said.

Even Gaby had to admit she was impressed.

And Dad would say, "I think it's better than last year. This is the best tree ever. Don't you think?"

Agreement was unanimous.

Even George liked the tree.

Perhaps too much.

To your typical cat, the appeal of a Christmas tree, beyond its alluring fragrance and the flavor of the needles, is the plethora of dangling objects hanging down from its lowermost branches. George, however, didn't immediately succumb to all these attractions. When first he beheld this astounding addition to his surrogate family's domain, George was apprehensive. He prowled gingerly all around its spreading perimeter, sniffing and twitching his tail. He winced and blinked at the glare of its lights. This immense tree suddenly erected inside the house might have confirmed George's suspicion that humans are crazy, but there's no telling because the mind of a cat is a black box.

By his next visit, George had adapted. The tree was there, perhaps permanently, and it clearly afforded him possibilities for amusement. The ornaments were particularly appealing. He discovered that when he batted a ball, or a Santa, or a dangling bell, it bobbed around and swung back at his face, which afforded him the pleasure of hitting it again, eventually turning the experience into a kittenweight title bout. When George got bored with this, he curled up on the flannel skirt beneath the tree, a bed scented with pine needles, for a yuletide snooze.

It was during one of these naps, on Christmas Eve, when George opened his eyes and spied the snake.

Living in a bungalow in the woods, George had experience with snakes. They lurked among leaves on the forest floor. They slid silently along the ground, menacing songbirds, rabbits, chipmunks and other critters that George regarded as his personal prey. George resented snakes, and he pounced on them whenever he saw one. Inevitably, however, the snake would elude George's first thrust and foil him with one of two tactics. Most times, the snake would just slither away at a surprising speed and disappear into undergrowth too dense for George to follow. A few times, however, the threatened snake curled into a ball, its head exposed and beady eyes glaring at George, its tongue licking in and out of its mouth, daring the cat to go ahead and come after it, but be ready for it to bite him in the face and swallow one of his eyes.

In those cases, George muted the call of the wild and retreated to the safety of human habitation.

So, George was suddenly alert and wary at the sight of a long green snake lurking beneath the wonderful giant shrub in the middle of his human habitation. This wasn't fair! Poised to attack the interloper and chase it back outdoors where serpents belong, George hesitated. Cautiously, he pawed it once, barely touching it, testing its reaction. Would it flee or stand its ground?

It remained motionless. This was all the assurance George needed. He had a snake cornered inside the house. There was no underbrush into which it could crawl. George finally had a snake, his woodland nemesis, as vulnerable as a sparrow.

George pounced. He had it. It didn't twist or turn. It didn't curl up or fight back. Was it dead? George didn't care. He was a predator. Dead or alive, the snake was his quarry. He wasn't letting go. He sank his teeth into the snake, unaware of its secret defense.

Electricity!

George had bitten into an electric snake. It wouldn't let him go! Its charge coursed through George's bloodstream like a tongue of flame. For a moment, if observed from a near vantage point, George resembled a Looney Tunes tabby, his legs splayed, his hair standing out in spikes, his eyes bulging, tendrils of smoke rising from his ears.

Unable to let go, George launched his second option. He ran and ran in circles, circumnavigating the immense Christmas tree, dragging behind him the electric cord that lit the thousand lights. With each circuit, the cord tightened around the base of the tree like a noose.

At last, the snake fell out of George's teeth, and the piercing, brain-numbing pain subsided. George crouched beneath the boughs, stricken with an all-consuming depth of paranoia possible only in cats. In its struggle, the snake had wrapped itself around George's throat. George's solution was to run. He didn't know why he had to run exactly. But he had to. It was a cat thing. Only another cat would understand.

He looked for a way out.

There!

George burst from beneath the tree, plowing through Dad's lovely hand-painted papier mâché Nativity diorama, trampling Joseph and shoving the Virgin into the manger. Cows and sheep flew every which way. By the time George had reached the menorah and knocked it aside, the snake around his neck had tightened. He scrambled all the harder to escape its grip. He scurried to the left, and it wouldn't let go. He tried sprinting to the right. The snake hung on.

As a matter of physics, it would seem inconceivable that a cat weighing perhaps ten pounds could tip the balance of a fifteen-foot balsam fir. But, as anyone knows who has tried to situate and straighten a Christmas tree, your typical tannenbaum is treacherously top heavy with trimmings and baubles. It teeters in delicate balance. So, just as George wrenched free from the serpentine cord, as flames from the fallen menorah set fire to the skirt—littered with dry needles—beneath the tree, Dad's mighty balsam lost its mooring and tipped into the great window, striking it with both a coniferous thump and an ominous crack.

George's antics had, of course, caught the attention of Dad and Mom, Jody and Gaby. Dozer was slower on the uptake and too close to the action. By the time Dozer realized that George was tangled in an electric cord, the tree was toppling, and flames were licking up into its branches, his tail was on fire. He began to gallop around the house, knocking things over.

"Jesus CHRIST!" shouted Dad.

In the next moments, as Jody chased Dozer with a glass of water and Dad rooted in the closet for a fire extinguisher, Mom stood gaping in horror. She watched the fire creep toward Christmas presents she had spread festively beneath the far boughs of the mighty evergreen. Gaby kept busy taking photos with her mobile phone.

Jody managed to douse Dozer's tail, which had shrunk somewhat and continued to smoke. Dad was poised to unleash the extinguisher when everyone in the family realized the meaning of that cracking sound they had heard when the tree leaned into the window. Dad's Brancusi angel, the heaviest and hardest ornament on the tree, had struck the window with hammerlike force. The window was made of sturdy stuff and it had held except for a little crack. A moment later, audible even over the carols crooning from his stereo, Dad heard the crack expanding. It spread outward and down in an erratic staccato as the family listened in frozen, dreadful suspense.

By the time the web of cracks reached just about Dad's height, the weight of the Christmas tree had finished off the window. With a sudden *whoosh* and a tinkling cascade of glass that magically reflected the colors of a thousand lights, the window collapsed. The tree went prostrate, rather gracefully, ending up half outside the house and welcoming inside a cold solstice wind, flecked with snowflakes.

The Christmas lights still gleamed. The fire beneath still burned. After a few minutes, Dad with the fire extinguisher, Jody and Mom with a brief bucket brigade, had stanched the flames. There was remarkably little damage to the structure of Dad's dream house—except for a scorched floor and the fallen window.

Gaby got pictures of the entire event.

George missed most of the drama. Once free from the devious electric snake, he had left his troubles behind, slipped through the skylight and headed home, wherever that might be.

Aftermath

That night, after the volunteer fire department had dropped by and checked for lingering embers, the family left everything pretty much as it was and spent the night in the Shady Rest Motel.

On Christmas day, Dad somehow found a local contractor willing to work triple-time. By afternoon, the fifteen-foot window frame in Dad's dream house had been filled by an expanse of plywood that shielded the family from the worst of the winter blast. The house was still freezing and unlikely to warm up for twenty-four hours.

Dad and Jody spent an hour salvaging ornaments and untangling Christmas lights. Then, without eulogy, Dad dumped the tree over the edge of the hill and into the rocky ravine. Back inside, the family faced a soggy pile of Christmas presents that the sympathetic volunteer firefighters had stacked in the atrium. The family decided to let the gifts dry out for a day or two before unwrapping Santa's bounty. Bravely, Mom applied herself to Christmas dinner, which wasn't ready to eat 'til long after dark. But the Noels kept a stiff upper lip, sat down to their holiday feast in their winter coats and mufflers, listened to Christmas music on the stereo and gave Dozer a big bowl of roast turkey and stuffing as consolation for his torched tail.

Over dessert, Dad started to smile, which prompted Gaby to giggle, which got Jody laughing. Mom rolled her eyes and Dozer, despite a little discomfort, wagged his bandage.

"This is one Christmas," said Mom, "that we'll never forget."

Around midnight, as Jody was drifting off to sleep, George

found an opening in the skylight just wide enough to squeeze his head through. Jody felt the familiar plop of little cat feet on his bed. George settled in beside Jody's face and began to purr. Together, on Christmas night, they fell guiltlessly asleep.

19 Dec. '23

Nobody says

Hark, the herald angels joke,
Santa's dead of a massive stroke.

I

At first, the Cratchits were convinced that their real estate agent, Jake Marley, was a con man, offering them a lovingly maintained two-story Victorian manor with a wraparound veranda for a price less than half its assessed value. They were even more suspicious when they visited the property, known locally as the Old Yoolis Mansion. Although left inexplicably vacant for more than fifty years, the house had been lovingly maintained, said Marley, by the local historical society, whose members had succeeded in getting it listed on the National Register of Historic Places.

The grand old pile stood isolated in a glorious setting. Meadows rampant with wildflowers filled the space between the house and the distant street. Woods surrounded the house and, on one side, behind an ancient stone wall, a picturesque ancient cemetery, more than two centuries old, contained weathered headstones beneath a canopy formed by the limbs of birch, sugar maples and gnarled oaks.

"This is beautiful," whispered Hermione Cratchit to her husband, Bob.

"There's something fishy here," replied Bob, as he roamed and probed the property in search of the fatal flaw—dry rot, termites, basement seepage, radon—that Marley had contrived to conceal.

"It's too good to be true," Bob whispered.

Most fishy of all had been Marley's reluctance to even show the house to the Cratchits. But they had seen photos in the listing and insisted on a viewing. A tour of the interior and a stroll through the grounds, plus the temptingly low price, overpowered the Cratchits' doubts and the realtor's unexplained misgivings. They bought the Old Yoolis Mansion just in time for their kids, Martha, Peter, Mary and Tim, to start school.

The first sign that something might be amiss was the neighbors, none of whom offered even a cursory welcome. They seemed to be actively avoiding the Cratchits and their mansion. To reach the nearest neighbors, Dave and Candy Jarndyce, required a five-minute walk out to the street and down the block. After a week or so, Hermione decided it was up to her to break the ice. On a Saturday morning, she baked a batch of blueberry muffins—one of her specialties—and, with Mary and Tim in tow, took it over to the Jarndyces. When she opened the door to Hermione's knock, Mrs. Jarndyce seemed alarmed at the sight of her new neighbors.

In response to Hermione's greeting and a cheery "hello" from the children, Candy Jarndyce gaped in silence for a long, uncomfortable spell before saying, "Oh, uh. My husband. He's … ill. I can't …"

With that, she shut the door. The muffins were still warm, so Hermione decided to try the next house, home of old Dan Havisham and his dog, Dammitall.

Old Dan opened his door, snatched up a muffin, bit into it and spewed crumbs as he muttered, "You people got no idea what you're in for."

As he was closing the door, he reached out for a second muffin. "For the dog," he said. Staring at old Dan's knocker, Hermione Cratchit decided to postpone further efforts at outreach to the immediate community. In the next few weeks, the neighbors maintained their boycott, not even deigning to acknowledge the Cratchits' presence. The family noticed, however, that occasionally a car would slow to a crawl as it passed on the street, its windows rolled up, its passengers' faces pressed to the glass.

In school, for the first month, the Cratchit children heard murmuring behind their backs. They had difficulty making even casual acquaintance with other kids. Almost all conversations began and ended with the question, "Did you really move into the Old Yoolis Mansion?"

When Martha, who was fourteen, responded by inviting a girl to come over after school and see inside the famous house, the girl went pale and hurried away.

"Mom," said Martha, "there's something about this house."

"I get that impression," said her mother. "But what?"

"Nobody will say," said Martha.

"Maybe it's haunted," said Tim.

Martha cuffed Tim upside the head.

Bob Cratchit managed to pick up a slight clue when he encountered old Dan Havisham at the hardware store. "Mr. Havisham," said Bob cordially, "hello! I'm you're new—"

"I know who you are," growled old Dan.

"Oh, good. Well, then—"

"They come every Christmas," old Dan broke in. "Yooou'll see."

"Christmas? But who?"

"Yooou'll see."

With that, old Dan left Bob standing in the shovel, spade and pitchfork department and departed the store without buying anything.

"*Who* comes every Christmas?" Hermione asked her husband after he had related the hardware incident.

"He didn't say," said Bob.

"Nobody says," added Martha, irritably.

"Ghosts?" asked Tim cautiously.

That year, over Thanksgiving dinner, the Cratchits resolved, as a family, to find out why they seemed to be outcasts in their subdivision, although they had done nothing to offend anyone. Something about their house, the beautiful Old Yoolis Mansion, was bothering a lot of people who absolutely refused to say what was the matter. The Cratchits had learned nothing from Jake Marley, their skittish realtor. Old Dan Havisham had been gleefully cryptic. Hermione, brimming with hope, had made a call to one Mrs. Dombey, president of the historical society, who had only said, "It's yours now. We've washed our hands of it. God help you."

"Why should God help us?" asked Peter.

"Nobody says," replied Martha, disconsolately.

As Bob carved the turkey that day, he proposed that the family throw a big Christmas party. They would invite the whole block, serve a lot of spiked punch, hot cider and boozy egg nog. People's tongues would loosen and somebody, sooner or later, would reveal the dark secret of the old house.

"Good idea," said Hermione.

"Jeez, ya think the house is haunted?" said Tim, renewing his theme.

"Have you seen any ghosts?" asked Martha sharply.

"No," said Tim.

"Well then," said Martha.

"If it's not ghosts that people are scared of," asked Mary, "what is it?"

"Nobody *says*," snarled Martha.

Two weeks later, after delivering more than fifty invitations by hand, Hermione Cratchit had not received a single RSVP, nor even a refusal. The entire neighborhood had simply resolved—without consultation—to ignore the Cratchit Christmas cotillion.

No one on the block, or in the whole tightlipped town, bothered to tell the Cratchits why they would not set foot in their house, drink their wine and eat Hermione's celebrated

Christmas cookies. The ostracized family was as mystified as ever.

2

Two weeks before Christmas, Peter scored a breakthrough. He made friends with a boy called Twist, an unpopular middle school classmate. Over hot chocolate at the village soda shop, Twist had unspooled a tale that stretched Peter's credulity.

"I don't believe it," he told Twist.

"You wait and see," replied Twist ominously. "But if you do, if you *see,* it'll be too late."

"Too late for what?" asked Tim when Peter got home that day.

"They'll get us," said Peter, ominously.

"Who'll get us?" demanded Martha, the big sister.

Peter lowered his voice. "The undead."

"The *what*?" snapped Martha.

"Zombies," whispered Peter. "Christmas zombies."

"Nonsense," said Martha.

"That's the stupidest thing I ever heard," added Mary.

"Okay, you asked for it," said Peter. "Come with me."

Without another word, Peter led his sisters and little brother out of the old mansion, over the stone wall and into the ancient graveyard.

Leading them to a shadowy corner of the lot beneath a scarred and scabrous beech, Peter said, "Twist said it was here, and I looked for it. There!"

He pointed at a grave marker, sunken into the forest floor and half buried under fallen leaves. It was chipped and weathered, but the letters etched into its surface were clear. It read:

HERE LIE

"Here lie who?" asked Tim, whose reading level was two grades higher than his actual grade.

Peter hastened to the stone and swept away the concealing

leaf litter. Quickly, Tim was able to read:

THE GHOSTS

Peter kept kicking leaves away.

OF CHRISTMAS PAST
OF PEACE ON EARTH, AND

The last line was half visible where the ground had swallowed the headstone. Tim scratched away the dirt and read:

CHRISTMAS YET TO FEAR

"Fear?" asked Mary

"Ya see?" said Peter.

"See what?" said Martha, dubiously.

"Okay, listen," said Peter. He plumped onto the grave and glowered commandingly at Martha, Mary and Tim, who arranged themselves around him. "Here's what Twist said everybody's scared to talk about."

Peter then unfolded a tale that first astounded his sisters and brother and finally left them trembling with terrible wonderment.

"Sometime in the middle of the nineteenth century," said Peter, "the original owners of the house, the Yoolises, began dabbling in the supernatural and trying to communicate with the dead. One Christmas, the family patriarch, Ebenezer Yoolis, brought together the most prominent spiritualists, mediums, diviners, sorcerers and necromancers from hundreds of miles around. One of them, a self-declared witch named Zhenshchina Smertaya—"

"Wha'd you say?" asked Tim.

"C'mon, don't ask me to say it again."

"What *did* you say?"

Peter dug a piece of paper out of his pocket. "Twist wrote it down for me. Here."

While Tim stared at the sesquipedalian name, his lips

struggling to form the strange syllables, Peter went on to say that on the night of the séance, the witch ordered the erection in the cemetery of an altar composed of fallen headstones. At the stroke of Christmas midnight, Madame Smertaya led the weird company in a chorus of summons to the spirits of Christmas past and all mortals who had died on the day that the Christchild was born.

"What happened?" asked Martha.

"Nothin'," Peter replied. "No spirits, no ghosts, no bodies crawling out of their graves. Just, y'know, snow. Everybody went home sayin' the old bag was full of crap.

But the story didn't end that night," said Peter.

Years passed, and old Ebenezer Yoolis' grand convocation of necromancy was forgotten. The cemetery sank back into weeds, gopher burrows, feral cats and decrepitude. The Yoolis family gradually died off until the only Yoolis left was Ebenezer III, namesake of his grandfather. True to family tradition, Eb—who never married—was a cantankerous recluse in his decaying castle. He was known at Christmastide to batter carolers with his cane and fling snowballs at them as they fled his doorstep.

"But then," said Peter, "there was a Christmas blizzard with snow so heavy that people couldn't leave their houses."

A great silence descended on the town as the sky and the earth, bonded by the blizzard, seemed to become a single vast organism. Almost by a sort of telepathy, townspeople came to believe that this union of the heavens and the depths below the snow-smothered ground had brought to full vigor the spell cast fifty years before in the old boneyard by Madame Swertaya, demon queen of the gypsies. It was said—although no one saw—that Ebenezer Yoolis was visited that Christmas not by ghosts of Christmas past, present and future but by the very hordes of moaning, staggering, clutching and creeping undead whom the convocation of necromancers had tried and failed to summon.

DAVID BENJAMIN

Save for old Eb, there were no witnesses to the invasion of the living dead into the Old Yoolis Mansion. But somehow the rumor arose. Ebenezer III was seen the next day in the village shopping for butter and eggs. He greeted townspeople cordially, which he had never done before. He stopped and chatted. He patted children on the head. He stuffed a ten-dollar bill into the Salvation Army bucket. From that day on, until he died on a Christmas morning a dozen years later, he proved to be a kindly soul, a regular churchgoer and a boon to his neighbors. This transformation from bitter curmudgeon to Uncle Eb only reinforced the unanimous conviction in town that something had happened that storm-battered Christmas Eve and, whatever it was, it was still going on—every Christmas since.

"They crawl out of the cemetery every Christmas, out of *that grave*," said Peter. "The whole town knows they do. They wander around the house and the yard and the woods, hungering for human flesh. That's why nobody's lived here for years and years. That's why the last people who lived here left everything behind—they just ran away at midnight on Christmas Eve. Mother, father, all the kids. They never went back, not even to get their money or their car. They never said a word about what happened, and they moved as far away as they could go. Disappeared. Just like the family before them, like all the families who lived here and went away. Screaming. On Christmas. At midnight."

"Aw, bullshit," said Tim.

"It's true!"

"Timmy!" said his big sister. "Language."

"Has anybody ever seen these zombies?" asked Bob Cratchit two hours later when Peter repeated Twist's wild story to his parents.

"Well, yeah," said Peter. "The families who lived here. They saw 'em and ran away."

"Fifty years ago," said Bob Cratchit. "And they never told

anyone what they supposedly saw. Right?"

"Yeah, I guess," said Peter, irresolutely. "But everybody says—"

"Everybody says?" scoffed Bob Cratchit. "If everybody said the moon was made of guacamole, you'd believe them?"

Peter couldn't challenge his father's obvious logic. But he insisted that there had to be some reason why nobody had lived in the Old Yoolis Mansion for so long and why the historical society only visited the house, sweeping and scrubbing and painting it, on the longest, sunniest days in the middle of the summer.

Despite the doubts of the Cratchit parents, the legend of the Christmas undead came back around the dinner table the next evening. When Tim said there just might be a tiny chance that the dead could rise up and walk the Earth, his mother dropped her fork with a clatter.

"There is no way that could happen, Tim," she said. "It's against science."

"Dead is dead," added Bob Cratchit.

"Okay," said Tim meekly. "So, why do all the neighbors stay away from us? We didn't do anything. Why are they all scared of us?"

"They're not scared of us, Timmy," said his mother. "They're scared of ... well, you know."

"Yes, we do know, Mother," said Martha. "The whole town thinks dead people are creeping and crawling all over our house at Christmas."

"Martha," said her father, "people believe a lot of things that aren't real."

"Especially," said Hermione Cratchit, "things that are terrible and frightening. People used to believe in witches, ghosts, vampires, werewolves and doppelgangers."

Peter said, "What's a doppelganger?"

Mary softly added, "I believe in vampires, Mom. I read about how—"

She was interrupted by her father, who knew Mary's vampire theories too well. "Okay, kids, just for fun, let's say it's true. Every Christmas, a parade of dead carolers and deceased department store elves come up out of the cemetery and attack us in our beds. If that happens—oooh!" he shuddered. "What do we do?"

A silence suddenly descended on the Cratchit dinner table.

Bob Cratchit pressed on. "Maybe we should give up. Pack up and leave before they come."

"No!" protested Tim.

"I like this house," said Mary softly.

"Timmy's right," said Hermione with a ring of finality. "We do nothing. We stay here—because there is no such thing as zombies."

Bob Cratchit stuck to his thesis. "No, no, we're still playing pretend here, sweetie. What if our closest neighbors really are a bunch of dead Christmas cannibals? If we don't get away before they come and get us, what's the plan? How do we defend our home?"

"This is ridiculous," said Hermione Cratchit, throwing up her hands.

"It's simple, Dad. We have to kill 'em," said Peter.

Martha rolled her eyes. "You can't kill them, butthead. They're already dead."

"Oh, come on, Martha," said Peter, "haven't you seen any zombie movies or *The Walking Dead*?"

"Of course not, Peter. I have an actual brain, unlike you."

Tim intervened. "You're both right. Zombies are dead. But you gotta kill 'em all over again."

"Right," said Peter, banging the table. "Shoot 'em in the head. Blow their actual brains out."

"Or cut off their heads," said Tim, helpfully demonstrating a horizontal karate chop.

Mary squeaked with alarm. "Wait. Peter said some of these are dead Santa Clauses from, like, Christmas parades a hundred years ago," she said. "Peter, you could shoot Santa Claus in the head?"

"Well, yeah, I could," replied Peter, "if Santa was tryin' to eat me."

"And reindeer?" Martha broke in. "You could kill Dancer and Prancer? By chopping off their heads. Innocent little deers?"

"Guns," offered Tim. "We're gonna need lots of guns!"

"I have a better idea," said Bob Cratchit, smiling.

This conversation was the birth of the Old Yoolis Mansion Christmas Spectacle. Neighbors passed by slowly—some even stopped, although they never approached closer than the street—as, night by night, Bob Cratchit's brainstorm turned the once gloomy manor house into a holiday light show so brilliant that it could be seen from space.

First, in letters twelve feet high, lit from within and bathed in the glow of a million-candlepower spotlight, Bob Cratchit mounted the words "MERRY CHRISTMAS!" atop the roof. He stuffed a mannequin dressed as Santa Claus waist-deep in the chimney and arranged Santa's sleigh, eight lifesize reindeer sparkling with lights—plus Rudolph with a dazzling, throbbing red nose—all along the eaves troughs. Above this, Bob Cratchit erected a star, twenty feet in diameter, so bright that the neighbors, the Baxters, across the street a quarter-mile away, had to pull down their shades as soon as the sun went down.

In the yard, Bob Cratchit staked down an inflatable Frosty the Snowman two stories tall. He spent more than a thousand dollars on a Nativity creche with a lifesize Virgin Mary, Joseph, the shepherds and angels, cows, oxen, sheep, a donkey. He rented several chickens and a live goose. He bought an authentic manger lined with straw, hand-carved out of olive wood, by a craftsman in Israel. He surrounded the creche with Christmas trees fifteen feet tall, strung with silvery garlands. He covered the trees and rimmed the entire periphery of the mansion with multicolored Christmas lights. He put in fenceposts all along the driveway, ran wire from post to post and festooned the wires with more lights. He worked past midnight every day in his basement workshop cutting and painting plywood effigies of Santa's elves, Victorian carolers, Clyde the Camel, the Grinch who stole Christmas and replicas of Father Christmas and Saint Nick from six different European nations. In the windows of the house, he placed copies of the lurid lamp won by Ralphie's old man as a "major award" in *A Christmas Story*.

Halfway through the project, the overload of powerful illumination blew out the circuit breakers and almost set the house on fire. Bob Cratchit solved this problem by renting a generator so powerful that the neighbors worried about a blackout caused by electromagnetic pulse. He mounted a pair of rock concert-issue speakers at the corners of the roof and pumped out Christmas music from nine in the morning 'til midnight. After the police cited the Cratchits for disturbing the peace, Bob cut the broadcast back by three hours.

When all the elements of this production—including a quarter-ton of artificial snow—were finally complete two days before Christmas, Hermione Cratchit stood in the trampled meadow facing the house. She was wearing sunglasses to shield her eyes from the glare. She said to Bob, "Well, you've done it, honey. But what on earth is the point?"

Bob Cratchit said, "Look around. Two weeks ago, our kids were scared of a zombie apocalypse, and the whole town was waiting for us to run for our lives. Now, the kids are popular in school, they're praying for snow and wondering what Santa's going to bring them for Christmas. And the town? Everybody's talking about Bob Cratchit, the Christmas maniac."

Hermione Cratchit nodded thoughtfully. "Well, I guess if there were zombies, this might be the sort of show that would scare them off."

She was kissing her husband when old Dan Havisham

emerged from the glow of the driveway lights, holding his dog on a leash. He shambled straight up to Bob Cratchit, peered into his eyes and growled, "You're all gonna die."

Dammitall licked Hermione's hand.

3

On the day before Christmas, just as a precaution, Bob Cratchit went to the hardware store and bought a pump-action shotgun, which Pickwick, the hardware guy, explained was the preferred ordnance for dispatching zombies. He gave Bob a hundred rounds of ammo on the house, asked him to return any leftover shells (if he was still alive) and said, "God be with you."

On Christmas Eve, the Cratchits enforced a mood of holiday normalcy. After dinner, Bob and Hermione drank mulled wine and heated up a pot full of spicy cider for the kids. The family watched *It's a Wonderful Life* on TV, and they all teared up when Harry Bailey raised a glass and said, "A toast to my big brother, George, the richest man in town." At eleven o'clock, the kids were sent to bed. Bob and Hermione piled all the presents beneath the tree and Hermione set out a plateful of her legendary Christmas cookies with a big glass of milk for Santa.

Of course, no one was asleep in the Old Yoolis Mansion when the cuckoo clock in the dining room noisily announced midnight. The four children were lying wide-eyed in bed as wall-eyed cadavers danced in their heads. Bob and Hermione huddled together on the sofa in a darkened living room, lit only by the twinkling of the Christmas tree.

Neither of them approached the door. It simply unlocked itself, with a resounding creak, and swung open. Beyond, garishly illuminated by Bob's light show, a yellowish mist rose from the ground and swirled into a dense, impenetrable cloud. Five minutes passed silently. The mist grew thicker.

The first sign that old Dan Havisham and their fearful

neighbors had been right all along was a hollow-voiced groan emanating from the sickly mist. Then, a banshee scream split the night. Bob Cratchit erupted from the sofa and lunged for his shotgun. Before he could notice their presence and hold them back, Martha, Peter, Mary and Tim were downstairs, frozen in place as they stared through the door.

Soon, the darkness and the miasma were alive with the sound of anguished voices, all of which seemed to have a cold.

"Why," whispered Mary, "do they sound like that?"

"Their throats are full of slime," Tim explained.

The shuffling of a hundred feet and cloven hooves, the dull tinkle of tarnished jingle bells filled the air and enveloped the ancient house. Bravely, Bob Cratchit moved forward through the door to the top of the steps that led up to the veranda. The children huddled 'round him, peering desperately into the pulsating fog.

"Oh my God!" cried Hermione. Emerging from the mist, she saw a bearded face, purplish with decay, its head a decrepit dome of matted hair and bald spots, above a body draped in rotting wool, one three-fingered hand—half flesh, half bone—reaching upward toward the Cratchits.

"What is it?" whispered Mary.

"Don't you mean, who is it?" said Martha, pedantically.

"I think he's a shepherd," said Tim.

"Dad, Dad," said Peter. "Quick. Blow his brains out."

As though directed by his son, Bob Cratchit clambered down the steps and placed the barrel of his shotgun an inch from the face of the undead thing that had crept from the mist. Although missing much of one cheek and an entire lip, the apparent shepherd suddenly turned a deeper purple and grew expressively—even eloquently—wide-eyed with terror.

Poised to squeeze the trigger, Bob Cratchit—who had never killed anything larger than a cockroach—hesitated. The shepherd stood immobile, trembling, locked in Bob's gaze. No one moved for a long moment as, slowly, the enveloping mist lifted and blew away on a wintry breeze.

And they saw.

Ebenezer Yoolis' legion of Christmas undead stood, crouched, knelt and leaned in haphazard formation, crowding the grounds between the crumbling cemetery and the old mansion. They rocked and reeled uneasily. Some of them wobbled alarmingly on rotten legs. One toppled in a cloud of dust, detached from its legs and scrambling at the ground with talons that had once been hands.

Dozens were Santa Clauses, their red costumes faded to brown or dusty rose, their bellies shrunk to emaciation, their beards clinging in dirt-matted clumps to naked chinbones and ragged lips.

As Bob Cratchit's brilliant light barrage exposed the creatures, the family gasped not just at their numbers and hideousness but at the breathtaking variety of this ghastly throng. Besides Santa, there were clusters of gray-skinned elves with missing limbs and absent eyes, earless reindeer by the dozen, none with antlers still intact. Shepherds, of course, were abundant, some still erect on bony feet, others crawling, some all but naked, threads of their robes hanging from ravaged arms. Carolers, buried over centuries, wore the moldy mufflers and worm-eaten overcoats of each era when they stopped harking the herald angels and joined the heavenly choir.

Mary noticed the little drummer boy, still strapped with his drums but without hands to hold the sticks. There were Magi, once-mighty kings reduced in death to hobos, trailing remnants of their silk raiment, stripped of their gifts, reeking not of frankincense but putrescence.

The horror of the scene left the children dizzy with disgust and fear. The stench of death was overwhelming. But, as long as Bob Cratchit held the gun to the half-face of the stertorous shepherd, the army of ghouls remained immobile, as though awaiting a sign known to no one, as though poised to attack but oblivious to their motive.

Suddenly, Tim said, "Look, it's Rudolph."

Indeed, partly concealed behind the lead shepherd, Rudolph the red-nosed reindeer, seeming to hear his name, lifted his head slightly in response. As he did this, his nose flickered and lost its glow. Then, as though in slow motion, his legendary nose fell from his face and bounced off the frozen ground.

"Oh no," cried Tim. He rushed down the stairs and retrieved Rudolph's truant part. Approaching the celebrated reindeer, Tim was not hesitant. While Rudolph stood motionless, his best eye peering askance at the intrusive child, Tim pressed the fallen nose into its senescent socket and tried to screw it in as though it were a light bulb. But when Tim stood back, it fell out of the reindeer's face.

"Oh darn. It won't go back."

"Wait, wait," cried Mary. She ran into the house and came back a moment later with her Little Becky Sewing Kit, which she had gotten for Christmas a year before. She hurried down the stairs, gathered up Rudolph's nose and, using her needle to probe for purchase in the wasted tissues of Rudy's kisser, she patiently, painstakingly restored the dead reindeer's most renowned feature. When Tim tapped the nose, and it flickered weakly back to life, the Cratchit family sent up a spontaneous cheer.

Hermione Cratchit spoke up. "Bob, back away," she said sternly. "I have an idea."

"Back away?" protested Martha. "Mom, these are still zombies. They eat people."

"Maybe," said Hermione. "But let's see if that's what they've come for."

"Us!" cried Martha.

But slowly, Bob Cratchit lowered his shotgun and stood aside, watching with hair-trigger vigilance the throng of yuletide undead.

The first sign that something was different about these Christmas zombies came when the first shepherd, haltingly, stepped past Bob Cratchit and headed toward the steps. The others followed, stumbling and shambling, but showing no interest in the Cratchits and no hunger for living flesh.

"Where are they going?" said Peter. "What do these freaks want? Why here? Why us?"

His mother, whose intuition had saved the shepherd, said, "Just wait. We'll see."

By the time the zombies reached the living room, one recently deceased Santa Claus, still with a spring in his step, had passed the shepherd. With outstretched clawlike hands and one bloodshot eye glowing greedily, he reached out for the plate of Hermione's sublime Christmas cookies. He began, disgustingly, to guzzle down the glass of milk.

"Oh my God," said Tim in a flash of revelation, "they're all cookie monsters!"

The next crisis dawned first on Martha, who cried out in fresh terror. "But look, they're almost gone already! We don't have enough cookies!"

"They'll tear the house apart," shouted Peter over the rustle of rotted costumes and toeless feet.

"There's hundreds of them," added Mary, gratuitously.

Bob Cratchit, recognizing the crisis, reluctantly chambered a shell in his shotgun and readied himself to begin the slaughter of the cookie-crazed living dead threatening to destroy his home.

"Wait," said Hermione, reaching out to stay her husband's gunplay. "Look there!"

While all the zombies paused their feeding frenzy, a long-dead Virgin Mary, her face a bilious green, her gown a ravaged shroud, held forth an exceptionally well-preserved infant child, his grayish skin unblemished, both eyes still in their orbs, his little pudgy fingers still numbering ten. Even his halo was in place, radiating a feeble but determined holiness.

The child reached out and, with a beatific expression that might have been a smile but was probably gas, laid one tiny finger on the cookie plate. Suddenly, there were cookies everywhere. A wave of milk swept across the floor, soaking into the dried-out flesh and dusty rags of the living dead. The voracity of the zombies turned the living room into bedlam. The Cratchits backed away helplessly as their undead guests swept up the miraculous, endless supply of cookies in ghoulish handfuls, stuffed them into toothless jaws, rolled on the floor in a muck of milk and crumbs, mistook one another for cookies and bit off brittle arms and mangled hands. The frenzy seemed as though it would never end.

But, as Tim noted, the zombies seemed to be having fun. They didn't seem to care how many limbs they lost or whether their face fell off while chewing. They were celebrating, perhaps for the last time—before decomposing into ashes and wormshit—the birthday of Jesus and the joyfully profligate Christmas spirit.

Trailing well behind the throng was a bent old man, missing a cheek, who seemed indifferent to the cookie riot. He caught Bob Cratchit's eye and, through split lips and gappy teeth, asked, "Got anything stronger than milk, friend?"

Bob Cratchit, nonplussed to be spoken to so directly by a walking corpse, stood stuck in place, speechless.

"Sorry," said the zombie, "I should introduce myself."

"Uh," muttered Bob Cratchit.

"Yoolis," said the crumbling husk. "Ebenezer III."

"Oh!" said Bob Cratchit, the light dawning in his eyes. "You were buried ... out there."

"Yep," said Ebenezer Yoolis III, "and every year, climbing out gets a little harder."

They were silent for a moment.

"About that drink," asked the former homeowner.

"Oh, yes," said Bob, coming out of his spell. "A little brandy?"

A dim twinkle lit the corpse's eye. He sighed. "It's been so long."

And so, while the feeding frenzy transpired, Bob Cratchit and the undead Ebenezer kept a discreet distance, conversing softly and sipping a civilized dram of Hennessy.

As the cuckoo announced one o'clock, the visit of the living ended as swiftly as it had commenced. The zombies stopped where they stood or lay, lost interest in the cookies—in Christmas itself—and shuffled out the door, down the steps and into a freshly rising mist.

As he was the last to arrive, Ebenezer Yoolis, handing the empty snifter to Bob Cratchit and whispering his haunting thanks, was the last to return to the graveyard.

"Oh crap," said Bob Cratchit as he surveyed the chaotic state of his living room, "did nobody remember to take a picture?"

Not one Cratchit had thought to film or photograph the astounding Christmas of the living dead.

"The neighbors are never gonna believe this," said Peter.

"Aah, who cares about them?" said Tim.

Before going to bed, the whole family pitched in to clean up after their weird new circle of friends. Besides mopping up a scum of spilt milk and cookie detritus, they swept up fingers, feet and arms, rags, hair and teeth, oxen horns, musty wool, a donkey's ear, as well as toes, lips, eyes and various body parts in numbers too great to count. With a squeal of surprise, Mary found, under the sofa, an elf's head trying to play "Barbara Allen" on a kazoo. Having been detached from its body, Mary knew the delinquent noggin would not last long. But it gave her the willies, so she took it up in two fingers and dropped it over the stone wall into the cemetery.

This proved only a partial solution. Forever after, anyone who entered the old boneyard could hear, faintly in the twilight, the off-key melody of the tragic folk song.

The next year, to Hermione's relief, Bob Cratchit scaled back his Christmas display and tucked his shotgun into a trunk in the attic. Ebenezer and the zombies returned, of course, this time with plastic on the floor. Hermione had baked so many cookies that no miracle was necessary. None of the Cratchits' adult neighbors ever got close to the Old Yoolis Mansion on Christmas, but some of their children came to watch the feast and take "zombie selfies."

Sadly, every year, the Cratchit family noticed that some of their familiar Santas, carolers and Orient kings were missing. They'd fallen apart, gone to dust, turned to ashes. Or maybe they just couldn't bring themselves to climb out of a nice warm grave in the dead of winter.

But new zombies arose to take their places, flocking to the old Yoolis place and devouring Hermione's cookies because, as little Tim Cratchit once wisely said, "Christmas only comes once a year … but death is every day."

25 Dec. '24

About the Author

David Benjamin is a lifelong storyteller, dating back to Mrs. Poss' second-grade class at St. Mary's School in Tomah, Wis. His loosely told memoir, *The Life and Times of the Last Kid Picked*, was originally published by Random House and has been reprinted in a revised version by Last Kid Books. His Last Kid Books include a collection of his essays, *Almost Killed by a Train of Thought*, a short story anthology, *The Melting Grandmother and Other Short Works*, and sixteen novels, *Three's a Crowd, A Sunday Kind of Love, Summer of '68, Skulduggery in the Latin Quarter, Black Dragon, Jailbait, Bastard's Bluff, They Shot Kennedy, Fat Vinny's Forbidden Love, Woman Trouble, Witness to the Crucifixion, Choose Moose, Dead Shot, Bistro Nights, The Voice of the Dog* and *Cheat*. As a journalist, Benjamin has edited newspapers, published and edited several magazines, and authored *SUMO: A Thinking Fan's Guide to Japan's National Sport*.

Since its launch in 2019, Benjamin's publishing imprint, Last Kid Books, has won more than forty independent-press awards. These include, for *They Shot Kennedy*, the Midwest Book Awards' 2021 grand prize for literary/historical/contemporary fiction, and a 2022 Silver Medal to *Fat Vinny's Forbidden Love* in the Independent Book Publishers Association's prestigious Benjamin Franklin Awards. His essays have appeared in publications that include the *Philadelphia Inquirer, San Francisco Examiner, Minneapolis Star-Tribune, Los Angeles Times, Chicago Tribune* and Bill Evjue's *Capital Times*.

Benjamin and his wife, Junko Yoshida, have been married for ages. They live sometimes in Madison, Wis., and the rest of the time in Paris.